A SPLENDID HAZARD

A
SPLENDID HAZARD

By
HAROLD MAC GRATH

AUTHOR OF
THE GOOSE GIRL, THE LURE OF THE MASK,
THE MAN ON THE BOX, ETC.

With Illustrations by
HOWARD CHANDLER CHRISTY

WILDSIDE PRESS

WILDSIDE PRESS

CONTENTS

A SPLENDID HAZARD

A SPLENDID HAZARD

CHAPTER I

A MEMORABLE DATE

A BLURRING rain fell upon Paris that day; a
rain so fine and cold that it penetrated the
soles of men's shoes and their hearts alike, a
dispiriting drizzle through which the pale, acrid
smoke of innumerable wood fires faltered upward
from the clustering chimney-pots, only to be rent
into fragments and beaten down upon the glistening
tiles of the mansard roofs. The wide asphalts reflected the horses and carriages and trains and
pedestrians in forms grotesque, zigzagging, flitting,
amusing, like a shadow-play upon a wrinkled, wind-
blown curtain. The sixteenth of June. To Fitzgerald there was something electric in the date, a
tingle of that ecstasy which frequently comes into
the blood of a man to whom the romance of a great
battle is more than its history or its effect upon the
destinies of human beings. Many years before,

this date had marked the end to a certain hundred days, the eclipse of a sun more dazzling than Rome, in the heyday of her august Cæsars, had ever known: Waterloo. A little corporal of artillery; from a cocked hat to a crown, from Corsica to St. Helena: Napoleon.

Fitzgerald, as he pressed his way along the *Boulevard des Invalides,* his umbrella swaying and snapping in the wind much like the sail of a derelict, could see in fancy that celebrated field whereon this eclipse had been supernally prearranged. He could hear the boom of cannon, the thunder of cavalry, the patter of musketry, now thick, now scattered, and again not unlike the subdued rattle of rain on the bulging silk careening before him. He held the handle of the umbrella under his arm, for the wind had a temper mawling and destructive, and veered into the *Place Vauban.* Another man, coming with equal haste from the opposite direction, from the entrance of the tomb itself, was also two parts hidden behind an umbrella. The two came together with a jolt as sounding as that of two old crusaders in a friendly just. Instantly they retreated, lowering their shields.

" I beg your pardon," said Fitzgerald in French.

" It is of no consequence," replied the stranger, laughing. " This is always a devil of a corner on a windy day." His French had a slight German twist to it.

Briefly they inspected each other, as strangers will, carelessly, with annoyance and amusement interplaying in their eyes and on their lips, all in a trifling moment. Then each raised his hat and proceeded, as tranquilly and unconcernedly as though destiny had no ulterior motive in bringing them thus really together. And yet, when they had passed and disappeared from each other's view, both were struck with the fact that somewhere they had met before.

Fitzgerald went into the tomb, his head bared. The marble underfoot bore the imprint of many shoes and rubbers and hobnails, of all sizes and — mayhap — of all nations. He recollected, with a burn on his cheeks, a sacrilege of his raw and eager youth, some twelve years since; he had forgotten to take off his hat. Never would he forget the embarrassment of that moment when the attendant peremptorily bade him remove it. He, to have forgotten! He, who held Napoleon above all heroes! The shame of it!

To-day many old soldiers were gathered meditatively round the heavy circular railing. They were always drawn hither on memorable anniversaries. Their sires and grandsires had carried some of those tattered flags, had won them. The tides of time might ebb and flow, but down there, in his block of Siberian porphyry, slept the hero. There were some few tourists about this afternoon, muttering over their guide-books, when nothing is needed on this spot but the imagination; and that solemn quiet of which the tomb is ever jealous pressed down sadly upon the living. Through the yellow panes at the back of the high altar came a glow suggesting sunshine, baffling the drab of the sky outside; and down in the crypt itself the misty blue was as effective as moonshine.

Napoleon had always been Fitzgerald's ideal hero; but he did not worship him blindly, no. He knew him to have been a brutal, domineering man, unscrupulous in politics, to whom woman was either a temporary toy or a stepping-stone, not over-particular whether she was a dairy-maid or an

Austrian princess; in fact, a rascal, but a great, inventive, splendid, courageous one, the kind which nature calls forth every score of years to purge her breast of the petty rascals, to the benefit of mankind in general. Notwithstanding that he was a rascal, there was an inextinguishable glamour about the man against which the bolts of truth, history, letters, biographers broke ineffectually. Oh, but he had shaken up all Europe; he had made precious kings rattle in their shoes; he had redrawn a hundred maps; and men had laughed as they died for him. It is something for a rascal to have evolved the Code Napoleon. What a queer satisfaction it must be, even at this late day, nearly a hundred years removed, to any Englishman, standing above this crypt, to recollect that upon English soil the Great Shadow had never set his iron heel!

Near to Fitzgerald stood an elderly man and a girl. The old fellow was a fine type of manhood; perhaps in the sixties, white-haired, and the ruddy enamel on his cheeks spoke eloquently of sea changes and many angles of the sun. There was a button in the lapel of his coat, and from this Fitzgerald assumed that he was a naval officer, probably retired.

The girl rested upon the railing, her hands folded, and dreamily her gaze wandered from trophy to trophy; from the sarcophagus to the encircling faces, from one window to another, and again to the porphyry beneath. And Fitzgerald's gaze wandered, too. For the girl's face was of that mold which invariably draws first the eye of a man, then his intellect, then his heart, and sometimes all three at once. The face was as lovely as a rose of Taormina. Dark brown were her eyes, dark brown was her hair. She was tall and lithe, too, with the subtle hint of the woman. There were good taste and sense in her garments. A bunch of Parma violets was pinned against her breast.

"A well-bred girl," was the grateful spectator's silent comment. "No new money there. I wish they'd send more of them over here. But it appears that, with few exceptions, only freaks can afford to travel."

Between Fitzgerald and the girl was a veteran. He had turned eighty if a day. His face was powder-blown, an empty sleeve was folded across his breast, and the medal of the Legion of Honor fell over the sleeve. As the girl and her elderly escort, presumably her father, turned about to leave, she unpinned the flowers and offered them impulsively to the aged hero.

"Take these, *mon brave*," she said lightly; "you have fought for France."

The old man was confused and his faded eyes filled. "For me, mademoiselle?"

"Surely!"

"Thanks, mademoiselle, thanks! I saw *him* when they brought him back from St. Helena, and the Old Guard waded out into the Seine. Those were days. Thanks, mademoiselle; an old soldier salutes you!" And the time-bent, withered form grew tall.

Fitzgerald cleared his throat, for just then something hard had formed there. Why, God bless her! She was the kind of girl who became the mother of soldiers.

With her departure his present interest here began to wane. He wondered who she might be and what part of his native land she adorned when not gracing European capitals. Well, this was no time for mooning. He had arrived from London the day preceeding, and was leaving for Corfu on the morrow, and perforce he must crowd many things into this short grace of time. He was only moderately fond of Paris as a city; the cafés and restaurants and theaters amused him, to be sure; but he was always hunting for romance here and never finding it. The Paris of his Dumas and Leloir no longer existed. In one way or another, the Louvre did not carry him back to the beloved days; he could not rouse his fancy to such height that he could see D'Artagnan ruffling it on the staircase, or Porthos sporting a gold baldric, which was only leather, under his cloak. So then, the tomb of Napoleon and the articles of clothing and warfare which had belonged to him and the toys of the poor little king of Rome were far more to him than all the rest of Paris put together. These things of the first great empire were tangible, visible, close to the touch of his hand. Therefore, never he came to Paris that he failed to visit the tomb and the two museums.

To-day his sight-seeing ended in the hall of Turenne, before the souvenirs of the Duc de Reichstadt, so-called the king of Rome. Poor, little lead soldiers, tarnished and broken; what a pathetic history! Abused, ignored, his childish aspirations trampled on, the name and glory of his father made sport of; worried as cruel children worry a puppy; tantalized; hoping against hope that this night or the next his father would dash in at the head of the Old Guard and take him back to Paris. A plaything for Metternich! Who can gaze upon these little toys without a thrill of pity?

"Poor little codger!" Fitzgerald murmured aloud.

"Yes, yes!" agreed a voice in good English, over his shoulder; "who will ever realize the misery of that boy?"

Fitzgerald at once recognized his justing opponent of the previous hour. Further, this second appearance refreshed his memory. He knew now where he had met the man; he even recalled his name.

"Are you not Karl Breitmann?" he asked with directness.

"Yes. And you are — let me think. Yes; I have it. You are the American correspondent, Fitzgerald."

"And we met in Macedonia during the Greek war."

"Right. And you and I, with a handful of other scribblers, slept that night under the same tent."

"By George!"

"I did not recall you when we bumped a while ago; but once I had gone by you, your face became singularly familiar."

"Funny, isn't it?" And Fitzgerald took hold of the extended hand. "The sight of these toys always gets into my heart."

"Into mine also. Who can say what might have been had they not crushed out the great spirit lying dormant in his little soul? I saw Bernhardt and Coquelin recently in *L'Aiglon*. Ah, but they play it! It drove me here to-day. But this three-cornered hat holds me longest," with a quick gesture toward the opposite wall. "Can't you see the lean face under it, the dark eyes, the dark hair falling upon his collar? What thoughts have run riot under this piece of felt? The brain, the brain! A lieutenant at this time; a short, wiry, cold-blooded youngster, but dreaming the greatest dream in the world!"

Fitzgerald smiled. "You are an enthusiast like myself."

"Who wouldn't be who has visited every battle-field, who has spent days wandering about Corsica, Elba, St. Helena? But you?"

"My word, I have done the same things."

They exchanged smiles.

"What written tale can compare with this living one?" continued Breitmann, his eyes brilliant, his voice eager and the tone rich. "Ah! How many times have I berated the day I was born! To have lived in that day, to have been a part of that be-wildering war panorama; from Toulon to Waterloo! Pardon; perhaps I bore you?"

"By George, no! I'm as bad, if not worse. I shall never forgive one of my forebears for serving under Wellington."

"Nor I one of mine for serving under Blücher!"

They laughed aloud this time. It is always pleasant to meet a person who waxes enthusiastic over the same things as oneself. And Fitzgerald was drawn toward this comparative stranger, who was not ashamed to speak from his heart. They drifted into a long conversation, and fought a dozen battles, compared this general and that, and built idle fancies upon what the outcome would have been had Napoleon won at Waterloo. This might have gone on indefinitely had not the patient attendant finally dandled his keys and yawned over his watch. It was four o'clock, and they had been talking for a full hour. They exchanged cards, and Fitzgerald, with his usual disregard of convention, invited Breitmann to dine with him that evening at the Meurice.

He selected a table by the window, dining at seven-thirty. Breitmann was prompt. In evening clothes there was something distinctive about the man. Fitzgerald, who was himself a wide traveler and a man of the world, instantly saw and was agreeably surprised that he had asked a gentleman to dine. Fitzgerald was no cad; he would have been just as much interested in Breitmann had he arrived in a cutaway sack. But chance acquaintances, as a rule, are rudimental experiments.

They sat down. Breitmann was full of surprises; and as the evening wore on, Fitzgerald remembered having seen Breitmann's name at the foot of big newspaper stories. The man had traveled everywhere, spoke five languages, had been a war correspondent, a sailor in the South Seas, and Heaven knew what else. He had ridden camels and polo ponies in the Soudan; he had been shot in the Græco-Turkish war, shortly after his having met Fitzgerald; he had played a part in the recent Spanish-American, and had fought against the English in the Transvaal.

" And now I am resting," he concluded, turning his chambertin round and round, giving the effect of a cluster of rubies on the table linen. " And all my adventures have been as profitable as these," indebted for the moment to the phantom rubies. " But it's all a great stage, whether you play behind the wings or before the lights. I am thirty-eight; into twenty of those years I have crowded a century."

" You don't look it."

" Ah, one does not need to dissipate to live quickly. The life I have led has kept me in health and vigor. But you? You are not a man who travels without gaining material."

" I have had a few adventures, something like

yours, only not so widely diversified. I wrote some successful short stories about China once. I have had some good sport, too, here and there."

" You live well for a newspaper correspondent," suggested Breitmann, nodding at the bottle of twenty-eight-year-old Burgundy.

" Oh, it's a habit we Americans have," amiably. " We rough it for a few months on bacon and liver, and then turn our attention to truffles and old wines and Cabanas at two-francs-fifty. We are collectively, a good sort of vagabond. I have a little besides my work; not much, but enough to loaf on when no newspaper or magazine cares to pay my expenses in Europe. Anyhow, I prefer this work to staying home to be hampered by intellectual boundaries. My vest will never reach the true proportions which would make me successful in politics."

" You are luckier than I am," Breitmann replied. He sipped his wine slowly and with relish. How long was it since he had tasted a good chambertin?

Perhaps Fitzgerald had noticed it when Breitmann came in. The latter's velvet collar was worn; there was a suspicious gloss at the elbows; the

cuff buttons were of cheap metal; his fingers were
without rings. But the American readily understood. There are lean years and fat years in
journalism, and he himself had known them. For
the present this man was a little down on his luck;
that was all.

A party came in and took the near table. There
were four; two elderly men, an elderly woman, and
a girl. Fitzgerald, as he side-glanced, was afforded
a shiver of pleasure. He recognized the girl. It
was she who had given the flowers to the veteran.

" That is a remarkably fine young woman," said
Breitmann, echoing Fitzgerald's thought.

The waiter opened the champagne.

" Yes. I saw her give some violets this afternoon to an old soldier in the tomb. It was a pretty
scene."

" Well," said Breitmann, raising his glass, " a
pretty woman and a bottle ! "

It was the first jarring note, and Fitzgerald
frowned.

" Pardon me," added Breitmann, observing the
impression he had made, smiling, and when he
smiled the student slashes in his cheeks weren't so

noticeable. "What I should have said is, a good
woman and a good bottle. For what greater delight than to sip a rare vintage with a woman of
beauty and intellect opposite? One glass is enough
to loose her laughter, her wit, her charm. Bah!
A man who knows how to drink his wine, a woman
who knows when to laugh, a story-teller who stops
when his point is told; these trifles add a little color
as we pass. Will you drink to my success?"

"In what?" with Yankee caution.

"In whatever the future sees fit to place under
my hand."

"With pleasure! And by the same token you
will wish me the same?"

"Gladly!"

Their glasses touched lightly; and then their
glances, drawn by some occult force, half-circled
till they paused on the face of the girl, who, perhaps compelled by the same invisible power, had
leveled her eyes in their direction. With well-bred
calm her interest returned to her companions, and
the incident was, to all outward sign, closed. Whatever took place behind that beautiful but indifferent

mask no one else ever learned; but simultaneously in the minds of these two adventurers — and surely, to call a man an adventurer does not necessarily imply that he is a *chevalier d'industrie* — a thought, tinged with regret and loneliness, was born; to have and to hold a maid like that. Love at first sight is the false metal sometimes offered by poets as gold, in quatrains, distiches, verses, and stanzas, tolerated because of the license which allows them to give passing interest the name of love. If these two men thought of love it was only as bystanders, witnessing the pomp and panoply — favored phrase! — of Venus and her court from a curbstone, might have thought of it. Doubtless they had had an affair here and there, over the broad face of the world, but there had never been any barbs on the arrows, thus easily plucked out.

"Sometimes, knowing that I shall never be rich, I have desired a title," remarked Fitzgerald humorously.

"And what would you do with it?" curiously.

"Oh, I'd use it against porters, and waiters, and officials. There's nothing like it. I have observed

a good deal. It has a magic sound, like Orpheus'
lyre; the stiffest back becomes supine at the first
twinkle of it."

"I should like to travel with you, Mr. Fitzgerald,"
said Breitmann musingly. "You would be good
company. Some day, perhaps, I'll try your pre-
scription; but I'm only a poor devil of a homeless,
landless baron."

Fitzgerald sat up. "You surprise me."

"Yes. However, neither my father nor my
grandfather used it, and as the pitiful few acres
which went with it is a sterile Bavarian hillside, I
have never used it, either. Besides, neither the
Peerage nor *he Almanac de Gotha* make mention
of it; but still the patent of nobility was legal, and I
could use it despite the negligence of those two au-
thorties."

"You could use it in America. There are not
many 'Burke's' there."

"It amuses me to think that I should confide this
secret to you. The wine is good, and perhaps —
perhaps I was hungry. Accept what I have told
you as a jest."

They both became untalkative as the coffee came.

Fitzgerald was musing over the impulse which had seized him in asking Breitmann to share his dinner. He was genuinely pleased that he had done so, however; but it forced itself upon him that sometime or other these impulses would land him in difficulties. On his part the recipient of this particular impulse was also meditating; Napoleon had been utterly forgotten, verbally at least. Well, perhaps they had threshed out that interesting topic during the afternoon. Finally he laid down the end of his cigarette.

"I have to thank you very much for a pleasant evening, Mr. Fitzgerald."

"Glad I ran into you. It has done me no end of good. I leave for the East to-morrow. Is there any possibility of seeing you in the Balkans this fall?"

"No. I am going to try my luck in America again."

"My club address you will find on my card. You must go? It's only the shank of the evening."

"I have a little work to do. Some day I hope I may be able to set as good a dinner before you."

" Better have a cigar."

" No, thank you."

And Fitzgerald liked him none the less for his firmness. So he went as far as the entrance with him.

" Don't bother about calling a cab," said Breitmann. " It has stopped raining, and the walk will tone me up. Good night and good luck."

And they parted, neither ever expecting to see the other again, and equally careless whether they did or not.

Breitmann walked rapidly toward the river, crossed, and at length entered a gloomy old *pension* over a restaurant frequented by bargemen, students, and human driftwood. As he climbed the badly lighted stairs, a little, gray-haired man, wearing spectacles, passed him, coming down. A " pardon " was mumbled, and the little man proceeded into the restaurant, picked a *Figaro* from the table littered with newspapers, ensconced himself in a comfortable chair, and ordered coffee. No one gave him more than a cursory glance. The quarter was indigent, but ordinarily respectable; and it was only when some noisy Americans invaded the place that the habitués took any unusual interest in the coming and going of strangers.

Up under the mansard roof there was neither gas nor electricity. Breitmann lighted his two candles, divested himself of his collar, tie, and coat, and flung them on the bed.

"Threadbare, almost! Ah, but I was hungry to-night. Did he know it? Why the devil should I care? To work! Up to this night I have tried to live more or less honestly. I have tried to take the good that is in me and to make the most of it. And," ironically, "this is the result. I have failed. Now we'll see what I can accomplish in the way of being a great rascal."

He knelt before a small steamer trunk, battered and plentifully labeled, and unscrewed the lock. From a cleverly concealed pocket he brought forth a packet of papers. These he placed on the table and unfolded with almost reverent care. Sometimes he shrugged, as one does who is confronted by huge obstacles, sometimes he laughed harshly, sometimes his jaws hardened and his fingers writhed. When he had done — and many and many a time he had repeated this performance, studied the faded ink, the great seal, the water-marks — he hid them away in the trunk again.

He now approached the open window and leaned out. Glittering Paris, wonderful city! How the lights from the bridges twinkled on the wind-wrinkled Seine! Over there lay the third wealth of the world; luxury, vice, pleasure. Eh, well, he could not fight it, but he could curse it deeply and violently, which he did.

"Wait, Moloch, wait; you and I are not done with each other yet! Wait! I shall come back, and when I do, look to yourself! Two million francs, and every one of them mine!"

He laid his head on his hands. It ached dully. Perhaps it was the wine.

CHAPTER II

THE BUTTERFLY MAN

THE passing and repassing shadows of craft gave a fitful luster to the river; so crisply white were the spanning highways that the eye grew quickly dim with looking; the brisk channel breeze which moved with rough gaiety through the trees in the gardens of the Tuileries, had, long hours before, blown away the storm. Bright sunshine, expanses of deep cerulean blue, towering banks of pleasant clouds, these made Paris happy to-day, in spots.

The great minister gazed across the river, his hands under the tails of his frock, and the perturbation of his mind expressed by the frequent flapping of those somber woolen wings. To the little man who watched him, there was a faint resemblance to a fiddling cricket.

23

" Sometimes I am minded to trust the whole thing to luck, and bother no more about him."

" Monsieur, I have obeyed orders for seven years, since we first recognized the unfortunate affair. Nothing he has done in this period is missing from my note-book; and up to the present time he has done — nothing. But just a little more patience. This very moment, when you are inclined to drop it, may be the one. One way or another, it is a matter of no real concern to me. There will always be plenty of work for me to do, in France, or elsewhere. But I am like an old soldier whose wound, twinging with rheumatism, announces the approach of damp weather. I have, then, monsieur, a kind of psychological rheumatism; prescience, bookmen call it. Presently we shall have damp weather."

" You speak with singular conviction."

" In my time I have made very few mistakes. You will recollect that. Twenty years have I served France. I was wrong to say that this affair does not concern me. I'm interested to see the end."

" But will there be an end?" impatiently. " If

I were certain of that! But seven years, and still no sign."

"Monsieur, he is to be feared; this inactivity, to my mind, proves it. He is waiting; the moment is not ripe. There are many sentimental fools in this world. One has only to step into the street and shout 'Down with!' or 'Long live!' to bring these fools clattering about."

"That is true enough," flapping the tails of his coat again.

"This fellow was born across the Rhine. He has served in the navy; he is a German, therefore we can not touch him unless he commits some overt act. He waits; there is where the danger, the real danger, lies. He waits; and it is his German blood which gives him this patience. A Frenchman would have exploded long since."

"You have searched his luggage and his rooms, times without number."

"And found nothing; nothing that I might use effectively. But there is this saving grace; he on his side knows nothing."

"I would I were sure of that also. Eh, well; I

leave the affair in your hands, and they are capable ones. When the time comes, act, act upon your own initiative. In this matter we shall give no accounting to Germany."

" No, because what I do must be done secretly. It will not matter that Germany also knows and waits. But this is true; if we do not circumvent him, she will make use of whatever he does."

" It has its whimsical side. Here is a man who may some day blow up France, and yet we can put no hand on him till he throws the bomb."

" But there is always time to stop the flight of the bomb. That shall be my concern; that is, if monsieur is not becoming discouraged and desires me to occupy myself with other things. I repeat: I have rheumatism, I apprehend the damp. He will go to America."

" Ah! It would be a very good plan if he remained there."

The little man did not reply.

" But you say in your reports that you have seen him going about with some of the Orleanists. What is your inference there? "

" I have not yet formed one. It is a bit of a rid-

dle there, for the crow and the eagle do not fly together."

"Well, follow him to America."

"Thanks.   The pay is good and the work is
congenial."   The tone of the little man was softly
given to irony.

Gray-haired, rosy-cheeked, a face smooth as a
boy's, twinkling eyes behind spectacles, he was one
of the most astute, learned, and patient of the
French secret police.   And he did not care the flip
of his strong brown fingers for the methods of
Vidocq or Lecoq.   His only disguise was that not
one of the criminal police of the world knew him or
had ever heard of him; and save his chief and three
ministers of war — for French cabinets are given
to change — his own immediate friends knew him
as a butterfly hunter, a searcher for beetles and
scarabs, who, indeed, was one of the first authorities
in France on the subjects: Anatole Ferraud, who
went about, hither and thither, with a little red button in his buttonhole and a tongue facile in a dozen
languages.

"Very well, monsieur.   I trust that in the near
future I may bring you good news."

" He will become nothing or the most desperate man in Europe."

" Admitted."

" He is a scholar, too."

" All the more interesting."

" As a student in Munich he has fought his three duels. He has been a war correspondent under fire. He is a great fencer, a fine shot, a daring rider."

" And penniless. What a country they have over there beyond the Rhine! He would never have troubled his head about it, had they not harried him. To stir up France, to wound her if possible! He will be a man of great courage and resource," said the secret agent, drawing the palms of his hands together.

" In the end, then, Germany will offer him money? "

" That is the possible outlook."

" But, suppose he went to work on his own responsibility? "

" In that case one would be justified in locking him up as a madman. Do you know anything about Alpine butterflies? "

" Very little," confessed the minister.

" There is often great danger in getting at them; but the pleasure is commensurate."

" Are there not rare butterflies in the Amazonian swamps? " cynically.

" Ah, but this man has good blood in him; and if he flies at all he will fly high. Think of this man fifty years ago; what a possibility he would have been! But it is out of fashion to-day. Well, monsieur, I must be off. There is an old manuscript at the Bibliothèque I wish to inspect."

" Concerning this matter? "

" Butterflies," softly; " or, I should say, chrysalides."

The subtle inference passed by the minister. There were many other things to-ing and fro-ing in the busy corridors of his brain. " I shall hear from you frequently? "

" As often as the situation requires. By the way, I have an idea. When I cable you the word butterfly, prepare yourself accordingly. It will mean that the bomb is ready."

" Good luck attend you, my savant," said the minister, with a friendliness which was deep and genuine. He had known Monsieur Ferraud in

other days. "And, above all, take care of yourself."

"Trust me, Count." And the secret agent departed, to appear again in these chambers only when
his work was done.

"A strange man," mused the minister when he
was alone. "A still stranger business for a genuine scholar. Is he really poor? Does he do this
work to afford him ease and time for his studies?
Or, better still, does he hide a great and singular
patriotism under butterfly wings? Patriotism?
More and more it becomes self-interest. It is only
when a foreign mob starts to tear down your house,
that you become a patriot."

Now the subject of these desultory musings went
directly to the Bibliothèque Nationale. The study
he pursued was of deep interest to him; it concerned a butterfly of vast proportions and kaleido-
scopic in color, long ago pinned away and labeled
among others of lesser brilliancy. It had cast a
fine shadow in its brief flight. But the species was
now extinct, at least so the historian of this particular butterfly declared. Hybrid? Such a con-
tingency was always possible.

"Suppose it does exist, as I and a few others very well know it does; what a fine joke it would be to see it fly into Paris! But, no. Idle dream! Still, I shall wait and watch. And now, suppose we pay a visit to Berlin and use blunt facts in place of diplomacy? It will surprise them."

Each German chancellor has become, in turn, the repository of such political secrets as fell under the eyes of his predecessor; and the chancellor who walked up and down before Monsieur Ferraud, possessed several which did not rest heavily upon his soul simply because he was incredulous, or affected that he was.

"The thing is preposterous."

"As your excellency has already declared."

"What has it to do with France?"

"Much or little. It depends upon this side of the Rhine."

"What imagination! But for your credentials, Monsieur Ferraud, I should not listen to you one moment."

"I have seen some documents."

"Forgeries!" contemptuously.

"Not in the least," suavely. "They are in every part genuine. They are his own."

The chancellor paused, frowning. "Well, even then?"

Monsieur Ferraud shrugged.

"This fellow, who was forced to resign from the navy because of his tricks at cards, why I doubt if he could stir up a brawl in a tavern. Really, if there was a word of truth in the affair, we should have acted before this. It is all idle newspaper talk that Germany wishes war; far from it. Still, we lose no point to fortify ourselves against the possibility of it. Some one has been telling you old-wives' tales."

"Ten thousand marks," almost inaudibly.

"What was that you said?" cried the chancellor, whirling round abruptly, for the words startled him.

"Pardon me! I was thinking out loud about a sum of money."

"Ah!" And yet the chancellor realized that the other was telling him as plainly as he dared that the German government had offered such a sum to forward the very intrigue which he was so emphatically denying. "Why not turn the matter over to your own ambassador here?"

The secret agent laughed. "Publicity is what neither your government nor mine desires. Thank you."

"I am sorry not to be of some service to you."

"I can readily believe that, your excellency," not to be outdone in the matter of duplicity. "I thank you for your time."

"I hadn't the least idea that you were in the service; butterflies and diplomacy!" with a hearty laugh.

"It is only temporary."

"Your *Alpine Butterflies* compares favorably with *The Life of the Bee.*"

"That is a very great compliment!"

And with this the interview, extraordinary in all ways, came to an end. Neither man had fooled the other, neither had made any mistake in his logical deductions; and, in a way, both were satisfied. The chancellor resumed his more definite labors, and the secret agent hurried away to the nearest telegraph office.

"So I am to stand on these two feet?" Monsieur

Ferraud ruminated, as he took the seat by the window in the second-class carriage for Munich. " All the finer the sport. Ten thousand marks! He forgot himself for a moment. And I might have gone further and said that ninety thousand marks would be added to those ten thousand if the bribe was accepted and the promise fulfilled."

Ah, it would be beautiful to untangle this snarl all alone. It would be the finest chase that had ever fallen to his lot. No grain of sand, however small, should escape him. There were fools in Berlin as well as in Paris; and he knew what he knew. " Never a move shall he make that I shan't make the same; and in one thing I shall move first. Two million francs! Handsome! It is I who must find this treasure, this fulcrum to the lever which is going to upheave France. There will be no difficulty then in pricking the pretty bubble. In the meantime we shall proceed to Munich and carefully inquire into the affairs of the grand opera singer, Hildegarde von Mitter."

He extracted a wallet from an inner pocket and opened it across his knees. It was full of butterflies.

CHAPTER III

FITZGERALD'S view from his club window
afforded the same impersonal outlook as
from a window in a car. It was the two living cur-
rents, moving in opposite directions, each making
toward a similar goal, only in a million different
ways, that absorbed him. Subconsciously he was
always counting, counting, now by fives, now by
tens, but invariably found new entertainment ere he
reached the respectable three numerals of an even
hundred. Sometimes it was a silk hat which he
followed till it became lost up the Avenue; and as
often as not he would single out a waiting cabman
and speculate on the quality of his fare; and other
whimsies.

That this was such and such a woman, or that
was such and such a man never led him into any of
that gossip so common among club-men who are

35

out of touch with the vital things in life. Even when he espied a friend in this mysterious flow of souls, there was only a transient flash of recognition in his eyes. When he wasn't in the tennis-courts, or the billiard- or card-rooms, he was generally to be found in this corner. He had seen all manner of crowds, armies pursuing and retreating, vast concords in public squares, at coronations, at catastrophes, at play, and he never lost interest in watching them; they were the great expressions of humanity. This is perhaps the reason why his articles were always so rich in color. No two crowds were ever alike to him, consequently he never was at loss for a fresh description.

To-day the Italian vender of plaster statuettes caught his eye. For an hour now the poor wretch hadn't even drawn the attention of one of the thousands passing. Fitzgerald felt sorry for him, and once the desire came to go over and buy out the Neapolitan; but he was too comfortable where he was, and beyond that he was expecting a friend.

Fitzgerald was thirty, with a clean-shaven, lean, and eager face, russet in tone, well offset by the fine blue eyes which had the faculty of seeing little and

big things at the same time. He had dissipated in
a trifling fashion, but the healthy, active life he
lived in the open more than counteracted the effects.
A lonely orphan, possessing a lively imagination,
is seldom free from some vice or other. There had
never been, however, what the world is pleased to
term entanglements. His guardian angel gave him
a light step whenever there was any social thin ice.
Oh, he had some relatives; but as they were neither
very rich nor very poor, they seldom annoyed one
another. He was, then, a free lance in all the
abused word implies; and he lived as he pleased,
spending his earnings freely and often carelessly,
knowing that the little his father had left him
would keep a moderately hungry wolf from the
door. He had been born to a golden spoon, but the
food from the pewter one he now used tasted just
as good.

"So here you are! I've been in the billiard-room,
and the card-room, and the bar-room."

"Talking of bar-rooms!" Fitzgerald reached for
the button. "Sit down, Hewitt, old boy. Glad to
see you. Now, I'll tell you right off the bat, nothing will persuade me. For years I've been jumping

to the four points of the compass at the beck of your old magazine and syndicate. I'm going to settle down and write a novel."

" Piffle! " growled the editor, dropping his lanky form into a chair. " Thank goodness, they haven't swivel chairs in the club. I've been whirling round in one all day — a long, tall Scotch, please — but a novel! I say, piffle! "

" Piffle it may be, but I'm going to have a whack at it. If I ever do another article it will be as a millionaire's private secretary. I should like to study his methods for saving his money. What is it this time? "

" A dash to the North Pole."

" Never again north of Berlin or south of Assuan for mine. No."

" Come, Fitz; a great chance."

" When you sent me to Manila I explored hell for you, but I've cooled off considerably since then. No ice for mine, except in silver buckets."

" You've made a pretty good thing out of us; something like five thousand a year and your expenses; and with the credentials we've always given

you, you have been able to see the world as few men
see it."

"That's just the trouble. You've spoiled me."

"Well, you may take my word for it, you won't
have the patience to sit down at home here and write
a hundred thousand words that mean anything.
There's no reason why you can't do my work and
write novels on the side. We both know a dozen
fellows who are doing it. We've got to have this
article, and you're the only man we dare trust alone
on it, if it will flatter you any to know it."

"Come, pussy, come!"

"If it's a question of more money —"

"Perish the thought!" cried Fitzgerald, clasping
his knees and rocking gently. "You know as well
as I do, Hewitt, that it's the game and not the cash.
I've found a new love, my boy."

"Double harness?" with real anxiety. Hewitt
bit his scrubby mustache. When a special correspondent married that was the end of him.

"There you go again!" warned the recalcitrant.
"If you don't stop eating that mustache you'll have
stomach trouble that no Scotch whisky will ever

cure. The whole thing is in a nutshell," a sly humor creeping into his eyes. " I am tired of writing ephemeral things. I want to write something that will last."

" Write your epitaph, Jack," drawled a deep voice from the reading table. " That's the only sure way, and even that is no good if your marble is spongy."

" Oh, Cathewe, this is not your funeral," retorted the editor.

" Perhaps not. All the same, I'll be chief mourner if Jack takes up novel writing. Critics don't like novels, because any one can write an average story; but it takes a genius to turn out first-class magazine copy. Anyhow, art becomes less and less particular every day. The only thing that never gains or loses is this *London Times*. Someday I'm going to match the *Congressional Record* and the *Times* for the heavyweight championship of the world, with seven to one on the *Record,* to weigh in at the ringside."

" You've been up north, Arthur," said Fitzgerald. " What's your advice? "

" Don't do it. You've often wondered how and

where I lost these two digits. Up there." The *Times* rattled, and Cathewe became absorbed in the budget.

Arthur Cathewe was a tall, loose-limbed man, forty-two or three, rather handsome, and a bit shy with most folk. Rarely any one saw him outside the club. He had few intimates, but to these he was all that friendship means, kindly, tender, loyal, generous, self-effacing. And Fitzgerald loved him best of all men. It did not matter that there were periods when they became separated for months at a time. They would some day turn up together in the same place. "Why, hello, Arthur!" "Glad to see you, Jack!" and that was all that was necessary. All the enthusiasm was down deep below. Cathewe was always in funds; Fitzgerald sometimes; but there was never any lending or borrowing between them. This will do much toward keeping friendship green. The elder man was a great hunter; he had been everywhere, north and south, east and west. He never fooled away his time at pigeons and traps; big game, where the betting was even, where the animal had almost the same chance as the man. He could be tolerably humorous upon occasions. The solemn cast to his comely face predestined him for this talent.

" Well, Fitz, what are you going to do? "

" Hewitt, give me a chance. I've been home but a week. I'm not going to dash to the Pole without having a ripping good time here first. Will a month do? "

" Oh, the expedition doesn't leave for two months yet. But we must sign the contract a month beforehand."

" To-day is the first of June; I promise to telegraph you yes or no this day month. You have had me over in Europe eighteen months. I'm tired of trains, and boats, and mules. I'm going fishing."

" Ah, bass! " murmured Cathewe from behind his journal.

" By the way, Hewitt," said Fitzgerald, " have you ever heard of a chap called Karl Breitmann? "

" Yes," answered Hewitt. " Never met him personally, though."

" I have," joined in Cathewe quietly. He laid down the *Times*. " What do you know about him? "

"Met him in Paris last year. Met him once before in Macedonia. Dined with me in Paris. Amazing lot of adventures. Rather down on his luck, I should judge."

"Couple of scars on his left cheek and a bit of the scalp gone; German student sort, rather good-looking, fine physique?"

"That's the man."

"I know him, but not very well." And Cathewe fumbled among the other newspapers.

"Dine with me to-night," urged Hewitt.

"I'll tell you what. See that Italian over there with the statues? I am going to buy him out; and if I don't make a sale in half an hour, I'll sign the the dinner checks."

"Done!"

"I'll take half of that bet," said Cathewe, rising. "It will be cheap."

Ten minutes later the two older men saw Fitzgerald hang the tray from his shoulders and take his position on the corner.

"I love that chap, Hewitt; he is what I always wanted to be, but couldn't be." Cathewe pulled the drooping ends of his mustache. "If he should write a novel, I'm afraid for your sake that it will be a good one. Keep him busy. Novel writing keeps a man indoors. But don't send him on any damn goose chase for the Pole."

" Why not? "

" Well, he might discover it. But, honestly, it's so God-forsaken and cold and useless. I have hunted musk-ox, and I know something about the place. North Poling, as I call it, must be a man's natural bent; otherwise you kill the best that's in him."

" Heaven on earth, will you look! A policeman is arguing with him." Hewitt shook with laughter.

" But I bought him out," protested Fitzgerald. " There's no law to prevent me selling these."

" Oh, I'm wise. We want no horse-play on this corner; no joyful college stunts," roughly.

Fitzgerald saw that frankness must be his card, so he played it. " Look here, do you see those two gentlemen in the window there? "

" The club? "

" Yes. I made a wager that I could sell one of these statues in half an hour. If you force me off I'll lose a dinner."

"Well, I'll make a bargain with you. You can stand here for half an hour; but if you open your mouth to a woman, I'll run you in. No fooling; I'm talking straight. I'm going to see what your game is."

"I agree."

So the policeman turned to his crossing and reassumed his authority over traffic, all the while never losing sight of the impromptu vender.

Many pedestrians paused. To see a well-dressed young man hawking plaster Venuses was no ordinary sight. They knew that some play was going on, but, with that inveterate suspicion of the city pedestrian, none of them stopped to speak or buy. Some newsboys gathered round and offered a few suggestions. Fitzgerald gave them back in kind. No woman spoke, but there wasn't one who passed that didn't look at him with more than ordinary curiosity. He was enjoying it. It reminded him of the man who offered sovereigns for shillings, and never exchanged a coin.

Once he turned to see if his friends were still watching him. They were, two among many; for the exploit had gone round, and there were other wagers being laid on the result. While his head was turned, and his grin was directed at the club window, a handsome young woman in blue came along. She paused, touched her lips with her gloved hand meditatingly, and then went right-about-face swiftly. Some one in the window motioned frantically to the vender, but he did not understand. Ten minutes left in which to win his bet. He hadn't made a very good bargain. Hm! The young woman in blue was stopping. Her exquisite face was perfectly serious as her eyes ran over the collection on the tray. They were all done execrably, something Fitzgerald hadn't noticed before.

" How much are these apiece? "

" Er — twenty-five cents, ma'am," he stammered. As a matter of fact he hadn't any idea what the current price list was.

" You seem very well dressed," doubtfully; " and you do not look hungry."

" I am doing this for charity's sake," finding his wits. The policeman hovered near, scowling. He was powerless, since the young woman had spoken first.

"Charity," in a half-articulated voice, as if the word to her possessed many angles, and she was endeavoring to find the proper one to fit the moment. "What organization?"

A blank pause. "My own, ma'am, of which I am the head." There was no levity in tone or expression.

By now every window in the club framed a dozen or more faces.

"I will take this Canova, I believe," she finally decided, opening her purse and producing the necessary silver. "Of course, it is quite impossible to send this?"

"Yes, ma'am. Sending it would eat up all the profits." But, with ill-concealed eagerness, "If you will leave your address I can send as many as you like."

"I will do that."

Incredible as it seemed, neither face lost its repose; he dared not smile, and the young woman did not care to. There was something familiar to his memory in the oval face, but this was no time for a diligent search.

"Hey, miss," yelled one of the newsboys, "you're

t'rowin' your money away. He's a fake; he ain't
no statoo seller. He's doing it for a joke!' "

Fitzgerald lost a little color, that was all. But
his customer ignored the imputation. She took out
a card and laid it on the tray, and without further
ado went serenely on her way. The policeman
stepped toward her as if to speak, but she turned
her delicate head aside. The crowd engulfed her
presently, and Fitzgerald picked up the card.
There was neither name nor definite address on it.
It was a message, hastily written; and it sent a
thrill of delight and speculation to his impression-
able heart. Still carrying the tray before him he
hastened over to the club, where there was something of an ovation. Instead of a dinner for three
it became one for a dozen, and Fitzgerald passed the
statuettes round as souvenirs of the most unique
bet of the year. There were lively times. Toward
midnight, as Fitzgerald was going out of the coat
room, Cathewe spoke to him.

"What was her name, Jack?"

"Hanged if I know."

"She dropped a card on your tray."

Fitzgerald scrubbed his chin. "There wasn't

any name on it. There was an address and something more. Now, wait a moment, Arthur; this is no ordinary affair. I would not show it to any one else. Here, read it yourself."

"Come to the house at the top of the hill, in Dalton, to-morrow night at eight o'clock. But do not come if you lack courage."

That was all. Cathewe ran a finger, comb-fashion, through his mustache. He almost smiled.

"Where the deuce *is* Dalton?" Fitzgerald inquired.

"It is a little village on the New Jersey coast; not more than forty houses, post-office, hotel, and general store; perhaps an hour out of town."

"What would you do in my place? It may be a joke, and then again it may not. She knew that I was a rank impostor."

"But she knew that a man must have a certain kind of daredevil courage to play the game you played. Well, you ask me what I should do in your place. I'd go."

"I shall. It will double discount fishing. And the more I think of it, the more certain I become that she and I have met somewhere. By-by!"

Cathewe lingered in the reading-room, pondering. Here was a twist to the wager he was rather unprepared for; and if the truth must be told, he was far more perplexed than Fitzgerald. He knew the girl, but he did not know and could not imagine what purpose she had in aiding Fitzgerald to win his wager or luring him out to an obscure village in this detective-story manner.

" Well, I shall hear all about it from her father," he concluded.

And all in good time he did.

CHAPTER IV

PIRATES AND PRIVATE SECRETARIES

IT was a little station made gloomy by a single light. Once in so often a fast train stopped, if properly flagged. Fitzgerald, feeling wholly unromantic, now that he had arrived, dropped his hand-bag on the damp platform and took his bearings. It was after sundown. The sea, but a few yards away, was a murmuring, heaving blackness, save where here and there a wave broke. The wind was chill, and there was the hint of a storm coming down from the northeast.

" Any hotel in this place? " he asked of the ticket agent, the telegraph operator, and the baggageman, who was pushing a crate of vegetables off a truck.

" Swan's Hotel; only one."

" Do people sleep and eat there? "

" If they have good digestions."

" Much obliged."

"Whisky's no good, either."

"Thanks again. This doesn't look much like a summer resort."

"Nobody ever said it was. I beg your pardon, but would you mind taking an end of this darned crate?"

"Not at all." Fitzgerald was beginning to enjoy himself. "Where do you want it?"

"In   here,"   indicating   the   baggage-room. "Thanks. Now, if there's anything I can do to help you in return, let her go."

"Is there a house hereabouts called the top o' the hill?"

"Come over here," said the agent. "See that hill back there, quarter of a mile above the village; those three lights? Well, that's it. They usually have a carriage down here when they're expecting any one."

"Who owns it?"

"Old Admiral Killigrew. Didn't you know it?"

"Oh, Admiral Killigrew; yes, of course. I'm not a guest. Just going up there on business. Worth about ten millions, isn't he?"

"That and more. There's his yacht in the har-

bor. Oh, he could burn up the village, pay the in-
surance, and not even knock down the quality of his
cigars. He's the best old chap out. None of your
red-faced, yo-hoing, growling seadogs; just a kindly,
generous old sailor, with only one bee in his bon-
net."

"What sort of bee?"

"Pirates!" in a ghostly whisper.

"Pirates? Oh, say, now!" with a protest.

"Straight as a die. He's got the finest library on
piracy in the world, everything from *The Pirates of
Penzance* to *The Life of Morgan.*"

"But there's no pirate afloat these days."

"Not on the high seas, no. It's just the old
man's pastime. Every so often, he coals up the
yacht, which is a seventeen-knotter, and goes off to
the South Seas, hunting for treasures."

"By George!" Fitzgerald whistled softly.
"Has he ever found any?"

"Not so much as a postage stamp, so far as I
know. Money's always been in the family, and his
Wall Street friends have shown him how to double
what he has, from time to time. Just for the sport
of the thing some old fellows go in for crockery,

some for pictures, and some for horses. The admiral just hunts treasures. Half-past six; you'll excuse me. There'll be some train despatches in a minute."

Fitzgerald gave him a good cigar, took up his bag, and started off for the main street; and once there he remembered with chagrin that he had not asked the agent the most important thing of all: Had the admiral a daughter? Well, at eight o'clock he would learn all about that. Pirates! It would be as good as a play. But where did he come in? And why was courage necessary? His interest found new life.

Swan's Hotel was one of those nondescript buildings of wood which are not worth more than a three-line paragraph even when they burn down. It was smelly. The kitchen joined the dining-room, and the dining-room the office, which was half a bar-room, with a few boxes of sawdust mathematically arranged along the walls. There were many like it up and down the coast. There were pictures on the walls of terrible wrecks at sea, naval battles, and a race horse or two.

The landlord himself lifted Fitzgerald's bag to the counter.

" A room for the night and supper, right away."

" Here, Jimmy," called the landlord to a growing, lumbering boy, " take this satchel up to number five."

The boy went his way, eying the labels respectfully and with some awe. This was the third of its kind he had ported up-stairs in the past twenty-four hours.

Fitzgerald cast an idle glance at the loungers. There were half a dozen of them, some of them playing cards and some displaying talent on a pool table, badly worn and beer-stained. There was nothing distinctive about any of them, excepting the little man who was reading an evening paper, and the only distinctive thing about him was a pair of bright eyes. Behind their gold-rimmed spectacles they did not waver under Fitzgerald's scrutiny; so the latter dismissed the room and its company from his mind and proceeded into dinner. As he was late, he dined alone on mildly warm chicken, greasy potatoes, and muddy coffee. He was used often to worse fare than this, and no complaint was even thought of. After he had changed his linen he took the road to the house at the top of the hill. Now, then, what sort of an affair was this going to be, such as would bend a girl of her bearing to speak to him on the street? Moreover, at a moment when he was playing a grown-up child's game? She had known that he was prevaricating when he had stated that he represented a charitable organization; and he knew that she knew he knew it. What, then? It could not be a joke; women never rise to such extravagant heights. Pirates and treasures; he wouldn't have been surprised at all had Old Long John Silver hobbled out from behind any one of those vine-grown fences, and demanded his purse.

The street was dim, and more than once he stumbled over a loose board in the wooden walk. If the admiral had been the right kind of philanthropist he would have furnished stone. But then, it was one thing to give a country town something and another to force the town council into accepting it. The lamp-posts, also of wood, stood irregularly apart, often less than a hundred feet, and

sometimes more, lighting nothing but their immediate vicinity. Fitzgerald could see the lamps
plainly, but could separate none of the objects round
or beneath. That is why he did not see the face of
the man who passed him in a hurry. He never forgot a face, if it were a man's; his only difficulty was
in placing it at once. Up to this time one woman
resembled another; feminine faces made no particular impression on his memory. He would have remembered the face of the man who had just passed,
for the very fact that he had thought of it often.
The man had come into the dim radiance of the far
light, then had melted into the blackness of the night
again, leaving as a sign of his presence the creak of
his shoes and the aroma of a cigarette.

Fitzgerald tramped on cheerfully. It was not
an unpleasant climb, only dark. The millionaire's
home seemed to grow up out of a fine park. There
was a great iron fence inclosing the grounds, and
the lights on top of the gates set the dull red trunks
of the pines a-glowing. There were no lights shining in the windows of the pretty lodge. Still, the
pedestrians' gate was ajar. He passed in, fully

expecting to be greeted by the growl of a dog. Instead, he heard mysterious footsteps on the gravel. He listened. Some one was running.

" Hello, there! " he called.

No answer. The sound ceased. The runner had evidently taken to the silent going of the turf. Fitzgerald came to a stand. Should he go on or return to the hotel? Whoever was running had no right here. Fitzgerald rarely carried arms, at least in civilized countries; a stout cane was the best weapon for general purposes. He swung this lightly.

" I am going on. I should like to see the library."

He was not overfond of unknown dangers in the night; but he possessed a keen ear and a sharp pair of eyes, being a good hunter. A poacher, possibly. At any rate, he determined to go forward and ring the bell.

Both the park and the house were old. Some of those well-trimmed pines had scored easily a hundred and fifty years, and the oak, standing before the house and dividing the view into halves, was older still. No iron deer or marble lion marred the lawn which he was now traversing; a sign of good taste.

Gardeners had been at work here, men who knew their business thoroughly. He breathed the odor of trampled pine needles mingled with the harsher essence of the sea. It was tonic.

In summer the place would be beautiful. The house itself was built on severe and simple lines. It was quite apparent that in no time of its history had it been left to run down. The hall and lower left wing were lighted, but the inner blinds and curtains were drawn. He did not waste any time. It was exactly eight o'clock when he stepped up to the door and pulled the ancient wire bell. At once he saw signs of life. The broad door opened, and an English butler, having scrutinized his face, silently motioned him to be seated. The young man in search of an adventure selected the far end of the hall seat and dandled his hat. An English butler was a good beginning. Perhaps three minutes passed, then the door to the library opened and a young woman came out. Fitzgerald stood up. Yes, it was she.

"So you have come?" There was welcome neither in her tone nor face, nor was there the suggestion of any other sentiment.

"Yes. I am not sure that I gave you my name, Miss Killigrew." He was secretly confused over this enigmatical reception.

She nodded. She had been certain that, did he come at all, he would come in the knowledge of who she was.

"I am John Fitzgerald," he said.

She thought for a space. "Are you the Mr. Fitzgerald who wrote the long article recently on the piracy in the Chinese Seas?"

"Yes," full of wonder.

Interest began to stir her face. "It turns out, then, rather better than I expected. I can see that you are puzzled. I picked you out of many yesterday, on impulse, because you had the sang-froid necessary to carry out your jest to the end."

"I am glad that I am not here under false colors. What I did yesterday was, as you say, a jest. But, on the other hand, are you not playing me one in kind? I have much curiosity."

"I shall proceed to allay it, somewhat. This will be no jest. Did you come armed?"

"Oh, indeed, no!" smiling.

She rather liked that.   " I was wondering if you did not believe this to be some silly intrigue."

" I gave thought to but two things : that you were jesting, or that you were in need of a gentleman as well as a man of courage.   Tell me, what is the danger, and why do you ask me if I am armed? " It occurred to him that her own charm and beauty might be the greatest danger he could possibly face. More and more grew the certainty that he had seen her somewhere in the past.

" Ah, if I only knew what the danger was.   But that it exists I am positive.   Within the past two weeks, on odd nights, there have been strange noises here and there about the house, especially in the chimney.   My father, being slightly deaf, believes that these sounds are wholly imaginative on my part. This is the first spring in years we have resided here.   It is really our summer home.   I am not more than normally timorous.   Some one we do not know enters the house at will.   How or why I can't unravel.   Nothing has ever disappeared, either money, jewels, or silver, though I have laid many traps.   There is the huge fireplace in the library,

and my room is above.   I have heard a tapping, like
some one hammering gently on stone.   I have examined the bricks and so has my father, but neither
of us has discovered anything.   Three days ago I
placed flour thinly on the flagstone before the fireplace.   There were footprints in the morning — of
rubber shoes.   When I called in my father, the
maid had unfortunately cleaned the stone without
observing anything.   So my father still holds that I
am subject to dreams.   His secretary, whom he had
for three years, has left him.   The butler's and servants' quarters are in the rear of the other wing.
They have never been disturbed."

"I am not a detective, Miss Killigrew," he remarked, as she paused.

"No, but you seem to be a man of invention and
of good spirit.   Will you help me?"

"In whatever way I can."   His opinion at that
moment perhaps agreed with that of her father.
Still, a test could be of no harm.   She was a charming young woman, and he was assured that beneath
this present concern there was a lively, humorous
disposition.   He had a month for idleness, and why
not play detective for a change?   Then he recalled

the trespasser in the park. By George, she might
be right!

"Come, then, and I will present you to my father.
His deafness is not so bad that one has to speak
loudly. To speak distinctly will be simplest."

She thereupon conducted him into the library.
His quick glance, thrown here and there absorb-
ingly, convinced him that there were at least five
thousand volumes in the cases, a magnificent private
collection, considering that the owner was not a
lawyer, and that these books were not dry and musty
precedents from the courts of appeals and supreme.
He was glad to see that some of his old friends were
here, too, and that the shelves were not wholly given
over to piracy. What a hobby to follow! What
adventures all within thirty square feet! And a
shiver passed over his spine as he saw several tattered black flags hanging from the walls; the real
articles, too, now faded to a rusty brown. Over
what smart and lively heeled brigs had they floated,
these sinister jolly-rogers? For in a room like
this they could not be other than genuine. All his
journalistic craving for stories awakened.

Behind a broad, flat, mahogany desk, with a

green-shaded student lamp at his elbow, sat a bright-cheeked, white-haired man, writing. Fitzgerald instantly recognized him. Abruptly his gaze returned to the girl. Yes, now he knew. It was stupid of him not to have remembered at once. Why, it was she who had given the bunch of violets that day to the old veteran in Napoleon's tomb. To have remembered the father and to have forgotten the daughter!

" I was wondering where I had seen you," he said lowly.

" Where was that? "

" In Napoleon's tomb, nearly a year ago. You gave an old French soldier a bouquet of violets. I was there."

" Were you? " As a matter of fact his face was absolutely new to her. " I am not very good at recalling faces. And in traveling one sees so many."

" That is true." Queer sort of girl, not to show just a little more interest. The moment was not ordinary by any means. He was disappointed.

" Father! " she called, in a clear, sweet voice, for the admiral had not heard them enter.

At the call he raised his head and took off his

Mandarin spectacles. Like all sailors, he never had any trouble in seeing distances clearly; the difficulty lay in books, letters, and small type.

" What is it, Laura? "

" This is Mr. Fitzgerald, the new secretary," she answered blandly.

" Aha! Bring a chair over and sit down. What did you say the name is, Laura? "

" Fitzgerald."

" Sit down, Mr. Fitzgerald," repeated the admiral cordially.

Fitzgerald desired but one thing; the privilege of laughter!

CHAPTER V

NO FALSE PRETENSES

A PRIVATE secretary, and only one way out! If the girl had been kind enough to stand her ground with him he would not have cared so much. But there she was vanishing beyond the door. There was a suggestion of feline cruelty in thus abandoning him. He dared not call her back. What the devil should he say to the admiral? There was one thing he knew absolutely nothing about, and this was the duties of a private secretary to a retired admiral who had riches, a yacht, a hobby, and a beautiful, though impulsive daughter. His thought became irrelevant, as is frequent when one faces a crisis, humorous or tragic; here indeed was the coveted opportunity to study at close range the habits of a man who spent less than his income.

"Come, come; draw up your chair, Mr. Fitzgerald."

66

"I beg your pardon; I — that is, I was looking at those flags, sir," stuttered the self-made victim of circumstances.

"Oh, those? Good examples of their kind; early part of the nineteenth century. Picked them up one cruise in the Indies. That faded one belonged to Morgan, the bloodthirsty ruffian. I've always regretted that I wasn't born a hundred years ago. Think of bottling them up in a shallow channel and raking 'em fore and aft!" With a bang of his fist on the desk, setting the ink-wells rattling like old bones, "That would have been sport!"

The keen, blue, sailor's eye seemed to bore right through Fitzgerald, who thought the best thing he could do was to sit down at once, which he did. The ticket agent had said that the admiral was of a quiet pattern, but this start wasn't much like it. The fire in the blue eyes suddenly gave way to a twinkle, and the old man laughed.

"Did I frighten you, Mr. Fitzgerald?"

"Not exactly."

"Well, every secretary I've had has expected to see a red-nosed, swearing, peg-legged sailor; so I

thought I'd soften the blow for you. Don't worry.
Sailor?"

"Not in the technical sense," answered Fitzgerald, warming. "I know a stanchion from an
anchor and a rope from a smoke-stack. But as for
travel, I believe that I have crossed all the high and
middle seas."

"Sounds good. Australia, East Indies, China,
the Antilles, Gulf, and the South Atlantic?"

"Yes; round the Horn, too, and East Africa."
Fitzgerald remembered his instructions and spoke
clearly.

"Well, well; you are a find. In what capacity
have you taken these voyages?"

Here was the young man's opportunity. This
was a likeable old sea-dog, and he determined not
to impose upon him another moment. Some men,
for the sake of the adventure, would have left the
truth to be found out later, to the disillusion of all
concerned. The abrupt manner in which Miss Killigrew had abandoned him merited some revenge.

"Admiral, I'm afraid there has been a mistake,
and before we go any further I'll be glad to explain.

I'm not a private secretary and never have been one. I should be less familiar with the work than a Chinaman. I am a special writer for the magazines, and have been at odd times a war correspondent." And then he went on to describe the little comedy of the statuettes, and it was not without some charm in the telling.

Plainly the admiral was nonplussed. That girl; that minx, with her innocent eyes and placid face! He got up, and Fitzgerald awaited the explosion. His expectancy missed fire. The admiral exploded, but with laughter.

" I beg pardon, Mr. Fitzgerald, and I beg it again on my daughter's behalf. What would you do in my place?"

" Show me the door at once and have done with it."

" I'm hanged if I do! You shall have a toddy for your pains, and, by cracky, Laura shall mix it." He pushed the butler's bell. " Tell Miss Laura that I wish to see her at once."

" Very well, sir."

She appeared shortly. If Fitzgerald admired

her beauty he yet more admired her perfect poise
and unconcern. Many another woman would have
evinced some embarrassment. Not she.

"Laura, what's the meaning of this hoax?" the
admiral demanded sternly. "Mr. Fitzgerald tells
me that he had no idea you were hiring him as my
secretary."

"I am sure he hadn't the slightest." The look
she sent Fitzgerald was full of approval. "He
hadn't any idea at all save that I asked him to come
here at eight this evening. And his confession
proves that I haven't made any mistake."

"But what in thunder —"

"Father!"

"My dear, give me credit for resisting the desire
to make the term stronger. Mr. Fitzgerald's joke,
I take it, bothered no one. Yours has put him in a
peculiar embarrassment. What does it mean?
You went to the city to get me a first-class secretary."

"Mr. Fitzgerald has the making of one, I believe."

"But on your word I sent a capable man away

half an hour gone. He could speak half a dozen languages."

"Mr. Fitzgerald is, perhaps, as efficient."

Fitzgerald's wonder grew and grew.

"But he doesn't want to be a secretary. He doesn't know anything about the work. And I haven't got the time to teach him, even if he wanted the place."

"Father," began the girl, the fun leaving her eyes and her lips becoming grave, "I do not like the noises at night. I have not suggested the police, because robbery is *not* the motive."

"Laura, that's all tommyrot. This is an old house, and the wood always creaks with a change of temperature. But this doesn't seem to touch Mr. Fitzgerald."

The girl shrugged.

"Well, I'm glad I told that German chap not to leave till he heard again from me. I'll hire him. He looks like a man who wouldn't let noises worry him. You will find your noises are entirely those of imagination."

"Have it that way," she agreed patiently.

"But here's Mr. Fitzgerald still," said the admiral pointedly.

"Not long ago you said to me that if ever I saw the son of David Fitzgerald to bring him home. Till yesterday I never saw him; only then because Mrs. Coldfield pointed him out and wondered what he was doing with a tray of statuettes around his neck. As I could not invite him to come home with me, I did the next best thing; I invited him to call on me. I was told that he was fond of adventures, so I gave the invitation as much color as I could. Do I stand pardoned?"

"Indeed you do!" cried Fitzgerald. So this was the Killigrew his father had known?

"David Fitzgerald, your father? That makes all the difference in the world." The admiral thrust out a hand. "Your father wasn't a good business man, nor was he in the navy, but he could draw charts of the Atlantic coast with his eyes shut. Laura, you get the whisky and sugar and hot water. You haven't brought me a secretary, but you have brought under my roof the son of an old friend."

She laughed. It was rich and free-toned laugh-

ter, good for any man to hear. As she went to prepare the toddy, the music echoed again through the
hall.

"Sometimes I wake up in the morning with a
new gray hair," sighed the admiral. "What would
you do with a girl like that?"

"I'd hang on to her as long as I could," earnestly.

"I shall," grimly. "Your father and I were old
friends. There wasn't a yacht on these waters
that could show him her heels, not even my own.
You don't mean to tell me you're no yachtsman!
Why, it ought to be in the blood."

"Oh, I can handle small craft, but I don't know
much about the engine-room. What time does the
next train return to New York?"

"For you there'll be no train under a week.
You're going to stay here, since you've been the victim of a hoax."

"Disabuse your mind there, sir. I don't know
when I've enjoyed anything so thoroughly."

"But you'll stay? Oh, yes!" as Fitzgerald
shook his head. "The secretary can do the work
here while you and I can take care of the rats in
the hold. Laura's just imagining things, but we'll

humor her. If there's any trouble with the chimney, why, we'll get a bricklayer and pull it down."

"Miss Killigrew may have some real cause for alarm. I saw a man, or rather, I heard him, running, as I came up the road from the gates. I called to him, but he did not answer."

"Is that so? Wasn't the porter at the gates when you came in?"

"No. The footpath was free."

"This begins to look serious. If the porter isn't there the gate bell rings, I can open it myself by wire. I never bother about it at night, unless I am expecting some one. But in the daytime I can see from here whether or not I wish to open the gate. A man running in the park, eh? Little good it will do him. The house is a network of burglar alarms."

"Wires can be cut and quickly repaired."

"But this is no house to rob. All my valuables, excepting these books, are in New York. The average burglar isn't of a literary turn of mind. Still, if Laura has really heard something, all the more reason why you should make us a visit. Wait a moment. I've an idea." The admiral set the burglar alarm and tried it. The expression on his face was blank. " Am I getting deafer? "

" No bell rang," said Fitzgerald quickly.

" By cracky, if Laura *is* right! But not a word to her, mind. When she goes up-stairs we'll take a trip into the cellar and have a look at the main wire. You've got to stay; that's all there is about it. This is serious. I hadn't tested the wires in a week."

" Perhaps it's only a fuse."

" We can soon find out about that. Sh! Not a word to her! "

She entered with a tray and two steaming toddies, as graceful a being as Hebe before she spilled the precious drop. The two men could not keep their eyes off her, the one with loving possession, the other with admiration not wholly free from unrest. The daring manner in which she had lured him here would never be forgetable. And she had known him at the start? And that merry Mrs. Coldfield in the plot!

" I hope this will cheer you, father."

" It always does," replied the admiral, as he took the second glass. " I have asked Mr. Fitzgerald to spend a week with us."

"Thank you, father. It was thoughtful of you. If you had not asked him, the pleasure of doing so would have been mine. Mrs. Coldfield pointed you out to me as a most ungrateful fellow, because you never called on your father's or mother's friends any more, but preferred to gallivant round the world. You will stay? We are very unconventional here."

"It is all very good of you. I *am* rather a lonesome chap. The newspapers and magazines have spoiled me. There's never a moment so happy to me as when I am ordered to some strange country, thousands of miles away. It is in the blood. Thanks, very much; I shall be very happy to stay. My hand-bag, however, is at Swan's Hotel, and there's very little in it."

"A trifling matter to send to New York for what you need," said the admiral, mightily pleased to have a man to talk to who was not paid to reply. "I'll have William bring the cart round and take you down."

"No, no; I had much rather walk. I'll turn up some time in the morning, say luncheon, if that will be agreeable to you."

" As you please. Only, I should like to save you an unpleasant walk in the dark."

" I don't mind. A dark street in a country village this side of the Atlantic holds little or no dan-ger."

" I offered to build a first-class lighting plant if the town would agree to pay the running expenses; but the council threw it over. They want me to build a library. Not much! Hold on," as Fitzgerald was rising. " You are not going right away. I shan't permit that. Just a little visit first."

Fitzgerald resumed his chair.

" Have a cigar. Laura is used to it."

" But does Miss Killigrew like it? " laughing.

" Cigars, and pipes, and cigarettes," she returned. " I am really fond of the aroma. I have tried to acquire the cigarette habit, but I have yet to learn what satisfaction you men get out of it."

Conversation veered in various directions, and finally rested upon the subject of piracy; and here the admiral proved himself a rare scholar. By some peculiar inadvertency, as he was in the middle of one of his own adventures, his finger touched the burglar alarm. Clang! Brrrr! From top to bottom of the house came the shock of differently voiced bells. The two men gazed at each other dumfounded. But the girl laughed merrily.

"You touched the alarm, father."

"I rather believe I did. And a few minutes before you came in with the toddies I tried it and it didn't work."

It took some time to quiet the servants; and when that was done Fitzgerald determined to go down to the village.

"Good night, Mr. Fitzgerald," said the girl. "Better beware; this house is haunted."

"We'll see if we can't lay that ghost, as they say," he responded.

The admiral came to the door. "What do you make of it?" he whispered.

"You possibly did not press the button squarely the first time." And that was Fitzgerald's genuine belief.

"By the way, will you take a note for me to Swan's? It will not take me a moment to scribble it."

"Certainly."

Finally the young man found himself in the park,

heading quickly toward the gates. He searched the night keenly, but this time he neither heard nor saw any one. Then he permitted his fancy to take short flights. Interesting situation! To find himself a guest here, when he had come keyed up for something strenuous! Pirates and jolly-rogers and mysterious trespassers and silent bells, to say nothing of a beautiful young woman with a leaning toward adventure! But the most surprising turn was yet to come.

In the office of Swan's hotel the landlord sat snoozing peacefully behind the desk. There was only one customer. He was a gray-haired, ruddy-visaged old salt in white duck — at this time of year! — and a blue sack-coat dotted with shining brass buttons, the whole five-foot-four topped by a gold-braided officer's cap. He was drinking what is jocularly called a " schooner " of beer, and finishing this he lurched from the room with a rolling, hiccoughing gait, due entirely to a wooden peg which extended from his right knee down to a highly polished brass ferrule.

Fitzgerald awakened the landlord and gave him the admiral's note.

"You will be sure and give this to the gentleman in the morning?"

"Certainly, sir. Mr. Karl Breitmann," reading the superscription aloud. "Yes, sir; first thing in the morning."

CHAPTER VI

SOME EXPLANATIONS

KARL BREITMANN! Fitzgerald pulled off a shoe, and carefully deposited it on the floor beside his chair. Private secretary to Rear Admiral Killigrew, retired; Karl Breitmann! He drew off the second shoe, and placed it, with military preciseness, close to the first. Absently, he rose, with the intention of putting the pair in the hall, but remembered before he got as far as the door that it was not customary in America to put one's shoes outside in the halls. Ultimately, they would have been stolen or have remained there till the trump of doom.

Could there be two Breitmanns by the name of Karl? Here and there, across the world, he had heard of Breitmann, but never had he seen him since that meeting in Paris. And, simply because he had proved to be an enthusiastic student of Napoleon, like himself, he had taken the man to dinner. But that was nothing. Under the same circumstances he would have done the same thing again. There had been something fascinating about the fellow, either his voice or his manner. And there could be no doubting that he had been at ebb tide; the shiny coat, the white, but ragged linen, the cracked patent leathers.

A baron, and to reach the humble grade of private secretary to an eccentric millionaire — for the admiral, with all his kindliness and common sense, *was* eccentric — this was a fall. Where were his newspapers? There was a dignity to foreign work, even though in Europe the pay is small. There was trouble going on here and there, petty wars and political squabbles. Yes, where were his newspapers? Had he tried New York? If not, in that case, he — Fitzgerald — could be of some solid assistance. And Cathewe knew him, or had met him.

Fitzgerald had buffeted the high and low places; he seldom made mistakes in judging men offhand, an art acquired only after many initial blunders. This man Breitmann was no sham; he was a scholar, a gentleman, a fine linguist, versed in politics and war. Well, the little mystery would be brushed aside in the morning. Breitmann would certainly recognize him.

But to have forgotten the girl! To have permitted a course of events to discover her! Shameful! He jumped into bed, and pulled the coverlet close to his nose, and was soon asleep, sleep broken by fantastic dreams, in which the past and present mixed with the improbable chances of the future.

Thump-thump, thump-thump! To Fitzgerald's fogged hearing, it was like the pulse beating in the bowels of a ship, only that it stopped and began at odd intervals, intermittently. At the fourth recurrence, he sat up, to find that it was early morning, and that the sea lay, gray and leaden, under the pearly haze of dawn. Thump-thump! He rubbed his eyes, and laughed. It could be no less a person than the old sailor in the summer-yachting toggery. Drat 'em! These sailors were always trying to beat sun-up. At length, the peg left the room above, and banged along the hall and bumped down the stairs. Then all became still once more, and the listener snuggled under the covers again, and slept soundly till eight. Outside, the day was full, clear, and windy.

On the way to the dining-room, he met the man. The scars were a little deeper in color and the face was thinner, but there was no shadow of doubt in Fitzgerald's mind.

" Breitmann? " he said, with a friendly hand.

The other stood still. There was no recognition in his eyes; at least, Fitzgerald saw none.

" Breitmann is my name, sir," he replied courteously.

" I am Fitzgerald; don't you remember me? We dined in Paris last year, after we had spent the afternoon with the Napoleonic relics. You haven't forgotten Macedonia? "

Breitmann took the speaker by the arm, and turned him round. Fitzgerald had been standing with his back to the light. The scrutiny was short. The eyes of the Bavarian softened, though the quizzical wrinkles at the corners remained unchanged. All at once his whole expression warmed.

" It is you? And what do you here? " extending both hands.

Some doubt lingered in Fitzgerald's mind; yet the welcome was perfect, from whichever point he chose to look. " Come in to breakfast," he said, " and I'll tell you."

" My table is here; sit by the window. Who was it said that the world is small? Do you know, that dinner in Paris was the first decent meal I had had in a week? And I didn't recognize you at once! *Herr Gott!* " with sudden weariness. " Perhaps I have had reason to forget many things. But you? "

Fitzgerald spread his napkin over his knees. There was only one other man breakfasting. He was a small, wiry person, white of hair, and spectacled, and was at that moment curiously employed. He had pinned to the table a small butterfly, yellow, with tiny dots on the wings. He was critically inspecting his find through a jeweler's glass.

" I am visiting friends here," began Fitzgerald. " Rear Admiral Killigrew was an old friend of my father's. I did not expect to remain, but the admiral and his daughter insisted; so I am sending to New York for my luggage, and will go up this morning." He saw no reason for giving fuller details.

" So it must have been you who brought the admiral's note. It is fate. Thanks. Some day that casual dinner may give you good interest."

The little man with the butterfly bent lower over his prize.

" Do you believe in curses? " asked Breitmann.

" Ordinary, every-day curses, yes; but not in Roman anathemas."

" Neither of those. I mean the curse that sometimes dogs a man, day and night; the curse of misfortune. I was hungry that night in Paris; I have been hungry many times since. I have held honorable places; to-day, I become a servant at seventy-five dollars a month and my bread and butter. A private secretary."

" But why aren't you with some newspaper? " asked Fitzgerald, breaking his eggs.

Breitmann drew up his shoulders. " For the same reason that I am renting my brains as a private secretary. It was the last thing I could find, and still retain a little self-respect. My heart was dead when the admiral told me he had already engaged a secretary. But your note brought me the position."

" But the newspapers? "

" None of them will employ me."

" In New York, with your credentials? "

" Even so."

" I don't quite understand."

" It would take too long to explain."

" I can give you some letters."

" Thank you. It would be useless. Secretly and subterraneously, I have had the bottom knocked out from under my feet. Why, God knows! But no more of that. Some day I will give you my version."

The little man smiled over his butterfly, took out a wallet, something on the pattern of a fisherman's, and put the new-found specimen into one of the mica compartments, in which other dead butterflies of variant beauty reposed.

" So I become a private secretary, till the time offers something better." Breitmann stared at the sea.

" I am sorry. I wish I could help you. Better let me try." Fitzgerald stirred his coffee. " You are convinced that there is some cabal working against you in the newspaper business? That seems strange. Some of them must have heard of your work — London, Paris, Berlin. Have you tried them all?"

"Yes. Nothing for me, but promises as thick as yonder sands."

The little man rose, and walked out of the room, smiling.

"Splendid!" he murmured. "What a specimen to add to my collection!"

"Do you know what your duties will be?" Fitzgerald inquired.

"They will consist of replying to begging letters from the needy and deserving, from crazy inventors, and ministers. In the meantime, I am to do translating, together with indexing a vast library devoted to pirates. Droll, isn't it?" Breitmann laughed, but this time without bitterness.

"It is a harmless hobby," rather resenting Breitmann's tone.

"More than that," quickly; "it is philanthropic, since it will employ me for some length of time."

"When do they expect you?"

"At half-after ten."

"We'll go up together, then. Did you see the admiral's daughter?"

"A daughter? Has he one?" Breitmann accepted this news with an expression of disfavor.

"Yes; and charming, I can tell you. It's all very odd. In Paris that night, they both sat at the next table."

"Why did you not speak to them?"

"Didn't know who they were. The admiral was one of my father's boyhood friends, and I did not meet them till very recently;" which was all true enough. For some unaccountable reason, Fitzgerald found that he was on guard. "I have ordered an open carriage. If you have any trunks, I can take them up for you."

"It will be good of you."

They proceeded to finish the repast, and then sought the office, for their reckoning. Later, they strolled toward the water front. Fitzgerald, during moments when the talk lagged, thought over the meeting. There was a false ring to it somewhere. If Breitmann had been turned down in all the offices in New York, there must have been some good cause. Newspapers were not passing over men of this fellow's experience, unless he had been proved untrustworthy. Breitmann had not told him everything; he had even told him too little. Still, he would withhold his judgment till he heard from New York on the subject. Cathewe hadn't been enthusiastic over the name; but Cathewe was never inclined to enthusiasms.

Passing the angle of the freight depot brought the little harbor into full view. A fine white yacht lay tugging at her cables.

"There's a beauty," said Fitzgerald admiringly.

"She looks as if she could take care of herself. How fresh the green water-line looks! She'll be fast in moderate weather; a fair thousand tons, perhaps."

"A close guess."

"I understand she belongs to my employer. I hope he takes the sea soon. I suppose you know that I have knocked about some as a sailor."

"That will help you into the good graces of the admiral."

"How dull and uninteresting the coast-lines are here! No gardens, no palms, nothing of beauty."

"You must remember the immensity of this coast and that our summers are really less than three months. Here comes one who can tell us about the yacht," cried Fitzgerald, espying the peg-legged sailor. "I say!" he hailed, as the old sailor, drew nigh; "you are on the *Laura,* are you not?"

"Yessir. An' I've bin on her since she wus commissioned as a pleasure yacht, sir. Capt'n."

"Ah!"

"Fought under th' commodore in th' war, sir; an' he knows me, an' I knows him; an' when Flanagan is on th' bridge, he doesn't signal no pilots between Key West an' St. Johns."

"I am visiting the admiral," said Fitzgerald, amused.

"Oh!" Captain Flanagan ducked, with his hand to his cap. On land, he was likely to imitate landsmen in manners and politeness; but on board he tipped his hat to nobody; leastwise, to nobody but Miss Laura, bless her heart! "I reckon one o' you is th' new sec'rety."

"Yes, I am the new secretary," replied Breitmann, unsmiling.

"Furrin parts?"

"Yes."

"Well, well!" as if, while he couldn't help the fact, it was none the less to be pitied. "You'll be comin' aboard soon, then. Off for th' Banks. Take my word for it, you'll find her as stiddy as one o' your floatin' hotels, sir, where you don't see no sailor but a deck hand as swabs th' scuppers when a beam sea's on. Good mornin'!" And Captain Flanagan stumped off toward the village.

Breitmann shrugged contemptuously.

"He may not be in European yachting form," admitted Fitzgerald, "but he's the kind of man who makes a navy a good fighting machine."

"But we usually pick out gentlemen to captain our private yachts."

"Oh, this Flanagan is an exception. There is probably a fighting bond between him and the admiral; that makes some difference. You observed, he called the owner by the title of commodore, as he did thirty-five years ago. Ten o'clock; we should be going up."

The carriage was at the hotel when they returned. They bundled in their traps, and drove away.

The little man now dropped into the railway sta-

tion, and stuck his head into the ticket aperture.
The agent, who was seated before the telegraph
keys, looked up.

" No tickets before half-past ten, sir."

" I am not wanting a ticket. I wish to know if
I can send a cable from here."

" A cable? Sure. Where to? "

" Paris."

" Yes, sir. I telegraph it to the cable office in
New York, and they do the rest. Here are some
blanks."

The other wrote some hieroglyphics, which made
the address impossible to decipher, save that it was
directed mainly to Paris. The body of the cable-
gram contained a single word. The writer paid the
toll, and went away.

" Now, what would you think of that? " murmured the operator, scratching his head in perplex-
ity. " Well, the company gets the money, so it's
all the same to me. Butterflies; and all the rest in
French. Next time it'll be bugs. All right; here
goes! "

CHAPTER VII

THE house at the top of the hill had two names. It had once been called The Watch Tower, for reasons but vaguely known by the present generation of villagers. To-day it was generally styled The Pines. Yet even this had fallen into disuse, save on the occupant's letter paper. When any one asked where Rear Admiral Killigrew lived, he was directed to " the big white house at the top o' the hill."

The Killigrews had not been born and bred there. Its builder had been a friend of King George; that is, his sympathies had been with taxation without representation. One day he sold the manor cheap. His reasons were sufficient. It then became the property of a wealthy trader, who died in it. This was in 1809. His heirs, living, and preferring to live, in Philadelphia, put up a sign; and being of

94

careful disposition, kept the place in excellent re-
pair.

In the year 1816, it passed into the hands of a
Frenchman, and during his day the villagers called
the house The Watch Tower; for the Frenchman
was always on the high balcony, telescope in hand,
gazing seaward. No one knew his name. He
dealt with the villagers through his servant, who
could speak English, himself professing that he
could not speak the language. He was a recluse,
almost a hermit. At odd times, a brig would be
seen dropping anchor in the offing. She was always
from across the water, from the old country, as villagers to this day insist upon calling Europe. The
manor during these peaceful invasions showed signs
of life. Men from the brig went up to the big
white house, and remained there for a week or a
month. And they were lean men, battle-scarred
and fierce of eye, some with armless sleeves, some
with stiff legs, some twisted with rheumatism. All
spoke French, and spat whenever they saw the per-
fidious flag of old England. This was not marked
against them as a demerit, for the War of 1812 was
yet smoking here and there along the Great Lakes.

Suddenly, they would up and away, and the manor would reassume its repellent aloofness. Each time they returned their number was diminished. Old age had succeeded war as a harvester. In 1822, the mysterious old recluse surrendered the ghost. His heirs — ignored and hated by him for their affiliation with the Bourbons — sold it to the father of the admiral.

The manor wasn't haunted. The hard-headed longshoremen and sailors who lived at the foot of the hill were a practical people, to whom spirits were something mostly and generally put up in bottles, and emptied on sunless, blustery days. Still, they wouldn't have been human if they had not done some romancing.

There were a dozen yarns, each at variance with the other. First, the old " monseer " was a fugitive from France; everybody granted that. Second, that he had helped to cut off King Lewis' head; but nobody could prove that. Third, that he was a retired pirate; but retired pirates always wound up their days in riotous living, so this theory died. Fourth, that he had been a great soldier in the Napoleonic wars, and this version had some basis, as the old man's face was slashed and cut, some of his fingers were missing, and he limped. Again, he had been banished from France for a share in the Hundred Days. But, all told, nothing was proved conclusively, though the villagers burrowed and delved and hunted and pried, as villagers are prone to do when a person appears among them and keeps his affairs strictly to himself.

'But the next generation partly forgot, and the present only indifferently remembered that, once upon a time, a French *emigré* had lived and died up there. They knew all there was to know about the present owner. It was all compactly written and pictured in a book of history, which book agents sold over the land, even here in Dalton.

All these things Fitzgerald and his companion learned from the driver on the journey up the incline.

" Where was this Frenchman buried? " inquired Breitmann softly.

" In th' cemet'ry jest over th' hill. But nobody knows jest *where* he is now. Stone's gone, an' th' ground's all level that end. He wus on'y a Frenchman. But th' admiral, now you're talkin'! He pays cash, an' don't make no bargain rates, when he wants a job done. Go wan, y' ol' nag; what y' dreamin' of?"

"There might be history in that corner of the graveyard," said Breitmann.

"Who knows? Good many strange bits of furniture found their way over here during those tremendous times. Beautiful place in the daytime; eh?" Fitzgerald added, with an inclination toward The Pines.

"More like an Italian villa than an Englishman's home. Good gardeners, I should say."

"Culture and money will make a bog attractive."

"Is the admiral cultured, then?"

"I should imagine so. But I am sure the daughter is. Not that veneer which passes for it, but that deep inner culture, which gives a deft, artistic touch to the hand, softens the voice, gives elegance to the carriage, with a heart and mind nicely balanced. Judge for yourself, when you see her. If there is any rare knickknack in the house, it will have been put there by the mother's hand or the daughter's. The admiral, I believe, occupies himself with his books, his butterflies, and his cruises."

" A daughter.   She is cultured, you say?   Ah, if culture would only take beauty in hand!   But always she selects the plainer of two women."

Fitzgerald smiled inwardly.   " I have told you she is not plain."

" Oh, beautiful," thoughtfully.   " Culture and beauty; I shall be pleased to observe."

" H'm!   If there is any marrow in your bones, my friend, you'll show more interest when you see her."   This was thought, not spoken.   Fitzgerald wasn't going to rhapsodize over Miss Killigrew's charms.   It would have been not only incautious, but suspicious.   Aloud, he said: " She has a will of her own, I take it; however, of a quiet, resolute order."

" So long as she is not capricious, and does not interfere with my work —"

" Or peace of mind!" interrupted Fitzgerald, with prophetic suddenness, which was modified by laughter.

" No, my friend; no woman has ever yet stirred my heart, though many have temporarily captured my senses.   A man in my position has no right to love," with a dignity which surprised his auditor.

Fitzgerald looked down at the wheels. There was something even more than dignity, an indefinable something, a superiority which Fitzgerald's present attitude of mind could not approach.

"This man," he mused, "will afford some interesting study. One would think that nothing less than a grand duke was riding in this rattling old carryall." There was silence for a time. "I must warn you, Breitmann, that, in all probability, you will have your meals at the table with the admiral and his daughter; at least, in this house."

"At the same table? It would hardly be so in Europe. But it pleases me. I have been alone so much that I grow moody; and that is not good."

There was always that trifling German accent, no matter what tongue he used, but it was perceptible only to the trained ear. And yet, to Fitzgerald's mind, the man was at times something Gallic in his liveliness.

"You will never use your title, then?"

Breitmann laughed. "No."

"You have made a great mistake. You should have fired the first shot with it. You would have married an heiress by this time," ironically, " and all your troubles would be over."

" Or begun," in the same spirit. " I'm no fortune hunter, in the sense you mean. Pah! I have no debts; no crumbling *schloss* to rebuild. All I ask is to be let alone," with a flash of that moodiness of which he had spoken. " How long will you be here?"

" Can't say. Three or four days, perhaps. It all depends. What shall I say about you to them?"

" As little as possible."

" And that's really about all I could say," with a suggestion.

But the other failed to meet the suggestion half-way.

" You might forget about my ragged linen in Paris," acridly.

" I'll omit that," good-naturedly. " Come, be cheerful; fortune's wheel will turn, and it pulls up as well as down. Remember that."

" I must be on the ascendancy, for God knows that I am at the nadir just at present." He breathed in the sweet freshness which still clung to the morning, and settled his shoulders like a recruiting sergeant.

"How well the man has studied his English!" thought Fitzgerald. He rarely hesitated for a word, and his idioms were always nicely adjusted.

The admiral was alone. He received them with an easy courtliness, which is more noticeable in the old world than in the new. He directed the servants to take charge of the luggage, and to Breitmann there was never a word about work. That had all been decided by letter. He urged the new secretary to return to the library as soon as he had established himself.

"Strange that you should know the man," said the admiral. "It comes in pat. From what you say, he must be a brilliant fellow. But this situation seems rather out of his line."

"We all have our ups and downs, admiral. I've known a pinch or two myself. We are an improvident lot, we writers, who wander round the globe; rich to-day, poor to-morrow. But on the other hand, it's something to set down on paper what a king says, the turn of a battle, to hobnob with famous men, explorers, novelists, painters, soldiers, scientists, to say nothing of the meat in the pie and the bottom crust. I'm going to write a novel some day myself."

" Here," said the admiral, with a sweep of the hand, which included the row upon row of books, " come here to do it. Make it a pirate story; there's always room for another."

" But it takes a Stevenson to write it. It is very good of you, though. Where is Miss Killigrew this morning? "

" She hasn't returned from her ride. Ah! Come in, Mr. Breitmann, and sit down. By the way, you two must be fair horsemen."

Breitmann smiled, and Fitzgerald laughed.

" I dare say," replied the latter, " that there's only one thing we two haven't ridden: ostriches. Camels and elephants and donkeys; we've done some warm sprinting. Eh, Breitmann? "

The secretary agreed with a nod. He was rather grateful for Fitzgerald's presence. This occupation was not going to be menial; at the least, there would be pleasant sides to it. And, then, it might not take him a week to complete his own affair.

There was no misreading the admiral; he was a gentleman, affable, kindly, and a good story-teller, too, crisp and to the point, sailor fashion. Breit-mann cleverly drew him out. Pirates! He dared not smile. Why, there was hardly such a thing in the pearl zone, and China was on the highway to respectability. And every once in so often there was a futile treasure hunt! He grew cold. If this old man but knew!

"Do you know butterflies, Mr. Fitzgerald?"

"Social?"

The admiral laughed. "No. The law doesn't permit you to stick pins in that kind. No; I mean that kind," indicating the cases.

Both young men admitted that this field had been left unexplored by either of them.

It was during a lull, when the talk had fallen to the desultory, that the hall door opened, and Laura came in. Her cheeks glowed like the sunny side of a Persian peach; her eyes sparkled; between her moist red lips there was a flash of firm, white teeth; the seal-brown hair glinted a Venetian red — for at that moment she stood in the path of the sunshine which poured in at the window — and blown tendrils in picturesque disorder escaped from under her hat.

The three men rose hastily; the father with pride, Fitzgerald with gladness, and Breitmann with doubt and wonder and fear.

CHAPTER VIII

SOME BIRDS IN A CHIMNEY

IT might be truthfully said that the tableau lasted as long as she willed it to last. Perhaps she read in the three masculine faces turned toward her a triangular admiration, since it emanated from three given points, and took from it a modest pinch for her vanity. Vain she never was; still, she was not without a share of vanity, that vanity of the artless, needing no sacrifices, which is gratified and appeased by a smile. It pleased her to know that she was lovely; and it doubled her pleasure to realize that her loveliness pleased others. She demanded no hearts; she craved no jewels, no flattery. She warmed when eyes told her she was beautiful; but she chilled whenever the lips took up the speech, and voiced it. She was one of those happy beings in either sex who can amuse themselves, who can hold pleasant communion with the inner self, who can find romance in old houses, and yet love books, who prefer sunrises and sunsets at first hand, still loving a good painting.

Perhaps this trend of character was the result of her inherited love of the open. With almost unlimited funds under her own hand, she lived simply. She was never happy in smart society, though it was always making demands upon her. When abroad, she was generally prowling through queer little shops instead of mingling with the dress parades on the grand-hotel terraces. There was no great battle-field in Europe she had not trod upon. She knew them so well that she could people each field with the familiar bright regiments, bayonets and sabers, pikes and broadswords, axes and crossbowmen, matchlock and catapult, rifles and cannon.

And what she did not know of naval warfare her father did. They were very companionable. There was never any jealousy on the part of the admiral. Indeed, he was always grateful when some young man evinced a deep regard for his daughter. He would have her always, married or unmarried. He was rich enough, and the son-in-law should live with him. He was so assured of

her good judgment, he knew that whenever this son-
in-law came along, there would be another man in
the family. He had long ceased to bother his head
about the flylike buzzing of fortune hunters. He
had been father and mother and brother to the
child, and with wisdom.

She smiled at her father, gave her hand to Fitzgerald, who found it warm and moist from the ride,
and glanced inquiringly at Breitmann.

"My dear," said her father, "this is Mr. Breitmann, my new secretary."

That gentleman bowed stiffly, and the scars faded
somewhat when he observed that her hand was extended in welcome. This unconventionality rather
confused him, and as he took the hand he almost
kissed it. She understood the innocence of the
gesture, and saved him from embarrassment by
withdrawing the hand casually.

"I hope you will like it here," was the pleasant
wish.

"Thank you, I shall."

"You are German?" quickly.

"I was born in Bavaria, Miss Killigrew."

"The name should have told me." She excused herself.

"Oho!" thought Fitzgerald, with malicious exultancy. "If she doesn't interfere with your work!"

But with introspection, this exultancy grew suddenly dim. How about himself? Yes. Here was a question that would bear some close inspection. Was it really the wish to capture a supposable burglar? He made short work of this analysis. He never lied to others — not even in his work, which every one knows is endowed with special licenses in regard to truth — nor did he every play the futile, if soothing, game of lying to himself. This girl was different from the ordinary run of girls; she might become dangerous. He determined then and there not to prolong his visit more than three or four days; just to satisfy her that there was no ghost in the chimney. Then he would return to New York. He had no more right than Breitmann to fall in love with the daughter of a millionaire. Loving her was not impossible, but leaving at an early day would go toward lessening the probability.

He was not afraid of Breitmann; he was foreigner enough to accept at once his place, and to appreciate that he and this girl stood at the two ends of the world.

And Breitmann's mind, which had, up to this time, been deep and unruffled as a pool, became strangely disturbed.

The time moved on to luncheon. Breitmann took the part of listener, and spoke only when addressed.

"I must tell you, Mr. Breitmann," said Laura, "that a ghost has returned to us."

"A ghost?" interestedly.

"Yes. My daughter," said the admiral tolerantly, "believes that she hears strange noises at night, tapping, and such like."

"Oh!" politely. Breitmann broke his bread idly. It was too bad. She had not produced upon him the impression that she was the sort of woman whose imagination embraced the belief in spirits. "Where does this ghost do its tapping?"

"In the big chimney in the library," she answered.

No one observed Breitmann's hand as it slid from the bread, some of which was scattered upon the floor. The scars, betraying emotion such as no mental effort could control, deepened, which is to say that the skin above and below them had paled.

"Might it not be some trial visit of your patron saint, Santa Claus?" he inquired, his voice well under control.

"Really, it is no jest," she affirmed. "For several nights I have heard the noise distinctly; a muffled tapping inside the chimney."

"Suppose we inspect it after luncheon?" suggested Fitzgerald.

"It has been done," said the admiral. Outwardly he was still skeptical, but a doubt was forming in his mind.

"It will do no harm to try it again," said Breitmann.

If Fitzgerald noted the subdued excitement in the man's voice, he charged it to the moment.

"Take my word for it," avowed the admiral, "you will find nothing. Bring the coffee into the library," he added to the butler.

The logs were taken out of the fireplace, and as soon as the smoke cleared the young men gave the inside of the chimney a thorough going over. They could see the blue sky away up above. The opening was large, but far too small for any human being to enter down it. The mortar between the bricks seemed for the most part undisturbed. Breitmann made the first discovery of any importance. Just above his height, standing in the chimney itself, he saw a single brick projecting beyond its mates. He reached up, and shook it. It was loose. He wrenched it out, and came back into the light.

"See! Nothing less than a chisel could have cut the mortar that way. Miss Killigrew is right." He went back, and with the aid of the tongs poked into the cavity. The wall of bricks was four deep, yet the tongs went through. This business had been done from the other side.

"Well!" exclaimed the admiral, for once at loss for a proper phrase.

"You see, father? I was right. Now, what can it mean? Who is digging out the bricks, and for what purpose? And how, with the alarms all over the house, to account for the footprints in the flour?"

"It is quite likely that something is hidden in the chimney, and some one knows that it is worth hunting for. This chimney is the original, I should judge." Fitzgerald addressed this observation to the admiral.

"Never been touched during my time or my father's. But we can soon find out. I'll have a man up here. If there is anything in the chimney that ought not to be there, he'll dig it out, and save our midnight visitor any further trouble."

"Why not wait a little while?" Fitzgerald ventured. "With Breitmann and me in the house, we might trap the man."

"A good scheme!"

"He comes from the outside, somewhere; from the cellar, probably. Let us try the cellar." Breitmann urged this with a gesture of his hands.

"There'll be sport," said Fitzgerald.

The coffee was cold in the little cups when they returned to it. The cellar, as far as any one could learn, was free from any signs of recent invasion. It was puzzling.

" And the servants?" Breitmann intimated.

" They have been in the family for years."
The admiral shook his head convincedly. " I ask
your pardon, my dear. My ears are not so keen
as might be. I'm an old blockhead to think that you
were having an attack of ghosts. But we'll solve
the riddle shortly, and then we shan't have any
trouble with our alarm bells," with a significant
glance at Fitzgerald. " Well, Mr. Breitmann, suppose we take a look at the work? Laura, you
show Mr. Fitzgerald the gardens. The view from
the terrace is excellent."

Fine weather. The orchard was pink with apple
blossoms, giving the far end of the park a tint not
unlike Sicilian almonds in bloom. And the intermittent breeze, as it waned or strengthened, carried
delicate perfumes to and fro. Yon was the sea,
with well-defined horizon, and down below were
the few smacks and the white yacht *Laura,* formally
bowing to one another, or tossing their noses im-
pudently; and, far away, was the following trail of
brown smoke from some ship which had dropped
down the horizon.

Fitzgerald stood silent, musing, at the girl's

side. He was fond of vistas. There was rest in them, a peace not to be found even in the twilight caverns of cathedrals; wind blowing over waters, the flutter of leaves, the bend in the grasses. To dwell in a haven like this. No care, no worry, no bother of grubbing about in one's pockets for overlooked coins, no flush of excitement! It is, after all, the homeless man who answers quickest the beckon of wanderlust. It is only when he comes into the shelter of such a roof that he draws into his heart the bitter truth of his loneliness.

" You must think me an odd girl."

" Pray why? "

" By the manner in which I brought you here."

" On the contrary, you are one of the few women I ever met who know something about scoring a good joke. Didn't your friend, Mrs. Coldfield, know my mother; and wasn't your father a great friend of my father's? As for being odd, what about me? I believe I stood on the corner, and tried to sell plaster casts, just to win a foolish club wager."

" Men can jest that way with impunity, but a woman may not. Still, I really couldn't help acting the way I did," with a tinkle in her voice and a twinkle in her eyes.

"Convention is made up of many idiotic laws. Why we feel obliged to obey is beyond offhand study. Of course, the main block is sensible; it holds humanity together. It's the irritating, burr-like amendments that one rages against. It's the same in politics. Some clear-headed fellow gets up and makes a just law. His enemies and his friends alike realize that if the law isn't passed there will be a roar from the public. So they pass the bill with amendments. In other words, they kill its usefulness. I suppose that's why I am always happy to leave convention behind, to be sent to the middle of Africa, to Patagonia, or sign an agreement to go to the North Pole."

"The North Pole? Have you been to the Arctic?"

"No; but I expect to go up in June with an Italian explorer."

"Isn't it terribly lonely up there?"

"It can't be worse than the Sahara or our own Death Valley. One extreme is as bad as the other.

Some time I hope your father will take me along on one of those treasure hunts.   I should like to be in at the finding of a pirate ship.   It would make a boy out of me again."

His eyes were very handsome when he smiled. Boy? she thought.   He was scarce more than that now.

" Pirates' gold!   What a lure it has been, is, and will be!   Blood money, brrr!   I can see no pleasure in touching it.   And the poor, pathetic trinkets, which once adorned some fair neck!   It takes a man's mind to pass over that side of the picture, and see only the fighting.   But humanity has gone on.   The pirate is no more, and the highwayman is a thing to laugh at."

" Thanks to railways and steamships.   It is beautiful here."

" We are nearly always here in the summer.   In the winter we cruise.   But this winter we remained at home.   It was splendid.   The snow was deep, and often I joined the village children on their bob-sleds.   I made father ride down once.   He grumbled about making a fool of himself.   After the first slide, I couldn't keep him off the hill. He wants to go to St. Moritz next winter." She laughed joyously.

"I shall take the Arctic trip," he said to himself irrelevantly.

"Let us go and pick some apple blossoms. They last such a little while, and they are so pretty on the table. So you were in Napoleon's tomb that day? I have cried over the king of Rome's toys. Did Mr. Breitmann receive those scars in battle?"

"Oh, no. It was a phase of his student life in Munich. But he has been under fire. He has had some hard luck." He wanted to add: "Poor devil!"

She did not reply, but walked down the terrace steps to the path leading to the orchard. The sturdy, warty old trees leaned toward the west, the single evidence of the years of punishment received at the hands of the winter sea tempests. It was a real orchard, composed of several hundred trees, well kept, as evenly matched as might be, out of weedless ground. From some hidden bough, a robin voiced his happiness, and yellowbirds flew hither and thither, and there was billing and cooing

and nesting.   Along the low stone wall a wee chip-
munk scampered.

"What place do you like best in this beautiful old
world?" she asked, drawing down a snowy bough.
Some of the blossoms fell and lay entrapped in her
hair.

"This," he answered frankly.   She met his gaze
quickly, and with suspicion.   His face was smiling,
but not so his eyes.   "Wherever I am, if content,
I like that place best.   And I am content here."

"You fought with Greece?"

"Yes."

"How that country always rouses our sympathies!   Isn't there a little too much poetry and not
enough truth about it?"

"There is.   I fought with the Greeks because I
disliked them less than the Turks."

"And Mr. Breitmann?"

He smiled.   "He fought with the Turks to
chastise Greece, which he loves."

"What adventures you two must have had!   To
be on opposing sides, like that!"

"Opposing newspapers.   The two angles of
vision made our copy interesting.   There was really

no romance about it. It was purely a business transaction. We offered our lives and our pencils for a hundred a week and our expenses. Rather sordid side to it, eh? And a fourth-rate order or two —"

"You were decorated?" excitedly. "I am sure it was for bravery."

"Don't you believe it. The king of Greece and the sultan both considered the honor conferred upon us as good advertising."

"You are laughing."

"Well, war in the Balkans is generally a laughing matter. Sounds brutal, I know, but it is true."

"I know," gaily. "You are conceited, and are trying to make me believe that you are modest."

"A bull's-eye!"

"And this Mr. Breitmann has been decorated for valor? And yet to-day he becomes my father's private secretary. The two do not connect."

"May I ask you to mention nothing of this to him? It would embarrass him. I had no business to bring him into it."

She grew meditative, brushing her lips with the blossoms. "He will be something of a mystery.

I am not overfond of mysteries outside of book covers."

"There is really no mystery; but it is human for a man in his position to wish to bury his past greatness."

By and by the sun touched the southwest shoulder of the hill, and the two strolled back to the house.

From his window, Breitmann could see them plainly.

"Damn those scars!" he murmured, striking with his fist the disfigured cheek, which upon a time had been a source of pride and honor. "Damn them!"

CHAPTER IX

THEY DRESS FOR DINNER

BREITMANN watched them as long as he could. There was no jealousy in his heart, but there was bitterness, discontent, a savage self-pillorying. He was genuinely sorry that this young woman was so pretty; still, had she the graces of Calypso, he must have come. She would distract him, and he desired at that time distraction least of all diversions. Concentration and singleness of purpose — upon these two attributes practically hung his life. How strangely fate had stepped with him. What if there had not been that advertisement for a private secretary? How then should he have gained a footing in this house? Well, here he was, and speculation was of no value, save in a congratulatory sense. The fly in the amber was the presence of the young American;

Fitzgerald, shrewd and clever, might stumble upon something. Well, till against that time!

His room was pleasant, a corner which gave two excellent views, one of the sea and the other of the orchard. There was no cluttering of furniture; it was simple, substantial, decently old. On the plain walls were some choice paintings. A landscape by Constable, a water color by Fortuny, and a rough sketch by Détaille; and the inevitable marines, such as one might expect in the house of a fighting sailor. He examined these closely, and was rather pleased to find them valuable old prints. And, better to his mind than all these, was the deft, mysterious touch or suggestion of a woman's hand. He saw it in the pillows on the lounge, in the curtains dropping from the windows, in the counterpane on the old four-poster.

Did Americans usually house their private secretaries in rooms fit for guests of long and intimate acquaintance? Ah, yes; this sailor was a rich man; and this mansion had not been erected yesterday. It amused him to think that these walls and richly polished floors were older than the French revolution. It seemed incredible, but it was true.

"Pirates!" His laughter broke forth, not loudly but deeply, fired by a broad and ready sense of humor — a perilous gift for a man who is seeking fine hazards. It was droll, it was even fantastic. To cruise about the world in search of pirate treasures, as if there remained a single isle, shore, promontory, known to have been the haunt of pirates, which had not been dug up and dug up again! And here, under the very hand — He struck his palms. "Why not?"

He ran to the window. The sleek white yacht lay tugging at her cables, like an eager hound in the leash. "Seaworthy from stem to stern. Why not? No better cloak than this. I may not make you a good secretary, admiral; but, the gods propitious, I can, if needs say must, take you treasure hunting. It will be a fine stroke. Is it possible that fortune begins to smile on me at last? Well, I have had the patience to wait. The hour has come, and fortune shall not find me laggard. It has been something to wait as I have, never to have spoken, never to have forgotten. France knows and Germany knows, but only me, not what I have.

They have even tried to drive me to crime.   Wait,
fools, wait ! "

He drew his arms tightly over his heaving breast,
for he was deeply moved, while over his face came
that indefinable light which, at times, illuminates the
countenance of a great man.   It came and went; as
a flash of lightning betrays the oncoming storm.

The chimney!   His heart missed a beat.   He had
forgotten the chimney.   The reaction affected him
like a blow.   A snarl twisted his mouth.   What was
this chimney to any other man?   Only he of all
men, knew.   And yet, here was some one stealthily
at work, forestalling him, knocking the bottom out
of his great dream.   There was nothing pleasant in
the growing expression in his face; it was the tiger,
waking.   There could be only one way.

Swiftly he dashed to his trunk, knelt and examined the lock, unscrewed it, and took out the
documents more precious to him than the treasures
of a hundred Captain Kidds.   Instantly, he returned to the window.   Nothing was missing.   But
here was something he had never noticed before.
On the face of the slip of parchment — a diagram,

dim and faded — was an oily thumb-mark. The oil from the lock; nothing more; doubtless he himself had touched it. How many times had he found an unknown touch among his few belongings? How often had he smiled? Still, to quell all rising doubts, he rubbed his right thumb on the lock, and made a second impression. The daylight was now insufficient, so he turned on the electricity, and compared them. Slowly, the scars deepened till they were the tint of cedar. Death's head itself could not have fascinated him more than the dissimilarity of these two thumb-prints. He said nothing, but a queer little strangling sound came through his lips.

Who? Where? His heart beat so violently that the veins in his throat swelled and threatened to burst. But he was no weakling. He summoned all his will. He must act, and act at once, immediately. Fitzgerald? No, not that clever, idling fool. But who, who? He replaced the papers and the lock. A hidden menace. Question as he would, there was never any answer.

He practised the pleasant deceit that the first mark had been there when the diagram had been given to him. It was not possible that any one had discovered his hiding-place. Had he not with his own hands contrived it, alone and without aid, under that accursed mansard roof? Not one of his co-adventurers knew; they had advanced him funds on his word. His other documents they had seen; these had sufficed them. Still, back it came, with deadly insistence; some one was digging at the bricks in the chimney. The drama was beginning to move. Had he waited too long?

Mechanically, he proceeded to dress for dinner. Since he was to sit at the family table, he must fit his dress and manners to the hour. He did not resist the sardonic smile as he put on his fresh patent leathers and his new dinner coat. He recalled Fitzgerald's half-concealed glances of pity the last time they had dined together.

In the room across the corridor, Fitzgerald was busy with a similar occupation. The only real worry he had was the doubt of his luggage arriving before he left. He had neither tennis clothes nor riding-habit, and these two pastimes were here among the regular events of the day. The admiral both played and rode with his daughter. She was

altogether too charming. Had she been an ordinary
society girl, he would have stayed his welcome
threadbare perhaps. But, he repeated, she was not
ordinary. She had evidently been brought up with
few illusions. These she possessed would always
be hers.

The world, in a kindly but mistaken spirit, fosters
all sorts of beliefs in the head of a child. True, it
makes childhood happy, but it leaves its skin tender. The moment a girl covers her slippers with
skirts and winds her hair about the top of her curious young head, things begin to jar. The men are
not what she dreamed them to be, there never was
such a person as Prince Charming; and the women
embrace her — if she is pretty and graceful — with
arms bristling with needles of envy and malice; and
the rosal tint that she saw in the approach is nothing more or less than jaundice; and, one day dis-
heartened and bewildered, she learns that the world
is only a jumble of futile, ill-made things. The
admiral had weeded out most of these illusions at
the start.

"So much for suppositions and analysis," panted
Fitzgerald, reknotting his silk tie. "As for me, I

go to the Arctic; cold, but safe. I have never fallen in love. I have enjoyed the society of many women, and to some I've been silly enough to write, but I have never been maudlin. I'm no fool. This is the place where it would be most likely to happen. Let us beat an orderly retreat. What the devil ails my fingers to-night? M'h! There; will you stay tied as I want you? She has traveled, she has studied, she is at home with grand dukes in Nice, and scribblers in a country village. She is wise without being solemn. She has courage, too, or I should not be here on a mere fluke. Now, my boy, you have given yourself due notice. Take care!"

He slipped his coat over his shoulders — and passably sturdy ones they were — and took a final look into the glass. Not for vanity's sake; sometimes a man's tie *will* show above the collar of his coat.

"Hm! I'll wager the trout are rising about this time." He imitated a cast which was supposed to land neatly in the corner. "Ha! Struck you that time, you beauty!" All of which proved to himself, conclusively, that he was in normal condition. "I should get a wire to-morrow about Breitmann.

I hate to do anything that looks underhand, but he puzzles me. There was something about the chimney to-day; I don't know what. This is no place for him — nor for me, either," was the shrewd supplement.

There was still some time before dinner, so he walked about, with his hands in his pockets, and viewed the four walls of his room. He examined the paints and admired the collection of bloodthirsty old weapons over the mantel, but with the indirect interest of a man who is thinking of other things. At the end, he paused before the window, which, like the one in Breitmann's room, afforded a clear outlook to the open waters. Night was already mistress of the sea; and below, the village lights twinkled from various points.

Laura tried on three gowns, to the very great surprise of her maid. Usually her mistress told her in the morning what to lay out for dinner. Here there were two fine-looking young men about, and yet she was for selecting the simplest gown of the three. The little French maid did not understand the reason, nor at that moment could her mistress have readily explained. It was easy to

dress for the critical eyes of rich young men, officers, gentlemen with titles; all that was required
was a fresh Parisian model, some jewels, and a
bundle of orchids or expensive roses. But these
two men belonged to a class she knew little of;
gentlemen adventurers, who had been in strange,
unfrequented places, who had helped to make history, who received decorations, and never wore
them, who remained to the world at large obscure
and unknown.

So, with that keen insight which is a part of a
well-bred, intelligent woman — and also rather inexplicable to the male understanding — she chose
the simplest gown. She was hazily conscious that
they would notice this dress, whereas the gleaming
satin would have passed as a matter of fact. Round
her graceful throat she placed an Indian turquoise
necklace; nothing in her hair, nothing on her fingers.
She went down-stairs perfectly content.

As she came into the hall, she heard soft music.
Some one was in the music-room, which was just
off the library. She stopped to listen. Chopin,
with light touch and tender feeling. Which of the
two wanderers was it? Quietly, she moved along

to the door. Breitmann; she rather expected to find him. Nearly all educated Germans played. The music stopped for a moment, then resumed. Another melody followed, a melody she had heard from one end of France to the other. She frowned, not with displeasure, but with puzzlement. For what purpose did a soldier of the German empire play the battle hymn of the French republic? *The Marseillaise!* She entered the music-room, and the low but vibrant chords ceased instantly. Breitmann had been playing these melodies standing. He turned quickly.

"I beg your pardon," he said, but perfectly free from embarrassment.

"I am very fond of music myself. Please play whenever the mood comes to you. *The Marseillaise—*"

"Ah!" he interrupted, laughing. "There was a bit of traitor in my fingers just then. But music should have no country; it should be universal."

"Perhaps, generally speaking; but every land should have an anthem of its own. The greatest composition of Beethoven or Wagner will never touch the heart as the ripple of a battle song."

And when Fitzgerald joined them they were seriously discussing Wagner and his ill-treatment in Munich, and of the mad king of Bavaria.

As she had planned, both men noticed the simplicity of her dress.

" It is because she doesn't care," thought Breitmann.

" It is because she knows we don't care," thought Fitzgerald. And he was nearer the truth than Breitmann.

The dinner was pleasant, and there was much talk of travel. The admiral had touched nearly every port, Fitzgerald had been round three times, and Breitmann four. The girl experienced a sense of elation as she listened. She knew most of her father's stories, but to-night he drew upon a half-forgotten store. Without embellishment, as if they were ordinary, every-day affairs, they exchanged tales of adventure in strange island wildernesses; and there were lion hunts and man hunts and fierce battles on land and sea. Never had any story-book opened a like world. She felt a longing for the Himalayas, the Indian jungles, the low-lying islands of the South Pacific.

So far as the admiral was concerned, he was very well pleased with the new secretary.

Fitzgerald was not asleep. He had an idea, and he smoked his yellow African gourd pipe till this same idea shaped itself into the form of a resolve. He laid the pipe on the mantel, turned over the logs — for the nights were yet chill, and a fire was a comfort — and raised a window. He would like to hear some of that tapping in the chimney. He was fully dressed, excepting that he had exchanged shoes for slippers.

He went out into the corridor. There was no light under Breitmann's door. So much the better; he was asleep. Fitzgerald crept down the stairs with the caution of a hunter who is trailing new game. As he arrived at the turn of the first landing, he hesitated. He could hear the old clock striking off the seconds in the lower hall. He cupped his ear. By George! Joining the sharp monotony of the clock was another sound, softer, intermittent. He was certain that it came from the library. That door was never closed. Click-click! Click-click! The mystery was close at hand.

He moved forward. He wanted to get as close as possible to the fireplace. He peered in. The fire was all but dead; only the corner of a log glowed dully. Suddenly, the glow died, only to reappear, unchanged. This phenomena could be due to one thing, a passing of something opaque. Fitzgerald had often seen this in camps, when some one's legs passed between him and the fire. Some one else was in the room. With a light bound, he leaped forward, to find himself locked in a pair of arms no less vigorous than his own.

And even in that lively moment he remembered that the sound in the chimney went on!

CHAPTER X

IT was a quick, silent struggle. The intruder wore no shoes. It would be a test of endurance. Fitzgerald recalled some tricks he had learned in Japan; but even as he stretched out his arm to perform one, the arm was caught by the wrist, while a second hand passed under his elbow.

"Don't!" he gasped lowly. "I'll give in." His arm would have snapped if he hadn't spoken.

A muttered oath in German. "Fitzgerald?" came the query, in a whisper.

"Yes. For God's sake, is this you, Breitmann?"

"Sh! Not so loud! What are you doing here?"

"And you?"

"Listen! It has stopped. He has heard our scuffling."

"It seems, then, that we are both here for the same purpose?" said Fitzgerald, pulling down his cuffs, and running his fingers round his collar.

"Yes. You came too late or too soon." Breitmann stooped, and ran his hands over the rug.

The other saw him but dimly. "What's the matter?"

"I have lost one of my studs," with the frugal spirit of his mother's forebears. "You are stronger than I thought."

"Much obliged."

"It's a good thing you did not get that hold first. You'd have broken my arm."

"Wouldn't have given in, eh? I simply cried quits in order to start over again. There's no fair fighting in the dark, you know."

"Well, we have frightened him away. It is too bad."

"What have you on your feet?"

"Felt slippers."

"Are you afraid of the cold?"

'A laugh. "Not I!"

"Come with me."

"Where?"

"First to the cellar. Remember that hot-air box from the furnace, that backs the chimney, way up?"

"I looked only at the bricks."

"We'll go and have a look at that box. It just occurred to me that there is a cellar window within two feet of that box."

"Let us hurry. Can you find the way?"

"I can try."

"But lights?"

Fitzgerald exhibited his electric pocket lamp. "This will do."

"You Americans!"

After some mistakes they found their way to the cellar. The window was closed, but not locked, and resting against the wall was a plank. It leaned obliquely, as if left in a hurry. Fitzgerald took it up, and bridged between the box and the window ledge. Breitmann gave him a leg up, and in another moment he was examining the brick wall of the great chimney under a circular white patch of light. A dozen rows of bricks had been cleverly loosened. There were also evidences of chalk marks, something on the order of a diagram; but it was rather uncertain, as it had been redrawn four or five times. The man hadn't been sure of his ground.

"Can you see?" asked Fitzgerald.

"Yes." Only Breitmann himself knew what wild rage lay back of that monosyllable. He was sure now; that diagram brushed away any lingering doubt. The lock had been trifled with, but the man who had done the work had not been sure of his dimensions.

"Clever piece of work. Took away the mortar in his pockets; no sign of it here. The admiral had better send for his bricklayer, for more reasons than one. There'll be a defective flue presently. Now, what the devil is the duffer expecting to find?" Fitzgerald coolly turned the light full into the other's face.

"It is beyond me," with equal coolness; "unless there's a pirate's treasure behind there." The eyes blinked a little, which was but natural.

"Pirate's treasure, you say?" Fitzgerald laughed. "That *would* be a joke, eh?"

"What now?" For Breitmann thought it best to leave the initiative with his friend.

" A little run out to the stables," recalling to mind the rumor of the night before.

" The stables? "

" Why, surely. The fellow never got in here without some local assistance, and I am rather certain that this comes from the stables. Besides, no one will be expecting us." He came down agilely.

Breitmann nodded approvingly at the ease with which the other made the descent. " It would be wiser to leave the cellar by the window," he suggested.

" My idea, too. We'll make a step out of this board. The stars are bright enough." Fitzgerald climbed out first, and then gave a hand to Breitmann.

" I understood there was a burglar alarm in the house."

" Yes; but this very window, being open, probably breaks the circuit. All cleverly planned. But I'm crazy to learn what he is looking for. Double your coat over your white shirt."

Breitmann was already proceeding with this task. A dog-trot brought them into the roadway, but they kept to the grass. They were within a yard of the

stable doors when a hound began bellowing.   Breitmann smothered a laugh and Fitzgerald a curse.

"The quicker we get back to the cellar the better," was the former's observation.

And they returned at a clip, scrambling into the
cellar as quickly and silently as they could, and
made for the upper floors.

"Come into my room," said Fitzgerald; "it's
only midnight."

Breitmann agreed.   If he had any reluctance, he
did not show it.   Fitzgerald produced cigars.

"Do my clothes look anything like yours?"
asked Breitmann dryly, striking a match.

"Possibly."

They looked themselves over for any real dam-
age.   There were no rents, but there were cobwebs
on the wool and streaks of coal dust on the linen.

"We shall have to send our clothes to the village
tailor.   The admiral's valet might think it odd."

"Where do you suppose he comes from?"

"I don't care where.   What's he after, to take
all this trouble?   Something big, I'll warrant."

And then, for a time, they smoked like Turks,
in silence.

"By George, it's a good joke; you and I trying to choke each other, while the real burglar makes off."

"It has some droll sides."

"And you all but broke my arm."

Breitmann chuckled. "You were making the same move. I was quicker, that was all."

Another pause.

"The admiral has seen some odd corners. Think of seeing, at close range, the Japanese-Chinese naval fight!"

"He tells a story well."

"And the daughter is a thoroughbred."

"Yes," non-committally.

"By the way, I'm going to the Pole in June or August."

"The Italian expedition?"

"Yes."

"That ought to make fine copy. You will not mind if I turn in? A bit sleepy."

"Not at all. Shall we tell the admiral?"

"The first thing in the morning. Good night."

Fitzgerald finished his cigar, and went to bed

also. "Intersting old place," wadding a pillow under his ear. "More interesting to-morrow."

Some time earlier, the individual who was the cause of this nocturnal exploit hurried down the hill, nursing a pair of skinned palms, and laughing gently to himself.

"Checkmate! I shall try the other way."

On the morrow, Fitzgerald recounted the adventure in a semi-humorous fashion, making a brisk melodrama out of it, to the quiet amusement of his small audience.

"I shall send for the mason this morning," said the admiral. "I've been dreaming of *The Black Cat* and all sorts of horrible things. I hate like sixty to spoil the old chimney, but we can't have this going on. We'll have it down at once. A fire these days is only a nice touch to the mahogany."

"But you must tell him to put back every brick in its place," said Laura. "I could not bear to have anything happen to that chimney. All the same, I am glad the matter is going to be cleared up. It has been nerve-racking; and I have been all alone, waiting for I know not what."

" You haven't been afraid? " said Fitzgerald.

" I'm not sure that I haven't." She sighed.

" Nonsense! " cried the admiral.

" I am not afraid of anything I can see; but I do not like the dark; I do not like mysteries."

" You're the bravest girl I know, Laura," her father declared. " Now, Mr. Breitmann, if you don't mind."

" Shall we begin at once, sir? "

" You will copy some of my notes, to begin with. Any time you're in doubt over a word, speak to me. There will not be much outside of manuscript work. Most of my mail is sorted at my bankers, and only important letters forwarded. There may be a social note occasionally. Do you read and write English as well as you speak it? "

" Oh, yes."

Laura invited Fitzgerald to the tennis court.

" In these shoes? " he protested.

" They will not matter; it is a cement court."

" But I shan't look the game. Tennis without flannels is like duck without apples."

" Bother! We'll play till the mason comes up.

'And mind your game. I've been runner-up in a dozen tournaments."

And he soon found that she had not overrated her skill. She served strongly, volleyed beautifully, and darted across the court with a fleetness and a surety both delightful to observe. So interested were they in the battle that they forgot all about the mason, till the butler came out, and announced that the desecration had begun.

In fact the broad marble top was on the floor, and the room full of impalpable dust. The admiral and the secretary were gravely stacking the bricks, one by one, as they came out.

"Found anything?" asked the girl breathlessly.

"Not yet; but Mr. Donovan here has just discovered a hollow space above the mantel line." The admiral sneezed.

Mr. Donovan, in his usual free and happy way, drew out two bricks, and dropped them on the polished floor.

"There's your holler, sir," he said, dusting his hands.

Unbidden, Breitmann pushed his hand into the

cavity. His arm went down to the elbow, and he was forced to stand on tiptoe. He was pale when he withdrew his arm, but in his hand was a square metal case, about the size and shape of a cigar box.

"By cracky! What's the matter, Mr. Breitmann?" The admiral stepped forward solicitously.

Breitmann swayed, and fell against the side of the fireplace. "It is nothing; lost my balance for a moment. Will you open it, sir?"

"Lost his balance?" muttered Fitzgerald. "He looks groggy. Why?"

This was not a time for speculation. All rushed after the admiral, who laid the case on his desk, and took out his keys. None of them would turn in the ancient lock. With an impatient gesture, which escaped the others, the secretary seized Mr. Donovan's hammer, inserted the claw between the lock and the catch, and gave a powerful wrench. The lid fell back, crooked and scarred.

The admiral put on his Mandarin spectacles. With his hands behind his back, he bent and critically examined the contents. Then, very carefully, he extracted a packet of papers, yellow and old, bound with heavy cording. Beneath this packet was a medal of the Legion of Honor, some rose leaves, and a small glove.

"Know what I think?" said the admiral, stilling the shake in his voice. "This belonged to that mysterious Frenchman who lived here eighty years ago. I'll wager that medal cost some blood. By cracky, what a find!"

"And the poor little glove and the rose leaves!" murmured the girl, in pity. "It seems like a crime to disturb them."

"We shan't, my child. Our midnight friend wasn't digging yonder for faded keepsakes. These papers are the things." The admiral cut the string, and opened one of the documents. "H'm! Written in French. So is this," looking at another, "and this. Here, Laura, cast your eye over these, and tell us why some one was hunting for them."

Fitzgerald eyed Breitmann thoughtfully. The whole countenance of the man had changed. Indeed, it resembled another face he had seen somewhere; and it grew in his mind, slowly but surely, as dawn grows, that Breitmann was not wholly ignorant in this affair. He had not known who had been working at night; but that dizziness of the moment gone, the haste in opening the case, the eagerness of the search last night; all these, to Fitzgerald's mind, pointed to one thing: Breitmann knew.

"I shall watch him."

Laura read the documents to herself first. Here and there was a word which confused her; but she gathered the full sense of the remarkable story. Her eyes shone like winter stars.

"Father!" she cried, dropping the papers, and spreading out her arms. "Father, it's the greatest thing in the world. A treasure!"

"What's that, Laura?" straining his ears.

"A treasure, hidden by the soldiers of Napoleon; put together, franc by franc, in the hope of some day rescuing the emperor from St. Helena. It is romance! A real treasure of two millions of francs!" clapping her hands.

"Where?" It was Breitmann who spoke. His voice was not clear.

"Corsica!"

"Corsica!" The admiral laughed like a child. Right under his very nose all these years, and he cruising all over the chart! "Laura, dear, there's no reason in the world why we shouldn't take the yacht and go and dig up this pretty sum."

"No reason in the world!" But the secretary did not pronounce these words aloud.

"A telegram for you, sir," said the butler, handing the yellow envelope to Fitzgerald.

"Will you pardon me?" he said drawing off to a window.

"Go ahead," said the admiral, fingering the medal of the Legion of Honor.

Fitzgerald read:

"Have made inquiries. Your man never applied to any of the metropolitan dailies. Few ever heard of him."

He jammed the message into a pocket, and returned to the group about the case. Where should he begin? Breitmann had lied.

CHAPTER XI

PREPARATIONS AND COGITATIONS

THE story itself was brief enough, but there was plenty of husk to the grain. The old expatriate was querulous, long-winded, not niggard with his ink when he cursed the English and damned the Prussians; and he obtained much gratification in jabbing his quill-bodkin into what he termed the sniveling nobility of the old régime. Dog of dogs! was he not himself noble? Had not his parents and his brothers gone to the guillotine with the rest of them? But he, thank God, had no wooden mind; he could look progress and change in the face and follow their bent. And now, all the crimes and heroisms of the Revolution, all the glorious pageantry of the empire, had come to nothing. A Bourbon, thick-skulled, sordid, worn-out, again sat upon the throne, while the Great Man languished on a rock in the Atlantic. Fools that they had been, not

to have hidden the little king of Rome as against
this very dog! It was pitiful. He never saw a
shower in June that he did not hail curses upon it.
To have lost Waterloo for a bucketful of water!
Thousand thunders! could he ever forget that terrible race back to Paris? Could he ever forget the
shame of it? Grouchy for a fool and Blücher for a
blundering ass. *Eh bien;* they would soon tumble
the Bourbons into oblivion again.

A rambling desultory tale. And there were rem-
iniscences of such and such a great lady's *salon;* the
flight from Moscow; the day of the Bastille; the
poor fool of a Louis who donned a red-bonnet and
wore the tricolor; some new opera dances; the flight
of his cowardly cousins to Austria; Austerlitz and
Jena; the mad dream in Egypt; the very day when
the Great Man pulled a crown out of his saddle-bag
and made himself an emperor. Just a little corporal from Corsica; think of it! And so on; all
jumbled but keyed with tremendous interest to the
listeners and to Laura herself. It was the golden
age of opportunity, of reward, of sudden generals
and princes and dukes. All gone, nothing left but
a few battle-flags; England no longer shaking in

her boots, and the rest of them dividing the spoils!
No! There were some left, and in their hands lay
the splendid enterprise.

Quietly they had pieced together this sum and
that, till there was now stored away two-million
francs. Two or three frigates and a corvette or
two; then the work would go forward. Only a
little while to wait, and then they would bring their
beloved chief back to France and to his own again.
Had he not written: "Come for me, *mon brave*.
They say they have orders to shoot me. Come;
better carry my corpse away than that I should rot
here for years to come." They would come. But
this year went by and another; one by one the Old
Guard died off, smaller and smaller had drawn the
circle. The vile rock called St. Helena still remained impregnable. On a certain day they came
to tell him that the emperor was no more. Soon
he was all alone but one; these brave soldiers who
had planned with him were no more. An alien,
an outcast, he too longed for night. And what
should he do with it, this vast treasure, every franc
of which meant sacrifice and unselfishness, bravery
and loyalty? Let the gold rot. He would bury all

knowledge of it in yonder chimney, confident that no one would ever find the treasure, since he alone possessed the key to it, having buried it himself. So passed the greatest Cæsar of them all, the most brilliant empire, the bravest army. Ah! had the king of Rome lived! Had there been some direct Napoleonic blood to take up the work! Vain dreams! The Great Man's brothers had been knaves and fools.

" And so to-night," the narrator ended, " I bury the casket in the chimney; within it, my hopes and few trinkets of the past of which I am an integral part. Good-by, little glove; good-by, brave old medal! I am sending a drawing of the chimney to the good Abbe le Fanu. He will outlive me. He lives on forty-centime the day; treasures mean nothing to him; his cry, his eternal cry, is always of the People. He will probably tear it up. The brig will never come again. So best. Death will come soon. 'And I shall die unknown, unloved, forgotten. *Bonne nuit!* "

Mr. Donovan alone remained in normal state of mind. 'Twas all faradiddle, this talk of finding treasures. The old Frenchman had been only half-baked. He dumped his tools into his bag, and, with the wisdom of his kind, departed. There would be another job to-morrow, putting the bricks back.

The others, however, were for the time but children, and like children they all talked at once; and there was laughter and thumping of fists and clapping of hands. The admiral had a new plan every five minutes. He would do this, or he would do that; and Fitzgerald would shake his head, or Breitmann would point out the unfeasibility of the plan. Above all, he urged, there must be no publicity (with a flash toward Fitzgerald); the world must know nothing till the treasure was in their hands. Otherwise, there would surely be piracy on the high-seas. Two million francs was a prize, even in these days. There were plenty of men and plenty of tramp ships. Even when they found the gold, secrecy would be best. There might be some difficulty with France. Close lips, then, till they returned to America; after that Mr. Fitzgerald would become famous as the teller of the exploit.

"I confess that, for all my excitement," said

Fitzgerald, "I am somewhat skeptical. Still, your suggestion, Mr. Breitmann, is good."

"Do you mean to say you doubt the existence of the treasure?" cried the admiral, something impatient.

"Oh, no doubt it once existed. But seventy-five or eighty years! There were others besides this refugee Frenchman. Who knows into what hands similar documents may have fallen?"

"And the unknown man who worked in the chimney?" put in the girl quietly.

"That simply proves what I say. He knows that this treasure once existed, but not where. Now, it is perfectly logical that some other man, years ago, might have discovered the same key as we have. He may have got away with it. The man might have plausibly declared that he had made the money somewhere. The sum is not so large as to create any wide comment."

"Ah, my boy, your father had more enthusiasm than that." The admiral looked reproachful.

"My dear admiral," and Fitzgerald laughed in that light-hearted way of his, "I would go into the heart of China on a treasure hunt, for the mere fun of it. Enthusiasm? Nothing would gratify me more than to strike a shovel into the spot where this treasure, this pot of gold, is supposed to lie. It will be great sport; nothing like it. I was merely supposing. I have never heard of, or come into contact with, a man who has found a hidden treasure. I am putting up these doubts because we are never sure of anything. Why, Mr. Breitmann knows; isn't it more fun to find a dollar in an old suit of clothes than to know you have ten in the suit you are wearing? It's not how much, it's the finding that gives the pleasure."

"That is true," echoed Breitmann generously. He fingered the papers with a touch that was almost a caress. "A pity that you will go to the Arctic instead."

"I am not quite sure that I shall go," replied Fitzgerald. That this man had deliberately lied to him rendered him indecisive. For the present he could not do or say anything, but he had a great desire to be on hand to watch.

"You are not your father's son if you refuse to

go with us; " and the Admiral sent home this charge
with fist against palm.

" ' Pieces of eight! Pieces of eight! ' " parroted
the girl drolly. " You will go, Mr. Fitzgerald."

" Do you really want me to? " cleverly putting
the decision with her.

" Yes." There was no coquetry in voice or eye.

" When do you expect to go? " Fitzgerald put
this question to the admiral.

" As soon as we can coal up and provision.
Laura, I've just got to smoke. Will you gentlemen
join me? " The two young men declined. " We
can go straight to Funchal in the Madieras and re-
coal. With the club-ensign up nobody will be asking questions. We can telegraph the *Herald* whenever we touch a port. Just a pleasure-cruise."
The admiral fingered the Legion of Honor. " And
here was Alladin's Lamp hanging up in my chimney! " He broke in laughter. " By cracky! that
man Donovan knows his business. He's gone
without putting back the bricks. He has mulcted
me for two days' work."

" But crossing in the yacht," hesitated Fitzgerald.

He wished to sound this man Breitmann. If he suggested obstacles and difficulties it would be a confirmation of the telegram and his own singular doubts.

"It is likely to be a rough passage," said Breitmann experimentally.

"He doesn't want me to go." Fitzgerald stroked his chin slyly.

"We have crossed the Atlantic twice in the yacht," Laura affirmed with a bit of pride; "once in March too, and a heavy sea half the way."

"Enter me as cabin-boy or supercargo," said Fitzgerald. "If you don't you'll find a stowaway before two days out."

"That's the spirit." The admiral drew strongly on his cigar. He had really never been so excited since his first sea-engagement. "And it comes in so pat, Laura. We were going away in a month anyway. Now we can notify the guests that we've cut down the time two weeks. I tell you what it is, this will be the greatest cruise *I* ever laid a course to."

"Guests?" murmured Fitzgerald, unconsciously poaching on Breitmann's thought.

"Yes. But they shall know nothing till we land in Corsica. And in a day or two this fellow would have laid hands on these things and we'd never been any the wiser."

"And may we not expect more of him?" said Breitmann.

"Small good it will do him."

"Corsica," repeated the girl dreamily.

"Ay, Napoleon. The Corsican Brothers' daggers and vendetta, the restless island! It is full of interest. I have been there." Breitmann smiled pleasantly at the girl, but his thought was unsmiling. Versed as he was in reading at a glance expression, whether it lay in the eyes, in the lips, or the hands, he realized with chagrin that he had made a misstep somewhere. For some reason he would have given much to know, Fitzgerald was covertly watching him.

"You have been there, too, have you not, Mr. Fitzgerald?" asked Laura.

"Oh, yes; but never north of Ajaccio."

"Laura, what a finishing touch this will give to my book." For the admiral was compiling a volume of treasures found, lost and still being hunted.

"All I can say is, that I am really sorry that the money wasn't used for the purpose intended."

"I do not agree there," said Fitzgerald.

"And why not?" asked Breitmann.

"France is better off as she is. She has had all the empires and monarchies she cares for. Wonderful country! See how she has lived in spite of them all. There will never be another kingdom in France, at least not in our generation. There's a Napoleon in Belgium and a Bourbon in England; the one drills mediocre soldiers and the other shoots grouse. They will never go any further."

The secretary spread his fingers and shrugged. "If there was only a direct descendant of Napoleon!"

"Well, there isn't," retorted Fitzgerald, dismissing the subject into limbo. "And much good it would do if there was."

"This treasure would rightly be his," insisted Breitmann.

"It was put together to bring Napoleon back. There is no Napoleon to bring back."

"In other words, the money belongs to the finder?"

"Exactly."

"Findings is keepings," the admiral determined.
"That's Captain Flanagan's rule."

The girl could bring together no reasons for the mind inclining to the thought that between the two young men there had risen an antagonism of some sort, nothing serious but still armed with spikes of light in the eyes and a semi-truculent angle to the chin. Fitzgerald was also aware of this apparency, and it annoyed him. Still, sometimes instinct guides more surely than logic. After all, he and Breitmann were only casual acquaintances. There had never been any real basis for friendship; and the possibility of this had been rendered nil by the telegram. One can not make a friend of a man who has lied gratuitously.

"Now, Mr. Breitmann," interposed the admiral pacifically, for he was too keen a sailor not to have noted the chill in the air, "suppose we send off those letters? Here, I'll write the names and addresses, and you can finish them up by yourself. Please call up Captain Flanagan at Swan's Hotel and tell him to report this afternoon." The admiral scribbled out the names of his guests, gathered up the precious documents, and put them into his pocket. " Come along now, my children; we'll take the air in the garden and picture the Frenchman's brig rocking in the harbor."

" It is all very good of you," said Fitzgerald, as the trio eyed the yacht from the terrace.

" Nonsense! The thing remains that all these years you ignored us."

" I have been, and still am, confoundedly poor. There is a little; I suppose I could get along in a hut in some country village; but the wandering life has spoiled me for that."

" Fake pride," rebuked the girl.

" I suppose it is."

" Your father had none. Long after the smash he'd hunt me up for a week's fishing. Isn't she a beauty? " pointing to the yacht.

" She is," the young man agreed, with his admiration leveled at the lovely profile of the girl.

" Let me see," began the admiral; " there will be Mr. and Mrs. Coldfield, first-class sailors, both of them. What's the name of that singer who is with them? "

" Hildegarde von Mitter."

"Of the Royal Opera in Munich?" asked Fitzgerald.

"Yes. Have you met her? Isn't she lovely?"

"I have only heard of her."

"And Arthur Cathewe," concluded the admiral.

"Cathewe? That will be fine," Fitzgerald agreed aloud. But in his heart he swore he would never forgive Arthur for this trick. And he knew all the time! "He's the best friend I have. A great hunter, with a reputation which reaches from the Carpathians to the Himalayas, from Abyssinia to the Congo."

"He is charming and amusing. Only, he is very shy."

At four that afternoon Captain Flanagan presented his respects. The admiral was fond of the old fellow, a friendship formed in the blur of battle-smoke. He had often been criticized for officering his yacht with such a gruff, rather illiterate man, when gentlemen were to be had for the asking. But Flanagan was a splendid seaman, and the admiral would not have exchanged him for the smartest English naval-reserve afloat. There was never a bend in Flanagan's back; royalty and commonalty

were all the same to him. And those who came to
criticize generally remained to admire; for Flanagan was the kind of sailor fast disappearing from
the waters, a man who had learned his seamanship
before the mast.

"Captain, how long will it take us to reach Funchal in the Madieras?"

"Well, Commodore, give us a decent sea an' we
can make 'er in fourteen days. But I thought we
wus goin' t' th' Banks, sir?"

"Changed my plans. We'll put out in twelve
days. Everything shipshape?"

"Up to the buntin', sir, and down to her keel.
I sh'd say about six-hundred tons; an' mebbe twelve
days instead of fourteen. An' what'll be our course
after Madeery, sir?"

"Ajaccio, Corsica."

"Yessir."

If the admiral had said the Antarctic, Flanagan
would never have batted an eye.

"You have spoken the crew?"

"Yessir; deep-sea men, too, sir. Halloran 'll
have th' injins as us'l, sir. Shall I run 'er up t' N'
York fer provisions? I got your list."

" Triple the order. I'll take care of the wine and tobacco."

" All right, sir."

" That will be all. Have a cigar."

" Thank you, sir. What's the trouble? " extending a pudgy hand toward the chimney.

" I'll tell you all about that later. Send up that man Donovan again." It occurred to the admiral that it would not be a bad plan to cover Mr. Donovan's palm. They had forgotten all about him. He had overheard.

Very carefully the captain put away the cigar and journeyed back to the village. He regretted Corsica. He hated Dagos, and Corsica was Dago; theives and cut-throats, all of them.

This long time Breitmann had despatched his letters and gone to his room, where he remained till dinner. He was a servant in the house. He must not forget that. He had been worse things than this, and still he had not forgotten. He had felt the blush of shame, yet he had remembered, and white anger had embossed the dull scars; it was impossible that he should forget.

He had grown accustomed, even in this short

time, to the window overlooking the sea, and he leaned that late afternoon with his arms resting on the part where the two frames joined and locked. The sea was blue and gentle breasted. Flocks of gulls circled the little harbor and land-birds ventured daringly forth.

With what infinite care and patience had he gained this place! What struggles had ensued! Like one of yonder birds he had been blown about, but even with his eyes hunting for this resting. He had found it and about lost it. A day or so later! He had come to rob, to lie, to pillage, any method to gain his end; and fate had led him over this threshold without dishonor, ironically. Even for that, thank God!

Dimly he heard Fitzgerald whistling in his room across. The sound entered his ear, but not his trend of thought. God in Heaven what a small place this earth was! In his hand, tightly clutched, was a ball of paper, damp from the sweat of his palm. He had gnawed it, he had pressed it in despair. Cathewe was a man, and he was not afraid of any man living. Besides, men rarely became tellers of tales. But the woman: Hildegarde von

Mitter! How to meet her, how to look into her great eyes, how to hear the sound of her voice!

He flung the ball of paper into the corner. She could break him as one breaks a dry and brittle reed.

CHAPTER XII

"YESSIR, Mr. Donovan," said Captain Flanagan, his peg-leg crossed and one hand ab-
stractedly polishing the brass ferrule; " Yessir, the
question is, what did y' hear? "

Mr. Donovan caressed his beer-glass and reflected. The two were seated in the office of Swan's
Hotel. " Well, I took them bricks out an' it seems
that loony ol' Frenchman our grandpas use to blow
about had hid a box in th' chimbley."

" A box in the chimbley. An what was in the
box? "

Mr. Donovan considered again. " I'll tell you the
truth, Cap'n. It wus a lot of rigermarole about
a treasure. I wanted t' laugh. Your commodore's
a hoodoo on pirates an' treasures, an' he ain't found
either yet."

" No jokin'; keep a clear course."

"No harm. Th' admiral's all right, and don't you forget it. As I wus sayin', they finds this 'ere box. The dockeyments wus in French, but th' daughter read 'em off sumpin wonderful. You've heard of Napoleon?"

"Yes; I recollects the name," replied the captain, with quiet ridicule.

"Well, this business pertained t' him. Seems some o' his friends got money t'gether t' rescue him from some island or other."

"St. Helena."

"That wus it. They left the cash in a box in Corsiker, 'nother island; I-talyan, I take it. But I'll bet a dollar you never find anythin' there."

"That is as may be." The captain liberated a full sigh and dug a hand into a trousers pocket. He looked cautiously about. The two of them were without witnesses. The landlord was always willing to serve beer to those in quest of it; but immediately on providing it, he resumed his interrupted perusal of the sporting column. At this moment his soul was flying around the track at Bennington. When the captain pulled out his hand it seemed full of bright autumn leaves. Donovan's glass was suspended midway between the table and his lips. Slowly the glass retraced the half-circle and resumed its perpendicular position upon the oak.

" Beauties; huh? " said the captain.

" Twenty-dollar bills! "

" Yessir; every one of 'em as good as gold; payable to bearer on demand, says your Uncle Sam."

" An' why are you makin' me envious this way? " said Donovan crossly.

" Donovan, you and me's been friends off an' on these ten years, ever since th' commodore bought th' *Laura*. Well, says he t' me ' Capt'n, we forgot that Mr. Donovan was in th' room at th' time o' th' discovery. Will you be so kind as to impress him with the fact that this expedition is on the Q. T.? Not that I think he will say anythin', but you might add these few bits o' paper to his promise not t' speak.' Says I, ' I'll trust Mr. Donovan.' An' I do. You never broke no promise yet."

" It pays in the long run," replied Mr. Donovan, vainly endeavoring to count the bills.

" Well, this 'ere little fortune is yours if you promise to abide by th' conditions."

" That I keeps my mouth shut."

" An' *not* open it even to th' Mrs."

Mr. Donovan permitted a doubt to wrinkle his brow. " That'll be a tough proposition."

" Put th' money in th' bank and say nothin' till you hear from me," advised the captain.

" That's a go."

" Then I give you these five nice ones with th' regards o' th' commodore." The captain stripped each bill and slowly laid it down on the table for the fear that by some curious circumstance there might be six.

" One hundred? Capt'n, I'm a —" Mr. Donovan emptied his glass with a few swift gulps and banged the table. " Two more."

The landlord lowered his paper wearily (would they never let him alone?) and stepped behind the bar. At the same time Mr. Donovan folded the bills and stowed them away.

" Not even t' th' Mrs.," he swore. " Here's luck, Capt'n."

" Same t' you; an' don't get drunk this side o' Jersey City."

And with this admonition the captain drank his beer and thumped off for the water front, satisfied that the village would hear nothing from Mr. Donovan. Nevertheless, it was shameful to let a hundred go that easy; twenty would have served. He was about to hail the skiff when he was accosted by the quiet little man he had recently observed sitting alone in the corner of Swan's office.

"Pardon, but you are Captain Flanagan of the yacht *Laura?*"

"Yessir," patiently. "But the owner never lets anybody aboard he don't know, sir."

"I do not desire to come aboard, my Captain. What I wish to know is if his excellency the admiral is at home."

"His excellency" rather confounded the captain for a moment; but he came about without "takin' more'n a bucketful," as he afterward expressed it to Halloran the engineer. "I knew right then he wus a furriner; I know 'em. They ain't no excellencies in th' navy. But I tells him that the commodore was snug in his berth up yonder, and with that he looks to me like I wus a lady. I've seen him in Swan's at night readin'; allus chasin' butterflies when he sees 'em in the street." And the captain rounded out this period by touching his forehead as a subtle hint that in his opinion the foreigner carried no ballast.

In the intervening time the subject of this light suggestion was climbing the hill with that tireless resiliant step of one born to mountains.   No task appeared visibly to weary this man.   Small as he was, his bones were as strong and his muscles as stringy as a wolf's.   If the butterfly was worth while he would follow till it fell to his net or daylight withdrew its support.   Never he lost patience, never his smile faltered, never his mild spectacled eyes wavered.   He was a savant by nature; he was a secret agent by choice.   Who knows anything about rare butterflies appreciates the peril of the pursuit; one never picks the going and often stumbles.   He was a hunter of butterflies by nature; but he possessed a something more than a mere smattering of other odd crafts.   He was familiar with precious gems, marbles he knew and cameos; he could point out the weakness in a drawing, the false effort in a symphony; he was something of mutual interest to every man and woman he met.

So it fell out very well that Admiral Killigrew was fond of butterflies.   Still, he should have been equally glad to know that the sailor's hobby inclined toward the exploits of pirates. M. Ferraud was a modest man. That his exquisite brochure on lepidopterous insects was in nearly all the public libraries of the world only gratified, but added nothing to his vanity.

As it oftentimes happens to a man whose mind is occupied with other things, the admiral, who received M. Ferraud in the library, saw nothing in the name to kindle his recollection. He bade the savant to be seated while he read the letter of introduction which had been written by the secretary of the navy.

" MY DEAR KILLIGREW:
" This will introduce to you Monsieur Ferraud, of the butterfly fame. He has learned of the success of your efforts in the West Indies and South America and is eager to see your collection. Do what you can for him. I know you will, for you certainly must have his book. I myself do not know a butterfly from a June-bug, but it will be a pleasure to bring you two together."

Breitmann arranged his papers neatly and waited to be dismissed. He had seen M. Ferraud at Swan's, but had formed no opinion regarding him;

in fact, the growth of his interest had stopped at indifference. On his part, the new arrival never so much as gave the secretary a seçond glance — the first was sufficient. And while the admiral read on, M. Ferraud examined the broken skin on his palms.

"Mr. Ferraud! Well, well; this is a great honor, I'm sure. It was very kind of them to send you here. Where is your luggage?"

"I am stopping at Swan's Hotel."

"We shall have your things up this very night."

"Oh!" said Ferraud, in protest; though this was the very thing he desired.

"Not a word!" The admiral summoned the butler, who was the general factotem at The Pines, and gave a dozen orders.

"Ah, you Americans!" laughed M. Ferraud, pyramiding his fingers. "You leave us breathless."

"Your book has delighted me. But I'm afraid my collection will not pay you for your trouble."

"That is for me to decide. My South American specimens are all seconds. On the other hand, you have netted yours yourself."

And straightway a bond of friendship was riveted

between these two men which still remains bright and untarnished by either absence or forgetfulness. They bent over the cases, agreed and disagreed, the one with the sharp gestures, the other with the rise and fall of the voice. For them nothing else existed; they were truly engrossed.

Breitmann, hiding a smile that was partly a yawn, stole quietly away. Butterflies did not excite his concern in the least.

M. Ferraud was charmed. He was voluble. Never had he entered a more homelike place, large enough to be called a château, yet as cheerful as a writer's fire. And the daughter! Her French was the elegant speech of Tours, her German Hanoverian. Incomparable! And she was not married? *Helas!* How many luckless fellows walked the world desolate? And this was M. Fitzgerald the journalist? And M. Breitmann had also been one? How delighted he was to be here! All this flowed on with perfect naturalness; there wasn't a false note anywhere. At dinner he diffused a warmth and geniality which were infectious. Laura was pleased and amused; and she adored her father for these impulses which brought to the board, unexpectedly, such men as M. Ferraud.

M. Ferraud did not smoke, but he dissipated to the extent of drinking three small cups of coffee after dinner.

"You are right," he acknowledged — there had been a slight dispute relative to the methods of roasting the berry —" Europe does not roast its coffee, it burns it. The aroma, the bouquet! I am beaten."

"So am I," Fitzgerald reflected sadly, snatching a vision of the girl's animated face.

Three days he had ridden into the country with her, or played tennis, or driven down to the village and inspected the yacht. He had been lonely so long and this beautiful girl was such a good comrade. One moment he blessed the prospective treasure hunt, another he execrated it. To be with this girl was to love her; and whither this pleasurable idleness would lead him he was neither blind nor self-deceiving. But with the semi-humorous recklessness which was the leaven of his success, he thrust prudence behind him and stuck to the primrose path. He had played with fire before, but never had the coals burned so brightly. He did not say that she was above him; mentally and by birth they were equals; simply, he was compelled to admit of the truth that she was beyond him. Money. That was the obstacle. For what man will live on his wife's bounty? Suppose they found the treasure (and with his old journalistic suspicion he was still skeptical), and divided it; why, the interest on his share would not pay for her dresses. To the ordinary male eye her gowns looked inexpensive, but to him who had picked up odd bits of information not usually in the pathway of man, to him there was no secret about it. That bodice and those sleeves of old Venetian point would have eaten up the gains of any three of his most prosperous months.

And Breitmann, dropping occasionally the ash of his cigarette on the tray, he, too, was pondering. But his German strain did not make it so easy for him as for Fitzgerald to give concrete form to his thought. The star, as he saw it, had a nebulous appearance.

M. Ferraud chatted gaily. Usually a man who

holds his audience is of single purpose. The little Frenchman had two aims: one, to keep the conversation on subjects of his own selection, and the other, to study without being observed. Among one of his own tales (butterflies) he told of a chase he once had made in the mountains of the Moors, in Abyssinia. To illustrate it he took up one of the nets standing in the corner. In his excitable way he was a very good actor. And when he swooped down the net to demonstrate the end of the story, it caught on a button on Breitmann's coat.

" Pardon! " said M. Ferraud, with a blithe laugh. " The butterfly I was describing was not so big."

Breitmann freed himself amid general laughter. And with Laura's rising the little after-dinner party became disorganized.

It was yet early; but perhaps she had some thought she wished to be alone with. This consideration was the veriest bud in growth; still, it was such that she desired the seclusion of her room. She swung across her shoulders the sleepy Angora and wished the men good night.

The wire bell in the hall clock vibrated twice;

two o'clock of the morning. A streak of moonshine fell aslant the floor and broke off abruptly.
Before the safe in the library stood Breitmann, a
small tape in his hand. For several minutes he
contemplated somberly the nickel combination
wheel. He *could* open it for he knew the combination. To open it would be the work of a moment.
Why, then, did he hesitate? Why not pluck it
forth and disappear on the morrow? The admiral
had not made a copy, and without the key he
might dig up Corsica till the crack of doom. The
flame on the taper crept down. The man gave a
quick movement to his shoulders; it was the shrug,
not of impatience but of resignation. He saw the
lock through the haze of a conjured face. He shut
his eyes, but the vision remained. Slowly he drew
his fingers over the flame.

Yet, before the flame died wholly it touched two
points of light in the doorway, the round crystals
of a pair of spectacles.

"Two souls with but a single thought!" the
secret agent murmured. "Poor devil! why does he
hesitate? Why does he not take it and be gone?

Is he still honest? *Peste!* I must be growing old. I shall not ruin him, I shall save him. It is not good politics, but it is good Christianity. *Schlafen Sie wohl, Hochwohl geboren!* ”

CHAPTER XIII

THE WOMAN WHO KNEW

"DON'T you sometimes grow weary for an abiding place?" Laura pulled off her gauntlets and laid her hot hands on the cool lichen-grown stones of the field-wall. The bridle-rein hung over her arm. Fitzgerald had drawn his through a stirrup. "Think of wandering here and there, with never a place to come back to."

"I have thought of it often in the few days I have been here. I have a home in New York, but I could not possibly afford to live in it; so I rent it; and when I want to go fishing there's enough under hand to pay the expenses. My poor old dad! He was always indorsing notes for his friends, or carrying stock for them; and nothing ever came back. I am afraid the disillusions broke his heart. And then, perhaps I was a bitter disappointment. I was expelled from college in my junior year. I had no head for figures other than that kind which inhabit the Louvre and the Vatican."

Her face became momentarily mirthful.

" So I couldn't take hold of the firm for him," he continued. " And I suppose the last straw was when I tried my hand at reporting on one of the newspapers. He knew that the gathering of riches, so far as I was concerned, was a closed door. But I found my level; the business was and is the only one that ever interested me or fused my energy with real work."

" But it *is* real work. You are one of those men who have done something. Most men these days rest on their fathers' laurels."

" It's the line of the least resistance. I never knew that the Jersey coast was so picturesque. What a sweep! Do you know, your house on that pine-grown crest reminds me of the Villa Serbelloni, only yonder is the sea instead of Como? "

" Como." Her eyes became dreamily half-shut. Recollection put on its seven-league boots and annihilated the space between the wall under her elbows and the gardens of Serbelloni. Fitzgerald half understood the thought. " Isn't Mr. Breit-

mann just a bit of a mystery to you?" she asked.
The seven-league boots had returned at a bound.

"In some ways, yes." He rather resented the
abrupt angle; it was not in poetic touch with the
time being.

"He is inclined to be too much reserved. But
last night Mr. Ferraud succeeded in tearing down
some of it. If I could put in a book what all you
men have seen and taken part in! Mr. Breitmann
would be almost handsome but for those scars."

He kicked the turf at the foot of the wall. "In
Germany they are considered beauty-spots."

"I am not in sympathy with that custom."

"Still, it requires courage of a kind."

"The noblest wounds are those that are carried
unseen. Student scars are merely patches of vanity."

"He has others besides those. He was nearly
killed in the Soudan." Fitzgerald was compelled to
offer some defense for the absent. That Breitmann had lied to him, that his appearance here had
been in the regular order of things, did not take
away the fact that the Bavarian was a man and a
brave one. Closely as he had watched, up to the

present he had learned absolutely nothing; and to have shown Breitmann the telegram would have accomplished nothing further than to have put him wholly on guard.

"Have you no scars?" mischief in her eyes.

"Not yet;" and the force of his gaze turned hers aside. "Yet I must not forget my conscience; 'tis pretty well battered up."

She greeted this with laughter. She had heard men talk like this before. "You have probably never done a mean or petty thing in all your life."

"Mean and petty things never disturb a man's conscience. It's the big things that scar."

"That's a platitude."

"Then my end of the conversation is becoming flat."

"Confess that you are eager to return to the great highways once more."

"I shall confess nothing of the sort. I should like to stay here for a hundred years."

"You would miss us all very much then," merrily. "And Napoleon's treasure would have gone in and out of innumerable pockets!"

"Do you really and truly believe that we shall

bring home a single franc of it?" facing her with incredulous eyes.

"Really and truly. And why not? Treasures have been found before. Fie on you for a Doubting Thomas!"

"We sometimes go many miles to find, in the end, that the treasure was all the time under our very eyes."

"Hyperbole!" But she looked down at the lichen again and began pealing it off the stone. She thought of a duke she knew. At this instant he would have been telling her that she was the most beautiful woman since Helen. What a relief this man at her side was! She was perfectly aware that he admired her, but he veiled his tributes with half-smiles and flashes of humor. "What a gay little man that Mr. Ferraud is!"

"Lively as a cricket. Your father, I understand, is to take him as far as Marseilles. After to-night everything will be quite formal, I suppose. Honestly, I feel ill at ease in accepting your splendid hospitality. I'm an interloper. I haven't even the claim of an ordinary introduction. It has been very, very kind of you."

"You know Mrs. Coldfield. I will, if you wish it, ask her to present you to me."

"I am really serious."

"So am I."

"They will be here to-morrow?"

"Yes. And in four days we sail. Oh, it is all so beautiful! A real treasure hunt."

"It does not seem possible that I have been here a week. It has been a long time since I enjoyed myself so thoroughly. Have you ever wondered what has become of the other man?"

"The other man?"

"Yes; the other one in or outside the chimney. I've been thinking about him this long while. Hasn't it occurred to you that he may have other devices?"

"If he has he will find that he has waited too long. But I would like to know how he found out. You see," triumphantly, "he believed that there is one." She shook the rein, for the sleek mare was nozzling her shoulder and pawing slightly. "Let us be off."

She put her small booted foot on his palm and vaulted into the saddle, and he swung on to his mount. He stuffed his cap into a pocket, for he was no fair-weather horseman, but loved the tingle of the wind rushing through his hair; and the two cantered down the clear sandy road.

"*En avant!*" she cried joyously, with a light stroke of her whip.

For half a mile they ran and drew in at the fork in the road. Exhilaration was in the eyes of both of them.

"There's nothing equal to it. You feel alive. And off there," with a wave of the whip toward the sea, "off there lies our fortunes. O happy day! to take part in a really truly adventure, without the assistance of a romancer!"

"I think you are one of the most charming women I have ever met," he replied.

"Some women would object to the modification, but I rather like it."

"I withdraw the modification." The smile on his lips was not reflected in his eyes.

The antithesis of the one expression to the other did not annoy her; rather she was sensitive to a tender exultance the recurrence of which, later in

the day, subdued her: for Breitmann at tea turned
a few phrases of a similar character. Fitzgerald
was light-hearted and boyish, Breitmann was grave
and dignified; but in the eyes of each there was a
force she had encountered so seldom as to forget
its being. Breitmann, in his capacity of secretary,
was not so often in her company as Fitzgerald;
nevertheless she was subtly attracted toward him.
When he was of the mind he could invent a happy
compliment with a felicity no less facile than Fitzgerald.   And the puzzling thing of it all was, both
men she knew from their histories had never been
ornaments at garden-parties where compliments are
current coin.   She liked Fitzgerald, but she admired
Breitmann, a differentiation which she had no inclination to resolve into first principles.   That
Breitmann was a secretary for hire drew no barrier
in her mind.   She had known many gentlemen of
fine families who had served in like situations.
There were no social distinctions.   On the other
hand, she never felt wholly comfortable with Breitmann.   There was not the least mistrust in this
feeling.   It was rather because she instinctively felt

that he was above his occupation. To sum it up briefly, Breitmann was difficult to understand and Fitzgerald wasn't.

Fitzgerald had an idea; boldly put, it was a grave suspicion. Not once had he forgotten the man in the chimney. Once the finger had pointed at Breitmann or some one with whom he was in understanding. This had proved to be groundless. But he kept turning over the incident and inspecting it from all sides. There were others a-treasure hunting; persons unknown; and a man might easily become desperate in the pursuit of two-million francs, almost half a million of American money, more, for some of these coins would be rare. He had thoroughly searched the ground outside the cellar-window, but the sea gravel held its secret with a tenacity as baffling as the mother-sea herself. There was a new under-groom, or rather there had been. He had left, and where he had gone no one knew. Fitzgerald dismissed the thought of him; at the most he could have been but an accomplice, one to unlock the cellar-window.

While Breitmann lingered near Laura, offering

what signs of admiration he dared, and while the admiral chatted to his country neighbors who were gathered round the tea-table, Fitzgerald and M. Ferraud were braced against the terrace wall, a few yards farther on, and exchanged views on various peoples.

"America is a wonderful country," said M. Ferraud, when they had exhausted half a dozen topics. He spread out his hands, Frenchman-wise.

"So it is." Fitzgerald threw away his cigarette.

"And how foolish England was over a pound of tea."

"Something like that."

"But see what she lost!" with a second gesture.

"In one way it would not have mattered. She would patronize us as she still does."

"Do you not resent it, this patronizing attitude?"

"Oh, no — we are very proud to be patronized by England," cynically. "It's a fine thing to have a lord tell you that you wear your clothes jolly well."

"I wonder if you are serious or jesting."

"I am very serious at this moment," said Fitzgerald quietly catching the other by the wrist and
turning the palm.

M. Ferraud looked into his face with an astonishment on his own, most genuine. But he did not
struggle. "Why do you do that?"

"I am curious, Mr. Ferraud, when I see a hand
like this. Would you mind letting me see the
other?"

"Not in the least." M. Ferraud offered the
other hand.

Fitzgerald let go. "What was your object?"

"*Mon dieu!* what object?"

Fitzgerald lowered his voice. "What was your
object in digging holes in yonder chimney? Did
you know what was there? And what do you propose to do now?"

M. Ferraud coolly took off his spectacles and
polished the lenses. It needed but a moment to
adjust them. "What are you talking about?"

"You are really M. Ferraud?" said the young
man coldly.

The Frenchman produced a wallet and took out
a letter. It was written by the president of France,

introducing M. Ferraud to the ambassador at Washington. Next, there was a passport, and far more important than either of these was the Legion of Honor. " Yes, I am Anatole Ferraud."

" That is all I desire to know."

" Shall we return to the ladies? " asked M. Ferraud, restoring his treasures.

" Since there is nothing more to be said at present. It seems strange to me that foreign politics should find its way here."

" Politics? I am only a butterfly hunter."

" There are varieties. But you are the man. I shall find out! "

" Possibly," returned M. Ferraud thinking hard.

" I give you fair warning that if anything is missing —"

" Oh, Mr. Fitzgerald! "

" I shall know where to look for it," with a smile which had no humor in it.

" Why not denounce me now? "

" Would it serve your purpose? "

" No," with deeper gravity. " It would be a great disaster; how great, I can not tell you."

" Then, I shall say nothing."

"About what?" dryly, even whimsically.

"About your being a secret agent from France."

This time M. Ferraud's glance proved that he was truly startled. Only three times in his career had his second life been questioned or suspected. He eyed his hands accusingly; they had betrayed him. This young man was clever, cleverer than he had thought. He had been too confident and had committed a blunder. Should he trust him? With that swift unerring instinct which makes the perfect student of character, he said: "You will do me a great favor not to impart this suspicion to any one else."

"Suspicion?"

"It is true: I am a secret agent;" and he said it proudly.

"You wish harm to none here?"

"*Mon dieu!* No. I am here for the very purpose of saving you all from heartaches and misfortune and disillusion. And had I set to work earlier I should have accomplished all this without a single one of you knowing it. Now the matter will have to go on to its end."

"Can you tell me anything?"

" Not now.   I trust you; will you trust me? "

Fitzgerald hesitated for a space.   " Yes."

" For that, thanks," and M. Ferraud put out a hand.   " It is clean, Mr. Fitzgerald, for all that the skin is broken."

" Of that I have no doubt."

" Before we reach Corsica you will know."

And so temporarily that ended the matter.   But as Fitzgerald went over to the chair just vacated by the secretary, he found that there was a double zest to life now.   This would be far more exciting than dodging ice-floes and freezing one's toes.

Laura told him the news.   Their guests would arrive that evening in time for dinner.

It was Breitmann's habit to come down first.   He would thrum a little on the piano or take down some old volume.   To-night it was Heine.   He had not met any of the guests yet, which he considered a piece of good fortune.   But God only knew what would happen when *she* saw him.   He dreaded the moment, dreaded it with anguish.   She was a woman, schooled in acting, but a time comes when the best acting is not sufficient.   If only in some way he might have warned her; but no way had opened. She would find him ready, however, ready with his eyes, his lips, his nerves. What would the others think or say if she lost her presence of mind? His teeth snapped. He read on. The lamp threw the light on the scarred side of his face.

He heard some one enter, and his gaze stole over the top of his book. This person was a woman, and her eyes traveled from object to object with a curiosity tinged with that incertitude which attacks us all when we enter an unfamiliar room. She was dressed in black, showing the white arms and neck. Her hair was like ripe wheat after a rainstorm: oh, but he knew well the color of her eyes, blue as the Adriatic. She was a woman of perhaps thirty, matured, graceful, handsome. The sight of her excited a thrill in his veins, deny it how he would.

She scanned the long rows of books, the strange weapons, the heroic and sinister flags, the cases of butterflies. With each inspection she stepped nearer and nearer, till by reaching out his hand he

might have touched her. Quietly he rose. It was
a critical moment.

She was startled. She had thought she was
alone.

" Pardon me," she said, in a low, musical voice;
" I did not know that any one was here."   And then
she saw his face.   Her own blanched and her hands
went to her heart. " Karl? "

CHAPTER XIV

THE DRAMA BEGINS

SHE swayed a little, but recovered as the pain of the shock was succeeded by numbness. That out of the dark of this room, into the light of that lamp, in this house so far removed from cities that it seemed not a part of the world . . . there should step this man! Why had there been no hint of his presence? Why had not the clair-voyance of despair warned her? One of her hands rose and pressed over her eyes, as if to sponge out this phantom. It was useless; it was no dream; he was still there, this man she had neither seen nor heard of for five years because her will was stronger than her desire, this man who had broken her heart as children break toys! And deep below all this present terror was the abiding truth that she still loved him and always would love him. The shame

198

of this knowledge did more than all else to rouse and to nerve her.

"Karl?" It was like an echo.

"Yes." There was war in his voice and attitude and not without reason. He had wronged this woman, not with direct intention it was true, but nevertheless he had wronged her; and her presence here could mean nothing less than that fate had selected this spot for the reckoning. She could topple down his carefully reared schemes with the same ease with which he had blown over hers. And to him these schemes were life to his breath and salt to his blood, everything. What was one woman? cynically. "Yes, it is I," in the tongue native to them both.

"And what do you here?"

"I am Admiral Killigrew's private secretary." He wet his lips. He was not so strong before this woman as he had expected to be. The glamour of the old days was faintly rekindled at the sight of her. And she *was* beautiful.

"Then, this is the house?" in a whisper.

"It is."

"You terrify me!"

"Hildegarde, this is your scheme," shrugging. "Tell them all you know; break me, ruin me. Here is a fair opportunity for revenge."

"God forbid!" she cried with a shiver. "Were you guilty of all crimes, I could only remember that once I loved you."

"You shame me," he replied frankly, but with infinite relief. "You have outdone me in magnanimity. Will you forgive me?"

"Oh, yes. Forgiveness is one of the few things you men can not rob us of." She spoke without bitterness, but her eyes were dim and her lips dropped. "What shall we do? They must not know that we have met."

"Cathewe knows," moodily.

"I had forgotten!"

"I leave all in your hands. Do what you will. If you break me — and God knows well that you can do it — it would be only an act of justice. I have been a damned scoundrel; I am man enough to admit of that."

She saw his face more clearly now. Time had marked it. There were new lines at the corners of his eyes and the cheek-bones were more prominent.

Perhaps he had suffered too. "You will always have the courage to do," she said, "right or wrong in a great manner."

"Am I wrong to seek —"

"Hush! I know. It is what you must thrust aside or break to reach it, Karl. The thing itself is not wrong, but you will go about it wrongly. You can not help that."

He did not reply. Perhaps she was right. Indeed, was she not herself an example of it? If there was one thing in his complex career that he regretted more than another it was the deception of this woman. He did not possess the usual vanity of the sex; there was nothing here to be proud of; his dream of conquest was not over the kingdom of women.

"Some one is coming," he said, listening.

"Leave it all to me."

"Ah! . . ." with a hand toward her.

"Do not say it. I understand the thought. If only you loved me, you would say!" the iron in her voice unmistakable.

He let his hand fall. He was sorry.

Presently the others made their entrance upon

the scene, a singular anticlimax.   The admiral rang
for the cocktails.   Introductions followed.

"Is it not strange?" said the singer to Laura.
"I stole in here to look at the trophies, when I dis-
covered Mr. Breitmann whom I once knew in
Munich."

"Mr. Cathewe," said the young hostess, "this
is Mr. Breitmann, who is aiding father in the com-
pilation of his book."

"Mr. Breitmann and I have met before," said
Cathewe soberly.

The two men bowed.   Cathewe never gave his
hand to any but his intimates.   But Laura, who was
not aware of this ancient reserve, thought that both
of them showed a lack of warmth.   And Fitzgerald,
who was watching all corners now, was sure that
the past of his friend and Breitmann interlaced in
some way.

"So, young man," said Mrs. Coldfield, a handsome motherly woman, "you have had the impu-
dence to let five years pass without darkening my
doors.   What excuse have you?"

"I'm guilty of anything you say," Fitzgerald answered humbly. "What shall be my punishment?"

"You shall take Miss Laura in and I shall sit at your left."

"For my sins it shall be as you say. But, really, I have been so little in New York," he added.

"I forgive you simply because you have not made a failure of your mother's son. And you look like her, too." It is one of the privileges of old persons to compare the young with this or that parent.

"You are flattering me. Dad used to say that I was as homely as a hedge-fence."

"Now you're fishing, and I'm too old a fish to rise to such a cast."

"I heard you sing in Paris a few years ago," said M. Ferraud.

"Yes?" Hildegarde von Mitter wondered who this little man could be.

"And you sing no more?"

"No. The bird has flown; only the woman remains." They were at the table now, and she absently plucked the flowers beside her plate.

"Ah, to sing as you did, and then to disappear,

to vanish! You had no right to do so. You belonged to the public," animatedly.

"The public is always selfish; it always demands more than any single person can give to it. Pardon?" she said as Cathewe leaned to speak to her. "I did not hear."

M. Ferraud nibbled his crisp celery.

"I asked, what will you do?" repeated Cathewe for her ear only.

"What do you mean?"

"Did you know that he was here?"

"I should not have been seated at this table had I known."

"Some day you are going to tell me all about it," he asserted; "and you are going to smile when you answer me."

"Thank you. I forgot. My dear friend, I am never going to tell you all about it. Why did you not come first?" her voice vibrating.

"You still love him."

"That is not kind," striving hard to keep the smile on her trembling lips. "Oh, I beg of you, do not make this friendship impossible. Do not rob me of the one man I trust."

Cathewe motioned aside the fish and reached for his sauterne. "I have loved you faithfully and loyally for seven years. I have tried to win you by all those roads a man may honorably traverse in quest of the one woman. For seven years; and for something like three I have stayed away at your command. Will you believe it? Sometimes my hands ache for his throat . . . Smile, they are looking."

It was a crooked smile. "Why did I ever tell you?"

"Why did you ever tell me . . . only part? It is the other part I wish to know. Till I learn what that is I shall never leave you. You will find that there is a difference between love and infatuation."

"As I have never known infatuation I can not tell the difference. Now, no more, unless you care to see me break down before them. For if you tell me that you have loved me seven years, I have loved him eight," cruelly, for Cathewe was pressing her cruelly.

"Devil take him! What do you find in the man?"

"What do you find in me?" her eyes filled with anger.

"Forgive me, Hildegarde; I am blind and mad to-night. I did not expect to find him here either."

Breitmann had tried ineffectually to read their lips. She had given her word, and once given he knew of old that she never broke it; but he was keenly alive that in some way he was the topic of the inaudible conversation. As he sat here to-night he knew why he had never loved Hildegarde, why in fact, he had never loved any woman. The one great passion which comes in the span of life was centered in the girl beside him, dividing her moments between him and Fitzgerald. Strange, but he had not known it till he saw the two women together. For once his nice calculations had ceased to run smoothly; there appeared now a knot in the thread for which he saw no untying.

"You do not sing now?" asked Laura across the table.

"No," Hildegarde answered, "my voice is gone."

"Oh, I am so sorry."

"It does not matter. I can hum a little to myself; there is yet some pleasure in that. But in opera, no, never again. Has not Mrs. Coldfield told you? No? Imagine! One night in Dresden, in the middle of the aria, my voice broke miserably and I could not go on."

"And her heart nearly broke with it," interposed Mrs. Coldfield, with the best intentions, nearer the truth than she knew. "I am sorry, Laura, that I never told you before."

Hildegarde laughed. "Sooner or later this must happen. I worked too hard, perhaps. At any rate, the opera will know me no more."

There was the hard blue of flint in Cathewe's eyes as they met and held Breitmann's. There was a duel, and the latter was routed. But hate burned fiercely in the breast against the man who could compel him to lower his eyes. Some day he would pay back that glance.

Now, M. Ferraud had missed nothing. He twisted the talk into other channels with his usual adroitness, but all the while there was bubbling in his mind the news that these two men had met before. The history of Hildegarde von Mitter was known to him. But how much did she know, or this man Cathewe? The woman was a thoroughbred. He, Anatole Ferraud, knew; it was his business to know; and that she should happen upon the scene he considered as one of these rare good pieces of luck that fall to the lot of few. There would be something more than treasure hunting here; an intricate comedy-drama, with as many well-defined sides as a diamond. He ate his endive with pleasure and sipped the old yellow *Pol Roger* with his eyes beaming toward the gods. To be, after a fashion, the prompter behind the scenes; to be able to read the final line before the curtain! Butterflies and butterflies and pins and pins.

Did Laura note any of the portentous glances, those exchanged between the singer and Cathewe and Breitmann? Perhaps. At all events she felt a curiosity to know how long Hildegarde von Mitter had known her father's secretary. There was no envy in her heart as again she acknowledged the beauty of the other woman; moreover, she liked her and was going to like her more. Impressions were made upon her almost instantly, for good or bad, and rarely changed.

She turned oftenest to Fitzgerald, for he made particular effort to entertain, and he succeeded bet-

ter than he dreamed. It kept turning over in her
mind what a whimsical, capricious, whirligig was
at work. It was droll, this man at her side, chatting
to her as if he had known her for years, when, seven
or eight days ago, he had stood, a man all unknown
to her, on a city corner, selling plaster of Paris
statuettes on a wager; and but for Mrs. Coldfield,
she had passed him for ever. Out upon the prude
who would look askance at her for harmless daring!

"Drop into my room before you turn in," urged
Fitzgerald to Cathewe.

"That I shall, my boy. I've some questions
to ask of you."

But a singular idea came into creation, and this
was for him, Cathewe, to pay Breitmann a visit on
the way to Fitzgerald's room. Not one man in a
thousand would have dared put this idea into a plan
of action. But neither externals nor conventions
deterred Cathewe when he sought a thing. He
rapped lightly on the door of the secretary's room.

"Come in."

Cathewe did so, gently closing the door behind
him. Breitmann was in his shirt-sleeves. He rose
from his chair and laid down his cigarette. A faint

smile broke the thin line of his mouth. He waited for his guest, or, rather, this intruder, to break the silence. And as Cathewe did not speak at once, there was a tableau during which each was speculatively busy with the eyes.

"The vicissitudes of time," said Cathewe, "have left no distinguishable marks upon you."

Breitmann bowed. He remained standing.

And Cathewe had no wish to sit. "I never expected to see you in this house."

"A compliment which I readily return."

"A private secretary; I never thought of you in that capacity."

"One must take what one can," tranquilly.

"A good precept." Cathewe rolled the ends of his mustache, a trifle perplexed how to put it. "But there should be exceptions. What," and his voice became crisp and cold, "what was Hildegarde von Mitter to you?"

"And what is that to you?"

"My question first."

"I choose not to answer it."

Again they eyed each other like fencers.

"Were you married?"

Breitmann laughed.   Here was his opportunity to wring this man's heart; for he knew that Cathewe loved the woman.   "You seem to be in her confidence.   Ask her."

"A poltroon would say as much.   There is a phase in your make-up I have never fully understood.   Physically you are a brave man, but morally you are a cad and a poltroon."

"Take care!"   Breitmann stepped forward menacingly.

"There will be no fisticuffs," contemptuously.

"Not if you are careful.   I have answered your questions; you had better leave at once."

"She is loyal to you.   It was not her voice that broke that night; it was her heart.   You have some hold over her."

"None that she can not throw off at any time." Breitmann's mind was working strangely.

"If she would have me I would marry her to-morrow," went on Cathewe, playing openly, "I would marry her to-morrow, priest or protestant, for her religion would be mine."

There was a spark of admiration in Breitmann's eyes.   This man Cathewe was out of the ordinary.

Well, as for that, so was he himself. He walked silently to the door and opened it, standing aside for the other to pass. "She is perfectly free. Marry her. She is all and more than you wish her to be. Will you go now?"

Cathewe bowed and turned on his heel. Breitmann had really got the better of him.

A peculiar interview, and only two strong men could have handled it in so few words. Not a word above normal tones; once or twice only, in the flutter of the eyelids or in the gesture of the hands, was there any sign that had these been primitive times the two would have gone joyously at each other's throats.

"I owed her that much," said Breitmann as he locked the door.

"It did not matter at all to me," was Cathewe's thought, as he knocked on Fitzgerald's door and heard his cheery call, "I only wanted to know what sort of man he is."

"Oh, I really don't know whether I like him or not," declared Fitzgerald. "I have run across him

two or three times, but we were both busy. He has
told me a little about himself. He's been knocked
about a good deal. Has a title, but doesn't use it."

"A title? That is news to me. Probably it is
true."

"I was surprised to learn that you knew him at
all."

"Not very well. Met him in Munich mostly."

A long pause.

"Isn't Miss Killigrew just rippin'? There's a
comrade for some man. Lucky devil, who gets
her! She is new to me every day."

"I think I warned you."

"You were a nice one, never to say a word that
you knew the admiral!"

"Are you complaining?"

Fitzgerald laughed; no not exactly; he wasn't
complaining.

"You remember the caravan trails in the Lybian
desert; the old ones on the way to Khartoum? The
pathway behind her is like that, marked with the
bleached bones of princely and ducal and common
hopes." Cathewe stretched out in his chair.

" Since she was eighteen, Jack, she has crossed the man-trail like a sandstorm, and quite as innocently, too."

" Oh, rot!   I'm no green and salad youth."

" Your bones will be only the tougher, that's all."

Another pause.

" But what's your opinion regarding Breit-mann? "

Cathewe laced his fingers and bent his chin on them.   " There's a great rascal or a great hero somewhere under his skin."

CHAPTER XV

THEY GO A-SAILING

FIVE o'clock in the afternoon, and a mild blue sea flashing under the ever-deepening orange of the falling sun. Golden castles and gray castles and castles of shadowed-white billowed in the east; turrets rose and subsided and spires of cloud-cities formed and re-formed. The yacht *Laura,* sleek and swan-white, her ensign and colors folding and unfolding, lifting and sinking, as the shore breeze stirred them, was making ready for sea; and many of the villagers had come down to the water front to see her off. Very few sea-going vessels, outside of freighters, ever stopped in this harbor; and naturally the departures of the yacht were events equalled only by her arrivals. The railroad station was close to the wharves, and the old sailors hated the sight of the bright rails; for the locomotive had robbed them of the excitement of the semi-weekly packets that used to coast up and down between New York and Philadelphia.

"Wonder what poor devil of a pirate is going to have his bones turned over this trip?" said the station-agent to Mr. Donovan, who, among others on the station platform, watched the drab anchor as it clanked jerkily upward to the bows, leaving a swivel and a boil on the waters which had released it so grudgingly.

"I guess it ain't goin' t' be any ol' pirate this time," replied Mr. Donovan, with a pleasurable squeeze of the pocket-book over his heart.

"Well, I hope he finds what he's going after," generously. "He is the mainstay of this old one-horse town. Say, she's a beauty, isn't she? Why, man, that anchor alone is worth more than we make in four months. And think of the good things to eat and drink. If I had a million, no pirates or butterflies for mine. I'd hie me to Monte Carlo and bat the tiger all over the place."

Mr. Donovan knew nothing definite about Monte Carlo, but he would have liked to back up against some of those New York contractors on their own grounds.

"Hi! There she goes. Good luck!" cried the station-agent, swinging his hat with gusto.

The yacht swam out gracefully. There was a freshening blow from the southwest, but it would take the yacht half an hour to reach the deep-sea swells outside. Her whistle blew cheerily and was answered by the single tug-boat moored to the railroad wharf. And after that the villagers straggled back to their various daily concerns. Even the landlord of Swan's Hotel sighed as he balanced up his books. Business would be slack for some days to come.

The voyagers were gathered about the stern-rail and a handkerchief or two fluttered in the wind. For an hour they tarried there, keeping in view the green-wooded hills and the white cottages nestling at their base. And turn by turn there were glimpses of the noble old house at the top of the hill. And some looked upon it for the last time.

"I've had a jolly time up there," said Fitzgerald. The gulls swooped, as they crossed and recrossed the milky wake. "Better time than I deserved."

"Are you still worried about that adventure?"

Laura demanded. " Dismiss it from your mind and let it be as if we had known each other for many years."

" Do you really mean that? "

" To be sure I do," promptly. " I have stepped to the time of convention so much that a lapse once in a while is a positive luxury. But Mrs. Coldfield had given me a guaranty before I addressed you, so the adventure was only a make-believe one after all."

There never was a girl quite like this one. He purloined a sidelong glance at her which embraced her wholly, from the chic gray cap on the top of her shapely head to the sensible little boots on her feet. She wore a heavy, plaid coat, with deep pockets into which her hands were snugly buried; and she stood braced against the swell and the wind which was turning out strong and cold. The rich pigment in the blood mantled her cheeks and in her eyes there was still a bit of captive sunshine. He knew now that what had been only a possibility was an assured fact. Never before had he cursed his father's friends, but he did so now, silently and earnestly; for their pilfering fingers and their plaus-

ible lies had robbed his father's son of a fine inheritance.   Money.   Never had he desired it so keenly.
A few weeks ago it had meant the wherewithal to
pay his club-dues and to support a decent table when
he traveled.   Now it was everything; for without
it he never could dare lift his eyes seriously to this
lovely picture so close to him, let alone dream of
winning her.   He recalled Cathewe's light warning
about the bones of ducal hopes.   What earthly
chance had he?   Unconsciously he shrugged.

"You are shrugging!" she cried, noting the
expression; for, if he was secretly observing her,
she was surreptitiously contemplating his own ad-
vantages.

"Did I shrug?"

"You certainly did."

"Well," candidly, "it was the thought of money
that made me do it."

"I detest it, too."

"Good heavens, I didn't say I detested it!   What
I shrugged about was my own dreary lack of it."

"Bachelors do not require much."

"That's true; but I no longer desire to remain
a bachelor."   The very thing that saved him was

the added laughter, forced, miserably forced. Fool! The words had slipped without his thinking.

"Gracious! That sounds horribly like a proposal." She beamed upon him merrily.

And his heart sank, for he had been earnest enough, for all his blunder. Manlike, he did not grasp the fact that under the circumstance merriment was all she could offer him, if she would save him from his own stupidity.

"But I do hate money," she reaffirmed

"I shouldn't. Think of what it brings."

"I do; begging letters, impostures, battle-scarred titles, humbugging shop-keepers, and perhaps one honest friend in a thousand. And if I married a title, what equivalent would I get for my money, to put it brutally? A château, which I should have to patch up, and tolerance from my husband's noble friends. Not an engaging prospect."

She threw a handful of biscuit to the gulls, and there was fighting and screaming almost in touch of the hands. Then of a sudden the red rim of the sun vanished behind the settling landscape, and all the grim loneliness of the sea rose up to greet them.

"It is lonely; let us go and prepare for dinner. Look!" pointing to a bright star far down the east. "And Corsica lies that way."

"And also madness!" was his thought.

"Oh, it seems not quite true that we are all going a-venturing as they do in the story-books. The others think we are just going to Funchal. Remember, you must not tell. Think of it; a real treasure, every franc of which must tell a story of its own; love, heroism and devotion."

"Beautiful! But there must be a rescuing of princesses and fighting and all that. I choose the part of remaining by the princess."

"It is yours." She tilted back her head and breathed and breathed. She knew the love of living.

"Lucky we are all good sailors," he said. "There will be a fair sea on all night. But how well she rides!"

"I love every beam and bolt of her."

Shoulder to shoulder they bore forward to the

companionway, and immediately the door banged after them.

Breitmann came out from behind the funnel and walked the deck for a time. He had studied the two from his shelter. What were they saying? Oh, Fitzgerald was clever and strong and good to look at, but . . . ! Breitmann straightened his arms before him, opened and shut his hands violently. Like that he would break him if he interfered with any of *his* desires. It would be fully twenty days before they made Ajaccio. Many things might happen before that time.

Two or three of the crew were lashing on the rail-canvas, and the snap and flap of it jarred on Breitmann's nerves. For a week or more his nerves had been very close to the surface, so close that it had required all his will to keep his voice and hands from shaking. As he passed, one of the sailors doffed his cap and bowed with great respect.

"That's not the admiral, Alphonse," whispered another of the crew, chuckling. "It's only his privit secretary."

"Ah, I haf meestake!"

But Alphonse had made no mistake. He knew

who it was. His mates did not see the smile of
irony, of sly ridicule, which stirred his lips as he
bowed to the passer. Immediately his rather handsome effeminate face resumed a stolid vacuity.

His name was not Alphonse; it was a captious
offering by the crew, which, on this yacht, never
went further than to tolerate the addition of a foreigner to their mess. He had signed a day or two
before sailing; he had even begged for the honor
to ship with Captain Flanagan; and he gave his
name as Pierre Picard, to which he had no more
right than to Alphonse. As Captain Flanagan was
too good a sailor himself to draw distinctions, he
was always glad to add a foreign tongue to his crew.
You never could tell when its use might come in
handy. That is why Pierre Picard was allowed to
drink his soup in the forecastle mess.

Breitmann continued on, oblivious to all things
save his cogitations. He swung round the bridge.
He believed that he and Cathewe could henceforth
proceed on parallel lines, and there was much to
be grateful for. Cathewe was quiet but deep; and
he, Breitmann, had knocked about among that sort
and knew that they were to be respected. In all,

he had made only one serious blunder. He should never have permitted the vision of a face to deter him. He should have taken the things from the safe and vanished. It had not been a matter of compunction. And yet . . . Ah, he was human, whatever his dream might be; and he loved this American girl with all his heart and mind. It was not lawless love, but it was ruthless. When the time was ripe he would speak. Only a little while now to wait. The course had smoothed out, the sailing was easy. The man in the chimney no longer bothered him. Whoever and whatever he was, he had not shot his bolt soon enough.

Hildegarde von Mitter. He stopped against the rail. The yacht was burying her nose now, and the white drift from her cut-water seemed strangely luminous as it swirled obliquely away in the fading twilight. Hildegarde von Mitter. Was she to be the flaw in the chain? No, no; there should be no regret; he had steeled his heart against any such weakness. She had been necessary, and he would be a fool to pause over a bit of sentimentality. Her appearance had disorganized his nerves, that was

all. Peering into his watch he found that he had
only half an hour before dinner. And it may be
added that he dressed with singular care.

So did Fitzgerald, for that matter.

It took Cathewe just as long, but he did not
make two or three selections of this or that before
finding what he wanted. He was engrossed most
of the time in the sober contemplation of the rubber
flooring or the running sea outside the port-hole.

And this night Hildegarde von Mitter was meditating on the last throw for her hopes. She determined to cast once more the full sun of her
beauty into the face of the man she loved; and if
she failed to win, the fault would not be hers. Why
could she not tear out this maddening heart of hers
and fling it to the sea? Why could she not turn it
toward the man who loved her? Why, why?
Why should God make her so unhappy? Why such
injustice? Why this twisted interlacing of lives?
And yet, amid all these futile seekings, with sub-
conscious deftness her hands went on with their
appointed work. Never again would the splendor
of her beauty burn as it did this night.

Laura, alone among them all, went serenely about her toilet. She was young, and love had not yet spread its puzzle before her feet.

As for the others, they were on the far side of the hill, whence the paths are smooth and gentle and the prospect is peacefulness and the retrospect is dimly rosal. They dressed as they had done those twenty odd years, plainly.

On the bridge the first officer was standing at the captain's side.

"Captain," he shouted, "where did you get that Frenchman?"

"Picked him up day before yestiddy. Speaks fair English an' a bit o' Dago. They're allus handy on a pleasure-boat. He c'n keep off th' riffraff boatmen. An' *you* know what persistent cusses they be in the Med'terranean. Why?"

"Oh, nothing, if he's a good sailor. Notice his hands?"

"Why, no!"

"Soft as a woman's."

"Y' don't say! Well, we'll see 'em tough enough before we sight Funchai. Smells good up here; huh?"

"Yes; but I don't mind three months on land, full pay. Not me. But this Frenchman?"

"Oh, he had good papers from a White Star liner; an' you can leave it to me regardin' his lily-white hands. By th' way, George, will you have them bring up my other leg? Th' salt takes th' color out o' this here brass ferrule, an' rubber's safer."

"Yes, sir."

There was one vacant chair in the dining-salon. M. Ferraud was indisposed. He could climb the highest peak, he could cross ice-ridges, with a sheer mile on either side of him, with never an attack of vertigo; but this heaving mystery under his feet always got the better of him the first day out. He considered it the one flaw in an otherwise perfect system. Thus, he missed the comedy and the tragedy of the eyes at dinner, nor saw a woman throw her all and lose it.

CHAPTER XVI

CROSS-PURPOSES

"IS there anything I can do for you?" asked Fitzgerald, venturing his head into M. Ferraud's cabin.

"Nothing; to-morrow it will all be gone. I am always so. The miserable water!" M. Ferraud drew the blanket under his chin.

"When you are better I should like to ask you some questions."

"My friend, you have been very good. I promise to tell you all when the time comes. It will interest you."

"Breitmann?"

"What makes you think I am interested in Mr. Breitmann?"

Fitzgerald could not exactly tell. "Perhaps I have noticed you watching him."

" Ah, you have good eyes, Mr. Fitzgerald.   Have
you observed that I have been watching you also? "

" Yes. You haven't been quite sure of me."
Fitzgerald smiled a little.   " But you may rest your
mind.   I never break my word."

" Nor do I, my friend.   Have patience.   Satan
take these small boats! "   He stiffled a groan.

" A little champagne? "

" Nothing, nothing; thank you."

" As you will.   Good night."

Fitzgerald shut the door and returned to the
smoking-room.   Something or other, concerning
Breitmann; he was sure of it.   What had he done,
or what was he going to do, that France should
watch him?   There was no doubt in his mind now;
Breitmann had known of this treasure and had come
to The Pines simply to put his hands on the casket.
M. Ferraud had tried to forestall him.   This much
of the riddle was plain.   But the pivots upon which
these things turned!   There was something more
than a treasure in the balance.   Well, M. Ferraud
had told him to wait.   There was nothing else for
him to do.

A little rubber at bridge was in progress.   The

admiral was playing with Mrs. Coldfield and
Cathewe sat opposite Hildegarde. The latter two
were losing. She was ordinarily a skilful player,
as Cathewe knew; but to-night she lost constantly,
was reckless with her leads, and played carelessly
into her opponents' hands. Cathewe watched her
gravely. Never had he seen her more beautiful;
and the apprehension that she would never be his
was like a hand straining over his heart.

Yes, she was beautiful; but he did not know that
there was death in her eyes and death in her smile.
Once upon a time he had believed that her heart
had broken; but she was learning that the heart
breaks, rebreaks, and breaks again.

How many times he stood on the precipice during the dinner hour, Breitmann doubtless would
never be told. A woman scorned is an old
story; still, the story goes on, retold each day.
Education may smooth the externals, but under-
neath the fire burns just as furiously as of old. To
this affront the average woman's mind leaps at once
to revenge; and that she does not always take it
depends upon two things: opportunity, and love,
which is more powerful than revenge. Sometimes,

on hot summer nights, clouds form angrily in the distance; vivid flashes dartle hither and about, which serve to intensify the evening darkness. Thus, a similar phenomenon was taking place in Hildegarde von Mitter's mind. The red fires of revenge danced before her eyes, blurring the spots on the cards, the blackness of despair crowding upon each flash. Let him beware! With a word she could shatter his dream; ay, and so she would. What! sit there and let him turn the knife in her heart and receive the pain meekly? No! It was the thoughtless brutality with which he went about this new affair that bit so poignantly. To show her, so indurately, that she was nothing, that, despite her magnificent sacrifice, she had never been more than a convenience, was maddening. There was no spontaneity in his heart; his life was a calculation to which various sums were added or subtracted. With all her beauty, intellect, genius and generosity, she had not been able to stir him as this young girl was unconsciously doing. She held no animosity for the daughter of her host; she was clear-visioned enough to put the wrong where it belonged.

"It is your lead," said the admiral patiently.

" Pardon me! " contritely.   The gentle reproach brought her back to the surroundings.

" It is the motion of the boat," hazarded Cathewe, as he saw her lead the ace.   " I often find myself losing count in waiting for the next roll."

" Mr. Cathewe is very kind," she replied.   " The truth is, however, I am simply stupid to-night."

Breitmann continued to speak lowly to Laura. He was evidently amusing, for she smiled frequently.   Nevertheless, she smiled as often upon Fitzgerald.   Never a glance toward the woman who held his fortunes, as they both believed, in the hollow of her hand.   Breitmann appeared to have forgotten her existence.

When the rubber was finished Cathewe came into the breach by suggesting that they two, he and his partner, should take the air for a while; and Hildegarde thanked him with her eyes.   They tramped the port side, saying nothing but thinking much. His arm was under hers to steady her, and he could feel the catch each time she breathed, as when one stifles sobs that are tearless.   Ah, to hold her close and to shield her; but a thousand arms may not intervene between the heart and the pain that stabs it. He knew; he knew all about it, and there was murder in his thought whenever his thought was of Breitmann. To be alone with him somewhere, and to fight it out with their bare hands.

She had been schooled in the art of acting, but not in the art of dissimulation; she had been of the world without having been worldly; and sometimes she was as frank and simple as a child. And worldliness makes a buffer in times like these. Cathewe thanked God for his own shell, toughened as it had been in the war of life.

"Look!" he exclaimed, thankful for the diversion. "There goes a big liner for Sandy Hook. How cheerful she looks with all her lights! Everybody's busy there. There will be greetings to-morrow, among the sundry curses of those who have not declared their Parisian models."

They paused by the rail and followed the great ship till all the lights had narrowed and melted into one; and then, almost at once, the limitless circle of pitching black water seemed tenanted by themselves alone.

Without warning she bent swiftly and kissed the hand which lay upon the rail. " How kind you are to me! "

" Oh, pshaw! " But the touch of her lips shook his soul.

Cathewe was one of those sure, quiet men, a staff to lean on, that a woman may find once in a life-time. They are, as a usual thing, always loving deeply and without success, but always invariably cheerful and buoyant, genuine philosophers. They are not given much to writing sonnets or posing; and they can stand aside with a brave heart as the other man takes the dream out of their lives. This is not to affirm that they do not fight stoutly to hold this dream; simply, that they accept defeat like good soldiers. There are many heroes who have never heard war's alarms. He knew that the whole heart of Hildegarde von Mitter had yielded to another. But it had been thrown, as it were, against a wall; there was this one hope, dimly burning, that some day he might catch it on the rebound.

" Why are not all men like you? " she asked.

" The world would not be half so interesting. Some men shall be fortunate and others shall not;

everything has to balance in some way. I am necessary to one side of the scales, as a weight." He spoke with a levity he by no means felt.

" You are always making sport of yourself."

" Would it be wise to weep? Not at all. I laugh because I enjoy it, just the same as I enjoy hunting or going on voyages of discovery."

" To have met *you!*" childishly.

" Don't talk like that. It always makes me less sad than furious. And how do you know? If it had been written that you should care for me, would any one else have mattered? No. It just is, that's all. So we'll go on as we have done in the past, good friends. Call me when you need me, and wherever I am I shall come."

" How pitifully weak I must seem to you! "

" You would be no happier if you wore a mask. Hildegarde, what has happened? What power has this adventurer over you? I can not understand. He was man enough to say that you were guiltless of any wrong."

" He said that? " turning upon him sharply. She could forgive much.

He could not see her face, but by the tone of her

voice he knew it had brightened. "Yes. I did a freakish thing the night we arrived at the Killigrews'. I forced him into a corner, but it did not pan out as I hoped. So far as it touched me, it wasn't necessary, as I have told you a thousand times. Your past is nothing to me; your future is everything, and I want it, God knows how I want it! Well, I wished to find out what kind of man he is, but I wasn't very successful. Hildegarde," and he pressed his hand down hard over hers, "I could find a priest the day we land if you would love me. You will always remember that."

"As if I could ever forget your kindness! But you forced him; there is no merit in such a confession. And I wonder how you forced him. It was not by fear. Much as I know him there are still some unfilled pages. I would call him a scoundrel did I not know that in parts he has been a hero. What sacrifices the man has made, and with what patience!"

"To what end?" quietly.

"No, no, Arthur! I have promised him."

He took her by the arm roughly. "Let us make

two or three rounds and go back.   We shan't grow any more cheerful talking this way."

" He loves her.   I saw it in his eyes; and I must stand aside and watch! "

" So must I," he said.   " Aren't you just a little selfish, Hildegarde? "

" I am wretched, Arthur; and I am a fool, besides.   Oh, that I were cold-blooded like your women, that I could eat out my heart in secret; but I can't, I can't! "

" But you have courage; only use it.   If what you say of him is true, rest easy.   She is not in his orbit.   She will not be impressed by an adventurer of his breed."

" Thank you! " with a broken laugh.   " I am only an opera-singer, here on suffrance."

" Oh, good Lord!   I did not mean it that way. Let us finish the walk," savagely.

On the afternoon of the second day out, tea was served under the awning, and Captain Flanagan condescended to leave his bridge for half an hour. Through a previous hint dropped by the admiral they lured the captain into spinning yarns; and well-salted hair-breadth escapes they were. He understood that the admiral's guests always expected these flights, and he was in nowise niggard. An ordinary sailor would have been dead these twenty years, under any one of the exploits.

"Marvelous!" said M. Ferraud from the depths of his rugs. "And he still lives to tell it?"

"It's the easiest thing in the world, sir, if y' know how," the captain declared complacently. Indeed, he had recounted these yarns so many times that he was beginning to regard them as facts. His statement, ambiguous as it was, passed unchallenged, however; for not one had the daring to inquire whether he referred to the telling or the living of them. So he believed that he was looked upon as an apostle of truth. Only the admiral had the temerity to look his captain squarely in the eye and wink.

"Captain, would you mind if I put these tales in a book?" Fitzgerald put this question with a seriousness which fooled no one but the captain.

"You come up t' the bridge some afternoon, when we've got a smooth sea, and I'll give y' some *real* ones." The captain's vanity was soothed, but he was not aware that he had put doubt upon his own veracity.

"That's kind of you."

"An' say!" went on the captain, drinking his tea, not because he liked it but because it was customary, "I've got a character forwards. I'm allus shippin' odds and ends. Got a Frenchman; hands like a lady."

Breitmann leaned forward, and M. Ferraud sat up.

"Yessir," continued the captain; "speaks I-taly-an an' English. An' if I ever meets a lady with long soft hands like his'n, I'm for a pert talk, straightway."

"What's the matter with his hands?" asked the admiral.

"Why, Commodore, they're as soft as Miss Laura's here, an' yet when th' big Swede who handles th' baggage was a-foolin' with him this mornin', it was the Swede who begs off. Nary a callous, an' yét he bowls the big one round the deck like he was a liner being pierced by a sassy tug. An' what gets me is, he knows every bolt from stem to stern, sir, an' an all-round good sailor int' th' bargain; an' it don' take me more'n twelve hours t' find that out. Well, I'm off t' th' bridge. Good day, ladies."

When he was out of earshot the admiral roared. " He's the dearest old liar since Münchhausen."

" Aren't they true stories? " asked Hildegarde.

" Bless you, no! And he knows we know it, too. But he tells them so well that I've never had the courage to sheer him off."

" It's amusing," said Laura; " but I do not think that it's always fair to him."

" Why, Laura, you're as good a listener as any I know. Read him a tract, if you wish."

Breitmann rose presently and sauntered forward, while M. Ferraud snuggled down in his rugs again. The others entered into a game of deck-cricket.

But M. Ferraud was not so ill that he was unable to steal from his cabin at half after nine, at night, without even the steward being aware of his departure. It can not be said that he roamed about the deck, for whenever he moved it was in the shadow, and always forward. By and by voices drifted down the wind. One he knew and expected, Breitmann's; of the other he was not sure, though the French he spoke was of classic smoothness. M. Ferraud was exceedingly interested. He had been waiting for this meeting. Only a phrase or two could be heard distinctly. But words were not necessary. What he desired above all things was a glimpse of this Frenchman's face. After several minutes Breitmann went aft. M. Ferraud stepped out cautiously, and luck was with him. The sailor to whom Breitmann had spoken so earnestly was lolling against the rail, in the act of lighting a cigarette. The light from the match was feeble, but it sufficed the keen eyes of the watcher. He gasped a little. Strong hands indeed! Here in the garb of a common sailor, was one of the foremost Orleanists in France!

CHAPTER XVII

BREITMANN and the admiral usually worked from ten till luncheon, unless it was too stormy; and then the admiral took the day off. The business under hand was of no great moment; it was rather an outlet for the admiral's energy, and gave him something to look forward to as each day came round. Many a morning he longed for the quarter-deck of his old battle-ship; the trig crew and marines lined up for inspection; the revelries of the foreign ports; the great manœuvres; the target practice. Never would his old heart swell again under the full-dress uniform nor his eyes sparkle under the plume of his rank. He was retired on half-pay. Only a few close friends knew how his half-pay was invested. There remained perhaps ten of the old war-crew, and among them every Christmas the admiral's half-pay was divided.

This and his daughter were the two unalloyed joys of his life.

Since his country had no further use for him, and as it was as necessary as air to his lungs that he tread the deck of a ship, he had purchased the *Laura;* and, when he was not stirring up the bones of dead pirates, he was at Cowes or at Brest or at Keil or on the Hudson, wherever the big fellows indulged in mimic warfare.

"That will be all this morning, Mr. Breitmann," he said, rising and looking out of the port-hole.

"Very well, sir. I believe that by the time we make Corsica we shall have the book ready for the printers. It is very interesting."

"Much obliged. You have been a good aid. As you know, I am writing this rubbish only because it is play and passable mental exercise."

"I do not agree with you there," returned the secretary, with his pleasant smile. "The book will be really a treasure of itself. It is far more interesting than any romance."

The admiral shook his head dubiously.

"No, no," Breitmann averred. "There is no flattery in what I say. Flattery was not in our agreement. And," with a slight lift of the jaw, "I never say what I do not honestly mean. It will be a good book, and I am proud to have had a hand, however light, in the making."

The admiral chuckled. "That is the kind of flattery no man may shut his ears to. It has been a great pleasure to me; it has kept me out-of-doors, in the open, where I belong. Come in, Laura, come in."

The girl stood framed in the low doorway, a charming picture to the old man and a lovely one to the secretary. She balanced herself with a hand on each side of the jam.

"Father, how can you work when the sun is so beautiful outside? Good morning, Mr. Breitmann," cordially.

"Good morning."

"Work is over, Laura. Come in." The admiral reached forth an arm and caught her, drawing her gently in and finally to his breast.

Breitmann would have given an eye for that right. The picture set his nerves twitching.

"I am not in the way?"

"Not at all," answered the secretary. "I was

just leaving." And with good foresight he passed out.

"A thing of beauty is a joy for ever," murmured the admiral.

"Fudge!" and she laughed.

"We are having a fine voyage."

"Splendid! Why is it that I am always happy?"

"It is because you do not depend upon others for it, my dear. I am happy, too. I am as happy as a boy with his first boat. But never has a ship gone slower than this one of mine. I am simply crazy to drop anchor in the Gulf of Ajaccio. I find it on the tip of my tongue, every night at dinner, to tell the others where we are bound."

"Why not? Where's the harm now?"

"I don't know, but something keeps it back. Laura," looking into her eyes, "did we ever cruise with brighter men on board?"

"What is it you wish to know, father?" merrily. "You dear old sailor, don't you understand that these men are different? They are men who accomplish things; they haven't time to bother about young women."

"You don't say!" pinching the ear nearest.

" This is the seventh day out, and not one of them has ceased to be interesting yet."

" Would they cease to be interesting if they proposed? " quizzing.

These two had no unshared secrets. They were sure of each other. He knew that when this child of his divided her affection with another man, that man would be deserving.

" I would rather have them all as they are. They make fine comrades."

He sighed thankfully. " Arthur seems to be out of the race."

" Rather say I am! " with laughter. " Why, a child could read Arthur Cathewe's face when he looks at her. Isn't she simply beautiful? "

" Very. But there are types and types."

" Am I really pretty? " Sometimes she grew shy under her father's open admiration. She was afraid it was his love rather than his judgment that made her beautiful in his eyes.

" My child, there's more than one man who will agree with me when I say that there is no one to compare with you. You are the living quotation from Keats."

"I shall kiss you for that." And straightway she did.

"What do you think of Mr. Breitmann?" soberly.

"He is charming sometimes; but he has a little too much reserve. Doubtless he sees his position too keenly. He should not."

"Do you like him?"

"Yes," frankly.

"So do I; and yet there are moments when I do not." The admiral filled his pipe carefully.

"But your reason?" surprised.

"That's just the trouble. I haven't any tangible reason. The doubt exists, and I can't explain it. The sea often looks smooth and mild, and the sky is cloudless; yet an old sailor will suddenly grow suspicious; he will see a storm, a heavy blow. And why, he couldn't say for the life of him. Flanagan will tell you."

The girl grew studious and grave. Had there not been an echo of this doubt in her own mind? Immediately she smiled.

"We are talking nonsense and wasting the sunshine."

" How about Fitzgerald? "

" Oh, he's the most sensible of them all. He proposed to me the first night out."

" What? "   The admiral dropped his pipe.

" Not so loud! " she warned.   And then the clear music of her laughter penetrated beyond the cabin; and Fitzgerald, wandering about without purpose, heard it and paused.

" You minx! " growled the admiral; " to scare your old father like that! "

" Dearest, weren't you fishing to be scared? "

" Let's get out into the sunshine. I never could get the besι of you. But you really don't mean —"

" I really do not. He's too busy telling me the plot of this novel he is going to write to make love to a girl who doesn't want more than one man in the family, and that's her foolish old father."

And they went outside, arm in arm, laughing together like the good comrades they were. M. Ferraud joined them.

" I wish," said he, " that I was a poet."

" What would you do? " she asked.

" I should write a sonnet to your eyebrows this morning, is it not? "

" Mercy, no!   That kind of poetry has long been *passé.*"

" *Helas!* " mournfully.

It was a beautiful morning, a sharp blue sky and a sea of running silver; warm, too, for they were bearing away into the southern seas now.   Every one had sea-legs by this time, and the larder dwindled in a respectable manner.

Fitzgerald viewed his case dispassionately.   But what to do?   A thousand times he had argued out the question, with a single result, that he was a fool for his pains.   He became possessed with sudden inexplicable longings for land.   He could not get away from this yacht; on land there would have been a hundred straight lines to the woods and the fisherman's philosophy.   Things were going directly to one end, and presently he would have no more power to stem the words.   At least one thing was certain, the admiral could not drop him overboard.

" The villain? "

He was moved suddenly out of his dream, for the object of it stood smiling at his side.   A wisp of hair was blowing across her eyes and she was endeavoring to adjust it under her cap.

"The villain?" making a fine effort to remarshal his thoughts.

"Yes. We were talking about him last night. Where did you leave him?"

"He was still pursuing, I believe."

"Why don't you make him a real villain, a man who never kills any one, but who makes every one unhappy?"

"But that's a problem-villain; what we must have is a romance-villain, the kind every one is sorry for. Look at that old Portuguese man-o'-war," pointing to the crest of a near-by wave. "Funny little codger!"

"When do you expect to begin the story on paper?"

"When I have *all* the material," not afraid of her eyes at that moment.

She propped her elbows on the rail. It was a seductive pose, and came very near being the young man's undoing.

"Does it seem impossible to you," she said, "that in these prosaic times we are treasure hunting? Must we not wake up and find it a dream?"

"Most dreams are perishable, but in this case

we have the dream tightly bound.   But what are we
going to do with all this money when we find it?"

"Divide it or start a soldiers' home.   I've never
thought of it as money."

"Heaven knows, I have!"

"Why?"

"Do you really wish to know?" in a voice new to
her ear.   "Do you wish to know why I want
money, lots and lots of it?"

She dropped her arms and turned.   The tone
agitated and alarmed her strangely.   "Why, yes.
With plenty of money you could devote all your
time to writing; and I am sure you could write
splendid stories."

"That was not my exact thought," he replied,
resolutely pulling himself together.   "But it will
serve."   By George! he thought, that was close
enough.

She did not ask him what his exact thought was,
but she suspected it.   There was a little shock of
pleasure and disappointment; the one rising from
the fact that he had stopped where he did and the
other that he had not gone on.   And she grew
angry over this second expression.   She liked him;

she had never met a young man whom she liked
more.   But liking is never loving, and her heart was
as free and unburdened as the wind.   As once remarked, many of the men with whom she had come
into contact had been bred in idleness, and her interest in them had never gone above friendly tolerance.   Her admiration was for men, young or old,
who cut their way roughly through the world's great
obstacles, who achieved things in pioneering, in history, in science; and she admired them because they
were rather difficult to draw out, being more familiar with startling journeys, wildernesses, strange
peoples, than with the gilded metaphors of the draw-
ing-room.

And here were three of them to meet daily, to
study and to ponder over.   And types as far apart
as the three points of a triangle; the man at
her side, young, witty, agreeable; Cathewe, grave,
kindly, and sometimes rather saturnine; Breitmann,
proud and reserved; and each of them having rung
true in some great crisis.   If ever she loved a man
. . .   The thought remained unfinished and she
glanced up and met Fitzgerald's eyes.   The   were
sad, with the line of a frown above them   How

was she to keep him under hand, and still erect an impassable barrier! It was the first time she had given the matter serious thought. The joy of the sea underfoot, the tang of the rushing air, the journey's end, these had occupied her volatile young mind. But now!

"I am dull," said he gloomily.

"Thank you!"

"I mean that I am stupid, doubly stupid," he corrected.

"Cricket will be a cure for that."

"I doubt it," approaching dangerous ground once more.

"Let's go and talk to Captain Flanagan, then."

"There!" with sudden spirit, "the very thing I've been wanting!"

It was of no importance that they both knew this to be a prevarication about which St. Peter would not trouble his hoary head nor take the pains to indite in his great book of demerits.

But all through that bright day the girl thought, and there were times when the others had to speak to her twice; not at all a reassuring sign.

CHAPTER XVIII

ONE day they dropped anchor in the sapphire
bay of Funchal, in the summer calm, hot and
glaring; Funchal, with its dense tropical growth, its
cloud-wreathed mountains, its amethystine sisters
in the faded southeast. And for two days, while
Captain Flanagan recoaled, they played like children, jolting round in the low bullock-carts, climbing the mountains or bumping down the corduroy
road. It was the strangest treasure hunt that ever
left a home port. It was more like a page out of
a boy's frolic than a sober quest by grown-ups.
That danger, menace and death hid in covert would
have appealed to them (those who knew) as ridicu-
lous, impossible, obsolete. The story of cutlass and
pistol and highboots had been molding in archives
these eighty-odd years. Dangers? From whom,
from what direction? No one suggested the pos-

sibility, even in jest; and the only man who could
have advanced, with reasonable assurance, that danger, real and serious, existed, was too busy apparently with his butterfly-net. Still, he had not yet
been consulted; he was not supposed to know that
this cruise was weighted with something more than
pleasure.

Fitzgerald waited with an impatience which often
choked him. A secret agent had not so adroitly
joined this expedition for the pleasure of seeing a
treasure dug up from some reluctant grave. What
was he after? If indeed Breitmann was directly
concerned, if he knew of the treasure's existence, of
what benefit now would be his knowledge? A
share in the finding at most. And was Breitmann
one who was conditioned of such easy stuff that
he would rather be sure and share than to strike out
for all the treasure and all the risks? The more
he gave his thought to Breitmann the more that
gentleman retracted into the fog, as it were. On
several occasions he had noticed signs of a preoc-
cupation, of suppressed excitement, of silence and
moroseness. Fitzgerald could join certain squares
of the puzzle, but this led forward scarce a step.

Breitmann had entered the employ of the admiral for the very purpose for which M. Ferraud had journeyed sundrily into the cellar and beaten futilely on the chimney. It resolved to one thing, and that was, the secretary had arrived too late. He was sure that Breitmann had no suspicion regarding M. Ferraud. But for a casual glance at the little man's hands, neither would he have had any. He determined to prod M. Ferraud. He was well trained in repression; so, while he often lost patience, there was never any external sign of it. Besides, there was another affair which over-shadowed it and at times engulfed it.

Love. The cross-tides of sense and sentiment made a pretty disturbance. And still further, there was another counter-tide. Love does not necessa-rily make a young man keen-sighted, but it generally highly develops his talent for suspicion. By subtle gradations, Breitmann had shifted in Fitzgerald's mind from a possible friend to a probable rival. Breitmann did not now court his society when the smoking bouts came round, or when the steward brought the whisky and soda after the ladies had retired. Breitmann was moody, and whatever

variance his moods had, they retained the gray tone.
This Fitzgerald saw and dilated upon; and it rankled
when he thought that this hypothetical adventurer
had rights, level and equal to his, always supposing
he had any.

In this state of mind he drooped idly over the
rail as the yacht drew out of the bay, the evening
of the second day. The glories of the southern
sunset lingered and vanished, a-begging, without his
senses being roused by them; and long after the sea,
chameleon-like, changed from rose to lavender,
from lavender to gray, the mountains yet jealously
clung to their vivid aureolas of phantom gold.
Fitzgerald saw nothing but writing on the water.

"Well, my boy," said Cathewe, lounging affec-
tionately against Fitzgerald, "here we are, rolled
over again."

"What?"

Cathewe described a circle with his finger lazily.

"Oh!" said Fitzgerald, listless. "Another day
more or less, crowded into the past, doesn't matter."

"Maybe. If we could only have the full days
and deposit the others and draw as we need them;

but we can't do it.   And yet each day means something; there ought always to be a little of it worth
remembering."

"Old parson!" cried Fitzgerald, with a jab of
his elbow.

"All bally rot, eh?   I wish I could look at it
that way.   Yet, when a man mopes as you are doing, when this sunset. . ."

"New one every day."

"What's the difficulty, Jack?"

"Am I walking around with a sign on my back?"
testily.

"Of a kind, yes."

Cathewe spoke so solemnly that Fitzgerald looked
round, and saw that which set his ears burning.
Immediately he lowered his gaze and sought the
water again.

"Have I been making an ass of myself, Arthur?"

"No, Jack; but you are laying yourself open to
some wonder.   For three or four days now, except
for the forty-eight hours on land there, you've been
a sort of killjoy.   Even the admiral has remarked
it."

"Tell him it's my liver," with a laugh not wholly

free of embarrassment. " Suppose," he continued, in a low voice; " suppose —" But he couldn't go on.

" Yes, suppose," said Cathewe, taking up the broken thread; " suppose there was a person who had a heap of money, or will have some day; and suppose there's another person who has but little and may have less in days to come. Is that the supposition, Jack? The presumption of an old friend, a right that ought never to be abrogated." Cathewe laid a hand on his young friend's shoulder; there was a silent speech of knowledge and brotherhood in it such as Fitzgerald could not mistake.

" That's the supposition," he admitted generously.

" Well, money counts only when you buy horses and yachts and houses, it never really matters in anything else."

" It is easy to say that."

" It is also easy to learn that it is true."

" Isn't there a good deal of buying these days where there should be giving? "

" Not among real people. You have had enough experience with both types to be competent to dis-

tinguish the one from the other. You have birth
and brains and industry; you're a decent sort of
chap besides," genially. "Can money buy these
things when grounded on self-respect as they are
in you? Come along now; for the admiral sent
me after you. It's the steward's champagne cocktail; and you know how good they are. And remember, if you will put your head into the clouds,
don't take your feet off the deck."

Fitzgerald expanded under his tactful interpreta-
tion. A long breath of relief issued from his heart,
and the rending doubt was dissipated: the vulture-
shadow spread its dark pennons and wheeled down
the west. A priceless thing is that friend upon
whom one may shift the part of a burden. It
seemed to be one of Cathewe's occupations in life
to absorb, in a kindly, unemotional manner, other
people's troubles. It is this type of man, too, who
rarely shares his own.

It would be rather graceless to say that after
drinking the cocktail Fitzgerald resumed his afore-
time rosal lenses. He was naturally at heart an
optimist, as are all men of action. And so the
admiral, who had begun to look upon him with

puzzled commiseration, came to the conclusion that
the young man's liver had resumed its normal
functions. An old woman would have diagnosed
the case as one of heart (as Mrs. Coldfield secretly
and readily and happily did); but an old fellow like
the admiral generally compromises on the liver.

When one has journeyed for days on the unquiet
sea, a touch of land underfoot renews, Antæus-
wise, one's strength and mental activity; so a festive
spirit presided at the dinner table. The admiral
determined to vault the enforced repression of his
secret. Inasmuch as it must be told, the present
seemed a propitious moment. He signed for the
attendants to leave the salon, and then rapped on
the table for silence. He obtained it easily enough.

"My friends," he began, "where do you think
this boat is really going?"

"Marseilles," answered Coldfield.

"Where else?" cried M. Ferraud, as if diversion
from that course was something of an improbability.

"Corsica. We can leave you at Marseilles, Mr.
Ferraud, if you wish; but I advise you to remain
with us. It will be something to tell in your old
age."

Cathewe glanced across to Fitzgerald, as if to ask: "Do you know anything about this?" Fitzgerald, catching the sense of this mute inquiry, nodded affirmatively.

"Corsica is a beautiful place," said Hildegarde. "I spent a spring in Ajaccio."

"Well, that is our port," confessed the admiral, laying his precious documents on the table. "The fact is, we are going to dig up a treasure," with a flourish.

Laughter and incredulous exclamations followed this statement.

"Pirates?" cried Coldfield, with a good-natured jeer. He had cruised with the admiral before. "Where's the cutlass and jolly-roger? Yo-ho! and a bottle o' rum!"

"Yes. And where's the other ship following at our heels, as they always do in treasure hunts, the rival pirates who will cut our throats when we have dug up the treasure?" — from Cathewe.

"Treasures!" mumbled M. Ferraud from behind his pineapple. Carefully he avoided Fitzgerald's gaze, but he noted the expression on Breitmann's face. It was not pleasant.

"Just a moment," the admiral requested patiently. "I know it smells fishy. Laura, go ahead and read the documents to the unbelieving giaours. Mr. Fitzgerald knows and so does Mr. Breitmann."

"Tell us about it, Laura. No joking, now," said Coldfield, surrendering his incredulity with some hesitance. "And if the treasure involves no fighting or diplomatic tangle, count me in. Think of it, Jane," turning to his wife; "two old church-goers like you and me, a-going after a pirate's treasure! Doesn't it make you laugh?"

Laura unfolded the story, and when she came to the end, the excitement was hot and Babylonic. Napoleon! What a word! A treasure put together to rescue him from St. Helena! Gold, French gold, English gold, Spanish and Austrian gold, all mildewing in a rotting chest somewhere back of Ajaccio! It was unbelievable, fantastic as one of those cinematograph pictures, running backward.

"But what are you going to do with it when you find it?"

"Findings is keepings," quoted the admiral.

" Perhaps divide it, perhaps turn it over to France, providing France agrees to use it for charitable purposes."

" A fine plan, is it not, Mr. Breitmann? " said M. Ferraud.

" Findings is keepings," repeated Breitmann, with a pale smile.

The eyes of Hildegarde von Mitter burned and burned. Could she but read what lay behind that impassive face! And he took it all with a smile! What would he do? what would he do now? kept recurring in her mind. She knew the man, or at least she thought she did; and she was aware that there existed in his soul dark caverns which she had never dared to explore. Yes, what would he do now? How would he put his hand upon this gold? She trembled with apprehension.

And later, when she found the courage to put the question boldly, he answered with a laugh, so low and yet so wild with fury that she drew away from him in dumb terror.

CHAPTER XIX

BREITMANN MAKES HIS FIRST BLUNDER

THE secretary nerved himself and waited; and yet he knew what her reply would be, even before she framed it, knew it with that indescribable certainty which prescience occasionally grants in the space of a moment. Before he had spoken there had been hope to stand upon, for she had always been gentle and kindly toward him, not a whit less than she had been to the others.

"Mr. Breitmann, I am sorry. I never dreamed of this;" nor had she. She had forgotten Europeans seldom understand the American girl as she is or believe that the natural buoyancy of spirit is as free from purpose or intent as the play of a child. But in this moment she remembered her little and perfectly inconsequent attentions toward this man, and seeing them from his viewpoint she readily forgave him. Abroad, she was always on

265

guard; but here, among her own compatriots who accepted her as she was, she had excusably forgotten. "I am sorry if you have misunderstood me in any way."

"I could no more help loving you than that those stars should cease to shine to-night," his voice heavy with emotion.

"I am sorry," she could only repeat. Men had spoken to her like this before, and always had the speech been new to her and always had a great and tender pity charged her heart. And perhaps her pity for this one was greater than any she had previously known; he seemed so lonely.

"Sorry, sorry! Does that mean there is no hope?"

"None, Mr. Breitmann, none."

"Is there another?" his throat swelling. But before she could answer: "Pardon me; I did not mean that. I have no right to ask such a question."

"And I should not have answered it to any but my father, Mr. Breitmann." She extended her hand. "Let us forget that you have spoken. I should like you for a friend."

Without a word he took the hand and kissed it. He made no effort to hold it, and it slipped from his clasp easily.

" Good night."

" Good night."   And he never lost sight of her till she entered the salon-cabin.   He saw a star fall out of nothing into nothing.   She was sorry!   The moment brewed a thousand wild suggestions.   To abduct her, to carry her away into the mountains, to cast his dream to the four winds, to take her in spite of herself.   He laid his hand on the teak railing, wondering at the sudden wracking pain, a pain which unlinked coherent thought and left his mind stagnant and inert.   For the first time he realized that his pain was a recurrence of former ones similar.   Why?   He did not know.   He only remembered that he had had the pain at the back of his head and that it was generally followed by a burning fury, a rage to rend and destroy things. What was the matter?

The damp rail was cool and refreshing, and after a spell the pain diminished.   He shook himself free and stood straight, his jaws hard and his eyes, absorbing what light there was from the stars, chatoyant. Sorry! So be it. To have humbled himself before this American girl and to be snubbed for his pains! But, patience! Two million francs and his friends awaiting the word from him. She was sorry! He laughed, and the laughter was not unlike that which a few nights gone had startled the ears of the other woman to whom he had once appealed in passionate tones and not without success.

"Karl!"

The sight of Hildegarde at this moment neither angered nor pleased him. He permitted her hand to lay upon his arm.

"My head aches," he said, as if replying to the unspoken question in her eyes.

"Karl, why not give it up?" she pleaded.

"Give it up? What! when I have come this far, when I have gone through what I have? Oh, no! Do not think so little of me as that."

"But it is a dream!"

He shook off her hand angrily. "If there is to be any reckoning I shall pay, never fear. But it will not, *shall* not fail!"

She would have liked to weep for him. "I

would gladly give you my eyes, Karl, if you might see it all as I see it. Ruin, ruin! Can you touch this money without violence? Ah, my God, what has blinded you to the real issues?"

"I have not asked you to share the difficulties."

"No. You have not been that kind to me."

To-night there were no places in his armor for any sentiment but his own. "I want nothing but revenge."

"I think I can read," her own bitterness getting the better of her tongue. "Miss Killigrew has declined."

"You have been listening?" with a snarl.

"It has not been necessary to listen; I needed only to watch."

"Well, what is it to you?"

"Take care, Karl! You can not talk to me like that."

"Don't drive me, then. Oh," with a sudden turn of mind, "I am sorry that you can not understand."

"If I hadn't I should never have given you my promise not to speak. There was a time when you had right on your side, but that time ceased to be when you lied to me. How little you understood me! Had you spoken frankly and generously at the start, God knows I shouldn't have refused you. But you set out to walk over my heart to get that miserable slip of paper. Ah! had I but known! I say to you, you will fail utterly and miserably. You are either blind or mad!"

Without a word in reply to this prophecy he turned and left her; and as soon as he had vanished she kissed the spot on the rail where his hand had rested and laid her own there. When at last she raised it, the rail was no longer merely damp, it was wet.

"Now there," began Fitzgerald, taking M. Ferraud firmly by the sleeve, "I have come to the end of my patience. What has Breitmann to do with all this business?"

"Will you permit me to polish my spectacles?" mildly asked M. Ferraud.

"It's the deuce of a job to get you into a corner," Fitzgerald declared. "But I have your promise, and you should recollect that I know things which might interest Mr. Breitmann."

"Croyez-vous qu'il pleuve? Il fait bien du vent," adjusting his spectacles and viewing the clear sky and the serene bosom of the Mediterranean. Then M. Ferraud turned round with: "Ah, Mr. Fitzgerald, this man Breitmann is what you call 'poor devil,' is it not? At dinner to-night I shall tell a story, at once marvelous past belief and pathetic. I shall tell this story against my best convictions because I wish him no harm, because I should like to save him from black ruin. But, attend me; my efforts shall be as wind blowing upon stone; and I shall not save him. An alienist would tell you better than I can. Listen. You have watched him, have you not? To you he seems like any other man? Yes? Keen-witted, gifted, a bit of a musician, a good deal of a scholar? Well, had I found that paper first, there would have been no treasure hunt. I should have torn it into one thousand pieces; I should have saved him in spite of himself and have done my duty also. He is mad, mad as a whirlwind, as a tempest, as a fire, as a sandstorm."

"About what?"

" To-night, to-night! "

And the wiry little man released himself and bustled away to his chair where he became buried in rugs and magazines.

CHAPTER XX

AN OLD SCANDAL

"CORSICA to-morrow," said the admiral.

"Napoleon," said Laura.

"Romance," said Cathewe.

"Treasures," said M. Ferraud.

Hildegarde felt uneasy. Breitmann toyed with the bread crumbs. He was inattentive besides.

"Napoleon. There is an old scandal," mused M. Ferraud. "I don't think that any of you have heard it."

"That will interest me," Fitzgerald cried. "Tell it."

M. Ferraud cleared his throat with a sharp ahem and proceeded to burnish his crystals. Specks and motes were ever adhering to them. He held them up to the light and pretended to look through them: he saw nothing but the secretary's abstraction.

"We were talking about treasures the other

night," began the Frenchman, "and I came near telling it then. It is a story of Napoleon."

"Never a better moment to tell it," said the admiral, rubbing his hands in pleasurable anticipation.

"I say to you at once that the tale is known to few, and has never had any publicity, and must never have any. Remember that, if you please, Mr. Fitzgerald, and you also, Mr. Breitmann."

"I beg your pardon," said Breitmann. "I was not listening."

M. Ferraud repeated his request clearly.

"I am no longer a newspaper writer," Breitmann affirmed, clearing the fog out of his head. "A story about Napoleon; will it be true?"

"Every word of it." M. Ferraud folded his arms and sat back.

During the pause Hildegarde shivered. Something made her desire madly to thrust a hand out and cover M. Ferraud's mouth.

"We have all read much about Napoleon. I can not recall how many lives range shoulder to shoulder on the booksellers' shelves. There have been letters and memoirs, anecdotes by celebrated men and

women who were his contemporaries.   But there is
one thing upon which we shall all agree, and that is
that the emperor was in private life something of
a beast.   As a soldier he was the peer of all the
Cæsars; as a husband he was vastly inferior to any
of them.   This story does not concern him as
emperor.   If in my narrative there occurs anything
offensive, correct me instantly.   I speak English
fluently, but there are still some idioms I trip on."

" I'll trust you to steer straight enough," said the
admiral.

" Thank you.   Well, then, once upon a time
Napoleon was in Bavaria.   The country was at that
time his ablest ally.   There was a pretty peasant
girl."

A knife clattered to the floor.   " Pardon! " whispered Hildegarde to Cathewe.   " I am clumsy."
She was as white as the linen.

Breitmann went on with his crumbs.

" I believe," continued M. Ferraud, " that it was
in the year 1813 that the emperor received a peculiar
letter.   It begged that a title be conferred upon a
pretty little peasant boy.   The emperor was a grim
humorist, I may say in passing; and for this infant

he created a baronetcy, threw in a parcel of land, and a purse. That was the end of it, as far as it related to the emperor. Waterloo came and with it vanished the empire; and it would be a long time before a baron of the empire returned to any degree of popularity. For years the matter was forgotten. The documents in the case, the letters of patent, the deeds and titles to the land, and a single Napoleonic scrawl, these gathered dust in the loft. When I heard this tale the thing which appealed to me most keenly was the thought that over in Bavaria there exists the only real direct strain of Napoleonic blood: a Teuton, one of those who had brought about the downfall of the empire."

"You say exists?" interjected Cathewe.

"Exists," laconically.

"You have proofs?" demanded Fitzgerald.

"The very best in the world. I have not only seen those patents, but I have seen the man."

"Very interesting," agreed Breitmann, brushing the crumbs into his hand and dropping them on his plate. "But, go on."

"What a man!" breathed Fitzgerald, who began to see the drift of things.

"I proceed, then. Two generations passed. I doubt if the third generation of this family has ever heard of the affair. One day the last of his race, in clearing up the salable things in his house — for he had decided to lease it — stumbled on the scant history of his forebears. He was at school then; a promising youngster, brave, cheerful, full of adventure and curiosity. Contrary to the natural sequence of events, he chose the navy, where he did very well. But in some way Germany found out what France already knew. Here was a fine chance for a stroke of politics. France had always watched; without fear, however, but with half-formed wonder. Germany considered the case: why not turn this young fellow loose on France, to worry and to harry her? So, quietly Germany bore on the youth in that cold-blooded, Teutonic way she has, and forced him out of the navy.

"He was poor, and poverty among German officers, in either branch, is a bad thing. Our young friend did not penetrate the cause of this at first; for he had no intention of utilizing his papers, save to dream over them. The blood of his great forebear refused to let him bow under this unjust stroke. He sought a craft, an interesting one. The net again closed in on him. He began to grow desperate, and desperation was what Germany desired. Desperation would make a tool of the young fellow. But our young Napoleon was not without wit. He plotted, but so cleverly and secretly that never a hand could reach out to stay him. Germany finally offered him an immense bribe. He threw it back, for now he hated Germany more than he hated France. You wonder why he hated France? If France had not discarded her empire — I do not refer to the second empire — he would have been a great personage to-day. At least this must be one of his ideas.

"And there you are," abruptly. "Here we have a Napoleon, indeed with all the patience of his great forebear. If Germany had left him alone he would to-day have been a good citizen, who would never have permitted futile dreams to enter his head, and who would have contemplated his greatness with the smile of a philosopher. And who can say where this will end? It is pitiful."

"Pitiful?" repeated Breitmann. "Why that?" calmly.

M. Ferraud repressed the admiration in his eyes. It was a singular duel. "When we see a madman rushing blindly over a precipice it is a human instinct to reach out a hand to save him."

"But how do you know he is rushing blindly?" Breitmann smiled this question.

Hildegarde sent him a terrified glance. But for the stiff back of her chair she must have fallen.

M. Ferraud demolished an olive before he answered the question. "He has allied himself with some of the noblest houses in France; that is to say, with the most heartless spendthrifts in Europe. Napoleon IV? They are laughing behind his back this very minute. They are making a cat's-paw of his really magnificent fight for their own ignoble ends, the Orleanist party. To wreak petty vengeance on France, for which none of them has any love; to embroil the government and the army that they may tell of it in the boudoirs. This is the aim they have in view. What is it to them that they break a strong man's heart? What is it to them if he be given over to perpetual imprisonment? Did a Bourbon ever love France as a country? Has not France always represented to them a purse into which they might thrust their dishonest hands to pay for their base pleasures? Oh, beware of the conspirator whose sole portion in life is that of pleasure! I wish that I could see this young man and tell him all I know. If I could only warn him."

Breitmann brushed his sleeve. " I am really disappointed in your climax, Mr. Ferraud."

" I said nothing about a climax," returned M. Ferraud. " That has yet to be enacted."

" Ah! "

" A descendant of Napoleon, direct! Poor devil! " The admiral was thunderstruck. " Why, the very spirit of Napoleon is dead. Nothing could ever revive it. It would not live even a hundred days."

" Less than that many hours," said M. Ferraud. " He will be arrested the moment he touches a French port."

" Father," cried Laura, with a burst of generosity which not only warmed her heart but her cheeks, " why not find this poor, deluded young man and give him the treasure? "

" What, and ruin him morally as well as politically? No, Laura; with money he might become a menace."

"On the contrary," put in M. Ferraud; "with money he might be made to put away his mad dream. But I'm afraid that my story has made you all gloomy."

"It has made me sad," Laura admitted. "Think of the struggle, the self-denial, and never a soul to tell him he is mad."

The scars faded a little, but Breitmann's eyes never wavered.

"The man hasn't a ghost of a chance." To Fitzgerald it was now no puzzle why Breitmann's resemblance to some one else had haunted him. He was rather bewildered, for he had not expected so large an order upon M. Ferraud's promise. "Fifty years ago. . ."

"Ah! Fifty years ago," interrupted M. Ferraud eagerly, "I should have thrown my little to the cause. Men and times were different then; the world was less sordid and more romantic."

"Well, I shall always hold that we have no right to that treasure."

"Fiddlesticks, Laura! This is no time for sentiment. The questions buzzing in my head are: Does this man know of the treasure's existence? Might he not already have put his hand upon it?"

"Your own papers discredit that supposition," replied Cathewe. "A stunning yarn, and rather hard to believe in these skeptical times. What is it?" he asked softly, noting the dead white on Hildegarde's cheeks.

"Perhaps it is the smoke," she answered with a brave attempt at a smile.

The admiral in his excitement had lighted a heavy cigar and was consuming it with jerky puffs, a bit of thoughtlessness rather pardonable under the stress of the moment. For he was beginning to entertain doubts. It was not impossible for this Napoleonic chap to have a chart, to know of the treasure's existence. He wished he had heard this story before. He would have left the women at home. Corsica was not wholly civilized, and who could tell what might happen there? Yes, the admiral had his doubts.

"I should like to know the end of the story," said Breitmann musingly.

"There is time," replied M. Ferraud; and of them

all, only Fitzgerald caught the sinister undercurrent.

"So, Miss Killigrew, you believe that this treasure should be handed over to its legal owner?" Breitmann looked into her eyes for the first time that evening.

"I have some doubt about the legal ownership, but the sentimental and moral ownership is his. A romance should always have a pleasant ending."

"You are thinking of books," was Cathewe's comment. "In life there is more adventure than romance, and there is seldom anything more incomplete in every-day life than romance."

"That would be my own exposition, Mr. Cathewe," said Breitmann.

The two fenced briefly. They understood each other tolerably well; only, Cathewe as yet did not know the manner of the man with whom he was matched.

The dinner came to an end, or, rather, the diners rose, the dinner having this hour or more been cleared from the table; and each went to his or her state-room mastered by various degrees of astonishment. Fitzgerald moved in a kind of waking sleep.

Napoleon IV! That there was a bar sinister did
not matter. The dazzle radiated from a single
point: a dream of empire! M. Ferraud had not
jested; Breitmann was mad, obsessed, a monomaniac. It was grotesque; it troubled the senses
as a Harlequin's dance troubles the eyes. A great-
grandson of Napoleon, and plotting to enter France!
And, good Lord! with what? Two million francs
and half a dozen spendthrifts. Never had there
been a wilder, more hopeless dreamer than this!
Whatever antagonism or anger he had harbored
against Breitmann evaporated. Poor devil, indeed!

He understood M. Ferraud now. Breitmann was
mad; but till he made a decisive stroke no man
could stay him. So many things were clear now.
He was after the treasure, and he meant to lay his
hands upon it, peacefully if he could, violently if
no other way opened. That day in the Invalides,
the old days in the field, his unaccountable appearance on the Jersey coast; each of these things
squared themselves in what had been a puzzle. But,
like the admiral, he wished that there were no
women on board. There would be a contest of some
order, going forward, where only men would be

needed.   Pirates!   He rolled into his bunk with a dry laugh.

Meantime M. Ferraud walked the deck alone, and finally when Breitmann approached him, it was no more than he had been expecting.

"Among other things," began the secretary, with ominous calm, "I should like to see the impression of your thumb."

"That lock was an ingenious contrivance.   It was only by the merest accident I discovered it."

"It must be a vile business."

"Serving one's country?   I do not agree with you. Wait a moment, Mr. Breitmann; let us not misunderstand each other.   I do not know what fear is; but I do know that I am one of the few living who put above all other things in the world, France: France with her wide and beautiful valleys, her splendid mountains, her present peace and prosperity.   And my life is nothing if in giving it I may confer a benefit."

"Why did you not tell the whole story?   A Frenchman, and to deny oneself a climax like this?"

M. Ferraud remained silent.

"If you had not meddled! Well, you have, and these others must bear the brunt with you, should anything serious happen."

"Without my permission you will not remain in Ajaccio a single hour. But that would not satisfy me. I wish to prove to you your blindness. I will make you a proposition. Tear up those papers, erase the memory from your mind, and I will place in your hands every franc of those two millions."

Breitmann laughed harshly. "You have said that I am mad; very well, I am. But I know what I know, and I shall go on to the end. You are clever. I do not know who you are nor why you are here with your warnings; but this will I say to you: to-morrow we land, and every hour you are there, death shall lurk at your elbow. Do you understand me?"

"Perfectly. So well, that I shall let you go freely."

"A warning for each, then; only mine has death in it."

"And mine, nothing but good-will and peace."

CHAPTER XXI

CAPTAIN FLANAGAN MEETS A DUKE

THE isle of Corsica, for all its fame in romance and history, is yet singularly isolated and unknown. It is an island whose people have stood still for a century, indolent, unobserving, thriftless. No smoke, that ensign of progress, hangs over her towns, which are squalid and unpicturesque, save they lie back among the mountains. But the country itself is wildly and magnificently beautiful: great mountains of granite as varied in colors as the palette of a painter, emerald streams that plunge over porphyry and marble, splendid forests of pine and birch and chestnut.

The password was, is, and ever will be, Napoleon. Speak that name and the native's eye will fire and his patois will rattle forth and tingle the ear like a snare-drum. Though he pays his tithe to France, he is Italian; but unlike the Italian of Italy, his predilection is neither for gardening, nor agriculture, nor horticulture. Nature gave him a few chestnuts, and he considers that sufficient. For the most part he subsists upon chestnut-bread, stringy mutton, sinister cheeses, and a horrid sour wine. As a variety he will shoot small birds and in the winter a wild pig or two; his toil extends no further, for his wife is the day-laborer. Viewing him as he is to-day, it does not seem possible that his ancestors came from Genoa la Superba.

Napoleon was born in Ajaccio, but the blood in his veins was Tuscan, and his mind Florentine.

These days the world takes little or no interest in the island, save for its wool, lumber and an inferior cork. Great ships pass it on the north and south, on the east and west, but only cranky packets and dismal freighters drop anchor in her ports.

The Gulf of Ajaccio lies at the southwest of the island and is half-moon in shape, with reaches of white sands, red crags, and brush covered dunes, and immediately back of these, an embracing range of bald mountains.

A little before sunrise the yacht *Laura* swam into the gulf. The mountains, their bulks in shadowy gray, their undulating crests threaded with yellow fire, cast their images upon the smooth tideless silver-dulled waters.   Forward a blur of white and red marked the town.

"Isn't it glorious?" said Laura, rubbing the dew from the teak rail.   "And oh! what a time we people waste in not getting up in the mornings with the sun."

"I don't know," replied Fitzgerald.   "Scenery and sleep; of the two I prefer the latter.   I have always been routed out at dawn and never allowed to turn in till midnight.   You can always find scenery, but sleep is a coy thing."

"There's a drop of commercial blood in your veins somewhere, the blood of the unromantic.   But this morning?"

"Oh, sleep doesn't count at all this morning. The scenery is everything."

And as he looked into her clear bright eyes he knew that before this quest came to its end he was going to tell this enchanting girl that he loved her "better than all the world"; and moreover, he intended to tell it to her with the daring hope of winning her, money or no money.   Had not some poet

written — some worldly wise poet who rather had
the hang of things —

> " He either fears his fate too much,
>   Or his deserts are small,
> Who dares not put it to the touch
>   To win or lose it all."

Money wasn't everything; she herself had made
that statement the first night out. He had been
afraid of Breitmann, but somehow that fear was
all gone now. Did she care, if ever so little?

He veered his gaze round and wondered where
Breitmann was. Could the man be asleep on a
morn so vital as this? No, there he was, on the
very bowsprit itself. The crew was busy about
him, some getting the motor-boat in trim, others
yanking away at pulleys, all the preparations of
landing. A sharp order rose now and then; a servant passed, carrying Captain Flanagan's breakfast
to the pilot-house. To all this subdued turmoil
Breitmann seemed apparently oblivious. What
mad dream was working in that brain? Did the
poor devil believe in himself; or did he have some
ulterior purpose, unknown to any but himself?
Fitzgerald determined, once they touched land,

never to let him go beyond sight. It would not be human for him to surrender any part of the treasure without making some kind of a fight for it, cunning or desperate. If only the women-folk remained on board!

Breitmann gazed toward the town motionless.

It was difficult for Fitzgerald not to tell the great secret then and there; but his caution whispered warningly. There was no knowing what effect it would have upon the impulsive girl at his side. And besides, there might have been a grain of selfishness in the repression. All is fair in love or war; and it would not have been politic to make a hero out of Breitmann.

"You haven't said a word for five minutes," she declared. How boyish he looked for a man of his experience!

"Silence is sometimes good for the soul," sententiously.

"Of what were you thinking?"

His heart struck hard against his breast. What an opening, what a moment in which to declare himself! But he said: "Perhaps I was thinking of breakfast. This getting up early always makes me ravenous. The smell of the captain's coffee may have had something to do with it."

"You were thinking of nothing of the sort," she cried. "I know. It was the treasure and this great-grandson of Napoleon. Sometimes I feel I only dreamed these things. Why? Because, who-ever started out on a treasure quest without having thrilling adventures, shots in the dark, footsteps outside the room, villains, and all the rest of the paraphernalia? I never read nor heard of such a thing."

"Nor I. But there's land yonder," he said, with-out an answering smile.

"Then," in an awed whisper, "you believe some-thing is going to happen there?"

"One thing I am certain of, but I can not tell you just at this moment."

A bit of color came to her cheeks. As if, reading his eyes, she did not know this thing he was so certain of! Should she let him tell her? Not a real eddy in the current, unless it was his fear of money. If only she could lose her money, tempo-rarily! If only she had an ogre for a parent, now! But she hadn't. He was so dear and so kind and so proud of her that if she told him she was going to be married that morning, his only questions would have been: At what time? Why, this sort of romance was against all accepted rules. She was inordinately happy.

"There is only one thing lacking; this great-grandson himself. He will be yonder somewhere. For the man in the chimney was he or his agent."

"And aren't you afraid?"

"Of what?" proudly.

"It will not be a comedy. It is in the blood of these Napoleons that nothing shall stand in the path of their desires, neither men's lives nor woman's honor."

"I am not afraid. There is the sun at last. What a picture! And the shame of it! I am hungry!"

At half after six the yacht let go her anchor a few hundred yards from the quay. Every one was astir by now; but at the breakfast table there was one vacant chair — Breitmann's. M. Ferraud and Fitzgerald exchanged significant glances. In fact, the Frenchman drank his coffee hurriedly and excused himself. Breitmann was not on deck; neither was he in his state-room. The door was open. M. Ferraud, without any unnecessary qualms of conscience, went in. One glance at the trunk was sufficient. The lock hung down, disclosing the secret hollow. For once the little man's suavity forsook him, and he swore like a sailor, but softly. He rushed again to the deck and sought Captain Flanagan, who was enjoying a pipe forward.

" Captain, where is Mr. Breitmann? "

" Breitmann? Oh, he went ashore in one of the fruit-boats. Missed th' motor."

" Did he take any luggage? "

" Baggage? " corrected Captain Flanagan. " Nothin' but his hat, sir. Anythin' wrong? "

" Oh, no! We missed him at breakfast." M. Ferraud turned about, painfully conscious that he had been careless.

Fitzgerald hove in sight. " Find him? "

" Ashore! " said M. Ferraud, with a violent gesture.

" Isn't it time to make known who he is? "

" Not yet. It would start too many complications. Besides, I doubt if he has the true measurements."

" There was ample time for him to make a copy."

" Perhaps."

" Mr. Ferraud? "

" Well? "

" I've an idea, and I have had it for some time, that you wouldn't feel horribly disappointed if our friend made away with the money."

M. Ferraud shrugged; then he laughed quietly.

" Well, neither would I," Fitzgerald added.

" My son, you are a man after my own heart. I was furious for the moment to think that he had outwitted me the first move. I did not want him to meet his confederates without my eyes on him. And there you have it. It is not the money, which is morally his; it is his friends, his lying, mocking friends."

" Are we fair to the admiral? He has set his heart on this thing."

" And shall we spoil his pleasure? Let him find it out later."

" Do you know Corsica? "

" As the palm of my hand."

" But the women? "

" They will never be in the danger zone. No

blood will be spilled, unless it be mine.   He has no
love for me, and I am his only friend, save one."

" Suppose this persecution of Germany's was only
a blind? "

" My admiration for you grows, Mr. Fitzgerald.
But I have dug too deeply into that end of it not
to be certain that Germany has tossed this bombshell
into France without holding a string to it.   Did
you know that Breitmann had once been hit by a
spent bullet?   Here," pointing to the side of his
head.   " He is always conscious of what he does
but not of the force that makes him do it.   Do you
understand me?   He is living in a dream, and I
must wake him."

The adventurers were now ready to disembark.
They took nothing but rugs and hand-bags, for
there would be no preening of fine feathers on hotel
verandas.   With the exception of Hildegarde all
were eager and excited.   Her breast was heavy
with forebodings.   Who and what was this man
Ferraud?   One thing she knew; he was a menace
to the man she loved, aye, with every throb of her
heart and every thought of her mind.

The admiral was like a boy starting out upon

his first fishing-excursion. To him there existed nothing else in the world beyond a chest of money hidden somewhere in the pine forest of Aïtone. He talked and laughed, pinched Laura's ears, shook Fitzgerald's shoulder, prodded Coldfield, and fussed because the motor wasn't sixty-horse power.

"Father," Laura asked suddenly, "where is Mr. Breitmann?"

"Oh, I told him last night to go ashore early, if he would, and arrange for rooms at the Grand Hotel d'Ajaccio. He knows all about the place."

M. Ferraud turned an empty face toward Fitzgerald, who laughed. The great-grandson of Napoleon, applying for hotel accommodations, as a gentleman's gentleman, and within a few blocks of the house in which the self-same historic forebear was born! It had its comic side.

"Are there any brigands?" inquired Mrs. Coldfield. She was beginning to doubt this expedition.

"Brigands? Plenty," said the admiral, "but they are all hotel proprietors these times, those that aren't conveniently buried. From here we go to Carghese, where we spend the night, then on to Evisa, and another night. The next morning we shall be on the ground. Isn't that the itinerary, Fitzgerald?"

"Yes."

"And be sure to take an empty carriage to carry canned food and bottled water," supplemented Cathewe. "The native food is frightful. The first time I took the journey I was ignorant. Happily it was in the autumn, when the chestnuts were ripe. Otherwise I should have starved."

"And you spent a winter or spring here, Hildegarde?" said Mrs. Coldfield.

"It was lovely then." There was a dream in Hildegarde's eyes.

The hotel omnibus was out of service, and they rode up in carriages. The season was over, and under ordinary circumstances the hotel would have been closed. A certain royal family had not yet left, and this fact made the arrangements possible. It was now very warm. Dust lay everywhere, on the huge palms, on the withered plants, on the chairs and railings, and swam palpable in the air. Breitmann was nowhere to be found, but he had seen the manager of the hotel and secured rooms facing the bay. Later, perhaps two hours after the arrival, he appeared. In this short time he had completed his plans. As he viewed them he could see no flaw.

Now it came about that Captain Flanagan, who had not left the ship once during the journey, found his one foot aching for a touch and feel of the land. So he and Holleran, the chief-engineer, came ashore a little before noon and decided to have a bite of maccaroni under the shade of the palms in the *Place des Palmiers*. A bottle of warm beer was divided between them. The captain said Faugh! as he drank it.

" Try th' native wine, Capt'n," suggested the chief-engineer.

" I have a picture of Capt'n Flanagan drinkin' the misnamed vinegar. No Dago's bare fut on the top o' mine, when I'm takin' a glass. An' that's th' way they make ut. This Napoleyun wus a fine man. He pushed 'em round some."

" Sure, he had Irish blood in 'im, somewheres," Holleran assented. " But I say," suddenly stretching his lean neck, " will ye look t' see who's comin' along! "

Flanagan stared. " If ut ain't that son-of-a-gun

ov a Picard, I'll eat my hat!" The captain grew purple. "An' leavin' th' ship without orders!"

"An' the togs!" murmured Holleran.

"Watch me!" said Flanagan, rising and squaring his peg.

Picard, arrayed in clean white flannels, white shoes, a panama set rakishly on his handsome head, his fingers twirling a cane, came head-on into the storm. The very jauntiness of his stride was as a red rag to the captain. So then, a hand, heavy and charged with righteous anger, descended upon Picard's shoulder.

"Right about face an' back to th' ship, fast as yer legs c'n make ut!"

Picard calmly shook off the hand, and, adding a vigorous push which sent the captain staggering among the little iron-tables, proceeded nonchalantly. Holleran leaped to his feet, but there was a glitter in Picard's eye that did not promise well for any rough-and-tumble fight. Picard's muscular shoulders moved off toward the vanishing point. Holleran turned to the captain, and with the assistance of a waiter, the two righted the old man.

"Do *you* speak English?" roared the old sailor.

" Yes, sir," respectfully.

" Who wus that? "

The waiter, in reverent tones, declared that the gentleman referred to was well known in Ajaccio, that he had spent the previous winter there, and that he was no less a person than the Duke of — But the waiter never completed the sentence. The title was enough for the irascible Flanagan.

" Th'— hell — he — is! " The captain subsided into the nearest chair, bereft of future speech, which is a deal of emphasis to put on the phrase. Picard, a duke, and only that morning his hands had been yellow with the stains of the donkey-engine oil! And by and by the question set alive his benumbed brain; what was a duke doing on the yacht *Laura?* " Holleran, we go t' the commodore. The devil's t' pay. What's a dook doin' on th' ship, and we expectin' to dig up gold in yonder mountains? Look alive, man; they's villany afoot! "

Holleran's jaw sagged.

CHAPTER XXII

THE ADMIRAL BEGINS TO DOUBT

"WHAT'S this you're telling me, Flanagan?"
said the admiral perturbed.

"Ask Holleran here, sir; he wus with me when th' waiter said Picard wus a dook. I've suspicioned his han's this long while, sir."

"Yes, sir; Picard it was," averred Holleran.

"Bah! Mistaken identity."

"I'm sure, sir," insisted Holleran. "Picard has a whisker-mole on his chin, sir, like these forriners grow, sir. Picard, sir, an' no mistake."

"But what would a duke . . ."

"Ay, sir; that's the question," interrupted Flanagan; and added in a whisper: "Y' c'n buy a dozen dooks for a couple o' million francs, sir. Th' first-officer, Holleran here, an' me; nobody else knows what we're after, sir; unless you gentlemen abaft, sir, talked careless. I say 'tis serious, Commodore. *He* knows what we're lookin' fer."

Holleran nudged his chief. "Tell th' commodore what we saw on th' way here."

"Picard hobnobbin' with Mr. Breitmann, sir."

Breitmann? The admiral's smile thinned and disappeared. There might be something in this. Two million francs did not appeal to him, but he realized that to others they stood for a great fortune, one worthy of hazards. He would talk this over with Cathewe and Fitzgerald and learn what they thought about the matter. If this fellow Picard was a duke and had shipped as an ordinary hand foreward . . . Peace went out of the admiral's jaw and Flanagan's heart beat high as he saw the old war-knots gather. Oh, for a row like old times! For twenty years he had fought nothing bigger than a drunken stevedore. Suppose this was the beginning of a fine rumpus? He grinned, and the admiral, noting the same, frowned. He wished he had left the women at Marseilles.

"Say nothing to any one," he warned. "But if this man Picard comes aboard again, keep him there."

" Yessir."

" That'll be all."

" What d' y' think? " asked Holleran, on the return to the *Place des Palmiers,* for the two were
still hungry.

" Think?   There's a fight, bucko! " jubilantly.

" These pleasure-boats sure become monotonous."
Holleran rubbed his dark hands.   " When d' y'
think it'll begin? "

" I wish ut wus t'day."

" I've seen y' do some fine work with th' peg."

They had really seen Picard and Breitmann talking together.   The acquaintanceship might have
dated from the sailing of the *Laura,* and again it
mightn't.   At least, M. Ferraud, who overheard
the major part of the conversation, later in the day,
was convinced that Picard had joined the crew of
the *Laura* for no other purpose than to be in touch
with Breitmann.   There were some details, however, which would be acceptable.   He followed
them to the Rue Fesch, to a *trattoria,* but entered
from the rear.   M. Ferraud never assumed any dis-
guises, but depended solely upon his adroitness in
occupying the smallest space possible.   So, while

the two conspirators sat at a table on the sidewalk, M. Ferraud chose his inside, under the grilled window which was directly above them.

" Everything is in readiness," said Picard.

" Thanks to you, duke."

" To-night you and your old boatman Pietro will leave for Aïtone. The admiral and his party will start early to-morrow morning. No matter what may happen, he will find no drivers till morning. The drivers all understand what they are to do on the way back from Evisa. I almost came to blows with that man Flanagan. I wasn't expecting him ashore. And I could not stand the grime and jeans a minute longer. Perhaps he will believe it a case of mistaken identity. At any rate he will not find out the truth till it's too late for him to make a disturbance. We have had wonderful luck!"

A cart rumbled past, and the listener missed a few sentences. What did the drivers understand? What was going to happen on the way back from Evisa? Surely, Breitmann did not intend that the admiral should do the work and then be held up later. The old American sailor wasn't afraid of any one, and he would shoot to kill. No, no;

Breitmann meant to secure the gold alone. But the drivers worried M. Ferraud. He might be forced to change his plans on their account. He wanted full details, not puzzling components. Quiet prevailed once more.

" Women in affairs of this sort are always in the way," said Picard.

M. Ferraud did not hear what Breitmann replied.

" Take my word for it," pursued Picard, " this one will trip you; and you can not afford to trip at this stage. We are all ready to strike, man. All we want is the money. Every ten francs of it will buy a man. We leave Marseilles in your care; the rest of us will carry the word on to Lyons, Dijon and Paris. With this unrest in the government, the army scandals, the dissatisfied employees, and the idle, we shall raise a whirlwind greater than '50 or '71. We shall reach Paris with half a million men."

Again Breitmann said something lowly. M. Ferraud would have liked to see his face.

" But what are you going to do with the other woman? "

Two women: M. Ferraud saw the ripple widen and draw near. One woman he could not understand, but two simplified everything. The drivers and two women.

" The other? " said Breitmann. " She is of no importance."

M. Ferraud shook his head.

" Oh, well; this will be your private affair. Captain Grasset will arrive from Nice to-morrow night. Two nights later we all should be on board and under way. Do you know, we have been very clever. Not a suspicion anywhere of what we are about."

" Do you recollect M. Ferraud? " inquired Breit-mann.

" That little fool of a butterfly-hunter? " the duke asked.

M. Ferraud smiled and gazed laughingly up at the grill.

" He is no fool," abruptly. " He is a secret agent, and not one move have we made that is unknown to him."

" Impossible! "

M. Ferraud could not tell whether the consternation in Picard's voice was real or assumed. He chose to believe the latter.

" And why hasn't he shown his hand? "

" He is waiting for us to show ours. But don't worry," went on Breitmann. " I have arranged to suppress him neatly."

And the possible victim murmured: " I wonder how? "

" Then we must not meet again until you return; and then only at the little house in the Rue St. Charles."

" Agreed. Now I must be off."

" Good luck! "

M. Ferraud heard the stir of a single chair and knew that the great-grandson was leaving. The wall might have been transparent, so sure was he of the smile upon Picard's face, a sinister speculating smile. But his imagination did not pursue Breitmann, whose lips also wore a smile, one of irony and bitterness. Neither did he hear Picard murmur " Dupe! " nor Breitmann mutter " Fools! "

When Breitmann saw Hildegarde in the hotel gardens he did not avoid her but stopped by her chair. She rose. She had been waiting all day for this moment.   She must speak out or suffocate with anxiety.

"Karl, what are you going to do?"

"Nothing," unsmilingly.

"You will let the admiral find and keep this money which is yours?"

Breitmann shrugged.

"You are killing me with suspense!"

"Nonsense!" briskly.

"You are contemplating violence of some order. I know it, I feel it!"

"Not so loud!" impatiently.

"You are!" she repeated, crushing her hands together.

"Well, all there remains to do is to tell the admiral.   He will, perhaps, divide with me."

"How can you be so cruel to me?   It is your safety; that is all I wish to be assured of.   Oh, I am pitifully weak!   I should despise you.   Take this chest of money; it is yours.   Go to England, to America, and be happy."

"Happy?   Do you wish me to be happy?"

"God knows!"

"And you?" curiously.

" I have no time to ask you to consider me,"
with a clear pride. " I do not wish to see you hurt.
You are courting death, Karl, death."

" Who cares? "

" I care! " with a sob.

The bitterness in his face died for a space.
" Hildegarde, I'm not worth it. Forget me as some
bad dream; for that is all I am or ever shall be.
Marry Cathewe; I'm not blind. He will make you
happy. I have made my bed, or rather certain
statesmen have, and I must lie in it. If I had
known what I know now," with regret, " this would
not have been. But I distrusted every one, myself, too."

She understood. " Karl, had you told me all in
the first place, I should have given you that diagram
without question, gladly."

" Well, I am sorry. I have been a beast. Have
we not always been such, from the first of us, down
to me? Forget me! "

And with that he left her standing by the side of
her chair and walked swiftly toward the hotel.
When next she realized or sensed anything she was
lying on her bed, her eyes dry and wide open. And

she did not go down to dinner, nor did she answer the various calls on her door.

Night rolled over the world, with a cool breeze driving under her million planets. The lights in the hotel flickered out one by one, and in the third corridor, where the adventurers were housed, only a wick, floating in a tumbler of oil, burned dimly.

Fitzgerald had waited in the shadow for nearly an hour, and he was growing restless and tired. All day long he had been obsessed with the conviction that if Breitmann ever made a start it would be some time that night. Distinctly he heard the light rattle of a carriage. It stopped outside the gardens. He pressed closer against the wall. The door to Breitmann's room opened gently and the man himself stepped out cautiously.

" So," began Fitzgerald lightly, " your majesty goes forth to-night ? "

But he overreached himself. Breitmann whirled, and all the hate in his breast went into his arm as he struck. Fitzgerald threw up his guard, but not soon enough. The blow hit him full on the side of the head and toppled him over; and as the back of his head bumped the floor, the world came to an end. When he regained his senses his head was pillowed on a woman's knees and the scared white face of a woman bent over his.

"What's happened?" he whispered. There were a thousand wicks where there had been one and these went round and round in a circle. Presently the effect wore away, and he recognized Laura. Then he remembered. "By George!"

"What is it?" she cried, the bands of terror about her heart loosening.

"As a hero I'm a picture," he answered. "Why, I had an idea that Breitmann was off to-night to dig up the treasure himself. Gone! And only one blow struck, and I in front of it!"

"Breitmann?" exclaimed Laura. She caught her dressing-gown closer about her throat.

"Yes. The temptation was too great. How did you get here?" He ought to have struggled to his feet at once, but it was very comfortable to feel her breath upon his forehead.

"I heard a fall and then some one running. Are you badly hurt?"

The anguish in her voice was as music to his ears.

"Dizzy, that's all. Better tell your father immediately. No, no; I can get up alone. I'm all right. Fine rescuer of princesses, eh?" with an unsteady laugh.

"You might have been killed!"

"Scarcely that. I tried to talk like they do in stories, with this result. The maxim is, always strike first and question afterward. You warn your father quietly while I hunt up Ferraud and Cathewe."

Seeing that he was really uninjured she turned and flew down the dark corridor and knocked at her father's door.

Fitzgerald stumbled along toward M. Ferraud's room, murmuring: "All right, Mr. Breitmann; all right. But hang me if I don't hand you back that one with interest. Where the devil is that Frenchman?" as he hammered on Ferraud's door and obtained no response. He tried the knob. The door opened. The room was black, and he struck a match. M. Ferraud, fully dressed, lay upon his bed. There was a handkerchief over his mouth and his hands and feet were securely bound. His eyes were open.

CHAPTER XXIII

CATHEWE ASKS QUESTIONS

THE hunter of butterflies rubbed his released
wrists and ankles, tried his collar, coughed,
and dropped his legs to the floor.

"I am getting old," he cried in self-communion;
"near-sighted and old. I've worn spectacles so long
in jest that now I must wear them in earnest."

"How long have you been here?" asked Fitzgerald.

"I should say about two hours. It was very simple. He came to the door. I opened it. He came
in. *Zut!* He is as powerful as a lion."

"Why didn't you call?"

"I was too busy, and suddenly it became too late.
Gone?"

"Yes." And Fitzgerald swore as he rubbed the
side of his head. Briefly he related what had befallen him.

" You have never hunted butterflies ? "

" No," sharply.   " Shall we start for him while his heels are hot ? "

" It is very exciting.   It is the one thing I really care for.   There is often danger, but it is the kind that does not steal round your back.   Hereafter I shall devote my time to butterflies.   You can make believe — is that what you call it ? — each butterfly is a great rascal.   The more difficult the netting, the more cunning the rascal . . . What did you say ? "

" Look here, Ferraud," cried Fitzgerald angrily; " do you want to catch him or not?   He's gone, and that means he has got the odd trick."

" But not the rubber, my son.   Listen.   When you set a trap for a rat or a lion, do you scare the animal into it, or do you lure him with a tempting bait?   I have laid the trap; he and his friend will walk into it.   I am not a police officer.   I make no arrests.   My business is to avert political calamities, without any one knowing that these calamities exist.   That is the real business of a secret agent. Let him dig up his fortune.   Who has a better right?   *Peste!*   The pope will not crown him in the gardens of the Tuileries. What!" with a ring in his voice Fitzgerald had never heard before; " am I one to be overcome without a struggle, without a call for help? The trap is set, and in forty-eight hours it will be sprung. Be calm, my son. To-night we should not find a horse or carriage in the whole town of Ajaccio."

" But what are you going to do? "

" Go to Aïtone, to find a hole in the ground."

" But the admiral!"

"Let him gaze into the hole, and then tell him what you will. I owe him that much. Come on!"

" Where? "

" To the admiral, to tell him his secretary is a fine rogue and that he has stolen the march on us. A good chase will soften his final disappointment."

" You're a strange man."

" No; only what you English and Americans call a game sport. To start on even terms with a man, to give him the odds, if necessary. What! have beaters for my rabbits, shoot pigeons from traps? *Fi donc!* "

" Hang it!" growled the young man, undecided.

" My son, give me my way. Some day you will

be glad.   I will tell you this: I am playing against
desperate men; and the liberty, perhaps honor, of
one you love is menaced."

"My God!"

"Sh! Ask me nothing; leave it all to me.
There! They are coming. Not a word."

The admiral's fury was boundless, and his ut-
terances were touched here and there by strong
sailor expressions. The scoundrel! The black-
leg! And he had trusted him without reservation.
He wanted to start at once. Laura finally succeeded in calming him, and the cold reason of M.
Ferraud convinced him of the folly of haste.
There was a comic side to the picture, too, but they
were all too serious to note it; the varied tints of
the dressing-gowns, the bath-slippers and bare feet,
the uncovered throats, the tousled hair, the eyes
still heavy with sleep. Every one of the party was
in Ferraud's room, and their voices hummed and
murmured and their arms waved. Only one of
them did Ferraud watch keenly; Hildegarde. How
would she act now?

Fitzgerald's head still rang, and now his mind
was being tortured. Laura in danger from this

madman? No, over his body first, over his dead
body. How often had he smiled at that phrase;
but there was no melodrama in it now. Her liberty
and perhaps her honor! His strong fingers worked
convulsively; to put them round the blackguard's
throat! And to do nothing himself, to wait upon
this Frenchman's own good time, was maddening.

"Your head is all right now?" as she turned to
follow the others from the room.

"It was nothing." He forced a smile to his lips.
"I'm as fit as a fiddle now; only, I'll never forgive
myself for letting him go. Will you tell me one
thing? Did he ever offend you in any way?"

"A woman would not call it an offense," a glint
of humor in her eyes. "Real offense, no."

"He proposed to you?"

The suppressed rage in his tone would have
amused if it hadn't thrilled her strangely. "It
would have been a proposal if I had not stopped it.
Good night."

He could not see her eyes very well; there was
only one candle burning. Impulsively he snatched
at her hand and kissed it. With his life, if need
be; ay, and gladly. And even as she disappeared

into the corridor the thought intruded: Where was the past, the days of wandering, the active and passive adventures, he had contemplated treasuring up for a club career in his old age? Why, they had vanished from his mind as thin ice vanishes in the spring sunshine. To love is to be borne again.

And Laura? She possessed a secret that terrified her one moment and enraptured her the next. And she marveled that there was no shame in her heart. Never in all her life before had she done such a thing; she, who had gone so calmly through her young years, wondering what it was that had made men turn away from her with agony written on their faces! She would never be the same again, and the hand she held softly against her cheek would never be the same hand. Where was the tranquillity of that morning?

Fitzgerald found himself alone with Ferraud again. There was going to be no dissembling; he was going to speak frankly.

"You have evidently discovered it. Yes, I love Miss Killigrew, well enough to die for her."

"*Zut!* She will be as safe as in her own house. Had Breitmann not gone to-night, had any of us

stopped him, I could not say. Unless you tell her,
she will never know that she stood in danger.
Don't you understand? If I marred one move
these men intend to make, if I showed a single card,
they would defeat me for the time; for they would
make new plans of which I should not have the least
idea. You comprehend?"

Fitzgerald nodded.

"It all lies in the hollow of my hand. Breitmann
made one mistake: he should have pushed me off
the boat, into the dark. *He* knows that I know.
And there he confuses me. But, I repeat, he is not
vicious, only mad."

"Where will it be?"

"It will *not* be;" and M. Ferraud smiled as he
livened up the burnt wick of his candle.

"Treachery on the part of the drivers? Oh,
don't you see that you can trust me wholly?"

"Well, it will be like this;" and reluctantly the
secret agent outlined his plan. "Now, go to bed
and sleep, for you and I shall need some to draw
upon during the next three or four days. Hunting
for buried treasures was never a junketing. The
admiral will tell you that. At dawn!" Then he

added whimsically: "I trust we haven't disturbed the royal family below."

"Hang the royal family!"

"Their own parliament, or Reichstag, will arrange for that!" and the little man laughed.

Dawn came soon enough, yellow and airless.

"My dear," said Mrs. Coldfield, "I really wish you wouldn't go."

"But Laura and Miss von Mitter insist on going. I can't back out now," protested Coldfield. "What are you worried about? Brigands, gunshots, and all that?"

"He will be a desperate man."

"To steal a chest full of money is one thing; to shoot a man is another. Besides, the admiral will go if he has to go alone; and I can't desert him."

"Very well. You will have to take me to Baden for nervous prostration."

"Humph! Baden; that'll mean about two-thousand in fresh gowns from Vienna or Paris. All right; I'm game. But, no nerves, no Baden."

"Go, if you will; but *do* take care of yourself; and let the admiral go *first,* when there's any sign of danger."

Coldfield chuckled. " I'll get behind him every time I think of it."

" Kiss me. They are waiting for you. And be careful."

It was only a little brave comedy. She knew this husband and partner of hers, hard-headed at times, but full of loyalty and courage; and she was confident that if danger arose the chances were he would be getting in front instead of behind the admiral. A pang touched her heart as she saw him spring into the carriage.

The admiral had argued himself hoarse about Laura's going; but he had to give in when she threatened to hire a carriage on her own account and follow. Thus, Coldfield went because he was loyal to his friends; Laura, because she would not leave her father; Hildegarde, because to remain without knowing what was happening would have driven her mad; M. Ferraud, because it was a trick in the game; and Cathewe and Fitzgerald, because they loved hazard, because they were going with the women they loved. The admiral alone went for the motive apparent to all: to lay hands on the scoundrel who had betrayed his confidence.

So the journey into the mountains began. In none of the admiral's documents was it explained why the old Frenchman had hidden the treasure so far inland, when at any moment a call might have been made on it. Ferraud put forward the supposition that they had been watched. As for hiding it in Corsica at all, every one understood that it was a matter of sentiment.

Fitzgerald keenly inspected the drivers, but found them of the ordinary breed, in velveteens, red-sashes, and soft felt hats. As they made the noon stop, one thing struck him as peculiar. The driver of the provision carriage had little or nothing to do with his companions. "That is because *he* is mine," explained M. Ferraud in a whisper. They were all capable horsemen, and on this journey spared their horses only when absolutely necessary. The great American *signori* were in a hurry. They arrived at Carghese at five in the afternoon. The admiral was for pushing on, driving all night. He stormed, but the drivers were obdurate. At Carghese they would remain till sunrise; that was final. Besides, it was not safe at night, without moonshine, for many a mile of the road lipping tremendous

precipices was without curb or parapet.   Not a foot
till dawn.

In the little *auberge,* dignified but not improved
by the name of Hôtel de France, there was room
only for the two women and the older men.   Fitzgerald and Cathewe had to bunk the best they
could in a tenement at the upper end of the town;
two cots in a single room, carpetless and ovenlike
for the heat.

Cathewe opened his rug-bag and spread out a rug
in front of his cot, for he wasn't fond at any time of
dirty, bare boards under his feet.   He began to un-
dress, silently, puffing his pipe as one unconscious of
the deed.   Cathewe looked old.   Fitzgerald hadn't
noticed the change before; but it certainly was a fact
that his face was thinner than when they put out to
sea.   Cathewe, his pipe still between his teeth, absently drew his shirt over his head.   The pipe fell
to the rug and he stamped out the coals, grumbling.

" You'll set yourself afire one of these fine days,"
laughed Fitzgerald from his side of the room.

" I'm safe enough, Jack, you can't set fire to
ashes, and that's about all I amount to."   Cathewe
got into his pajamas and sat upon the bed.   " Jack,

I thought I knew something about this fellow Breit-mann; but it seems I've something to learn."

The younger man said nothing.

" Was that yarn of Ferraud's fact or tommy-rot?"

" Fact."

" The great-grandson of Napoleon! Here! Nothing will ever surprise me again. But why didn't he lay the matter before Killigrew, like a man?"

Fitzgerald patted and poked the wool-filled pillow, but without success. It remained as hard and as uninviting as ever. " I've thought it over, Arthur. I'd have done the same as Breitmann," as if reluctant to give his due to the missing man.

" But why didn't this butterfly man tell the admiral all?"

" He had excellent reasons. He's a secret agent, and has the idea that Breitmann wants to go into France and make an emperor of himself."

" Do men dream of such things to-day, let alone try to enact them?" incredulously.

" Breitmann's an example."

" Are you taking his part?"

"No, damn him! May I ask you a pertinent question?"

"Yes."

"Did he know Miss von Mitter very well in Munich?"

"He did."

"Was he quite square?"

"I am beginning to believe that he was something between a cad and a scoundrel."

"Did you know that among her forebears on her mother's side was the Abbe Fanu, who left among other things the diagram of the chimney?"

"So that was it?" Cathewe's jaws hardened.

Fitzgerald understood. Poor old Cathewe!

"Most women are fools!" said Cathewe, as if reading his friend's thought. "Pick out all the brutes in history; they were always better loved than decent men. Why? God knows! Well, good night;" and Cathewe blew out his candle.

So did Fitzgerald; but it was long before he fell asleep. He was straining his ears for the sound of a carriage coming down from Evisa. But none came.

CHAPTER XXIV

THE PINES OF AITONE

BEFORE sun-up they were on the way again. They circled through magnificent gorges now, of deep red and salmon tinted granite, storm-worn, strangely hollowed out, as if some Titan's hand had been at work; and always the sudden disappearance and reappearance of the blue Mediterranean.

The two young women rode in the same carriage. Occasionally the men got down out of theirs and walked on either side of them. Whenever an abrupt turn showed forward, Fitzgerald put his hand in his pocket. From whichever way it came, he, at least, was not going to be found unprepared. Sometimes, when he heard M. Ferraud's laughter drift back from the admiral's carriage, he longed to throttle the aggravating little man. Yet, his admiration of him was genuine. What a chap to have wandered round with, in the old days! He began

327

to realize what Frenchmen must have been a hundred years gone. And the strongest point in his
armor was his humanity; he wished no one ill.
Gradually the weight on Fitzgerald's shoulders
lightened. If M. Ferraud could laugh, why not he?

"Isn't that view lovely!" exclaimed Laura, as
the *Capo di Rosso* glowed in the sun with all the
beauty of a fabulous ruby. "Are you afraid at all,
Hildegarde?"

"No, Laura; I am only sad. I wish we were
safely on the yacht. Yes, yes; I *am* afraid, of
something I know not what."

"I never dreamed that he could be dishonest.
He *was* a gentleman, somewhere in his past. I do
not quite understand it all. The money does not
interest my father so much as the mere sport of
finding it. You know it was agreed to divide, his
share among the officers and seamen, and the balance to our guests. It would have been such fun."

And the woman who knew everything must perforce remain silent. With what eloquence she could
have defended him!

"Do you think we shall find it?" wistfully.

"No, Laura."

" How can he find his way back without passing
us? "

" For a desperate man who has thrown his all on
this one chance, he will find a hundred ways of re-
turning."

A carriage came round one of the pinnacled
calenches. It was empty. M. Ferraud casually
noted the number. He was not surprised. He had
been waiting for this same vehicle. It was Breitmann's, but the man driving it was not the
man who had driven it out of Ajaccio. He was an
Evisan. A small butterfly fluttered alongside.
M. Ferraud jumped out and swooped with his hat.
He decided not to impart his discovery to the others.
He was assured that the man from Evisa knew absolutely nothing, and that to question him would
be a waste of time. At this very moment it was
not unlikely that Breitmann and his confederate
were crossing the mountains; perhaps with three or
four sturdy donkeys, their panniers packed with
precious metal. And the dupe would go straight
to his fellow-conspirators and share his millions.
Curious old world!

They saw Evisa at sunset, one of the seven glories of the earth. The little village rests on the side of a mountain, nearly three-thousand feet above the sea, the sea itself lying miles away to the west, V-shaped between two enormous shafts of burning granite. Even the admiral forgot his smoldering wrath.

The hotel was neat and cool, and all the cook had to do was to furnish dishes and hot water for tea. There was very little jesting, and what there was of it fell to the lot of Coldfield and the Frenchman. The spirit in them all was tense. Given his way, the admiral would have gone out that very night with lanterns.

"Folly! To find a given point in an unknown forest at night; impossible! Am I not right, Mr. Cathewe? Of course. Breitmann's man knew Aïtone from his youth. Suppose," continued M. Ferraud, "that we spend two days here?"

"What? Give him all the leeway?" The admiral was amazed that M. Ferraud could suggest such a stupidity. "No. In the morning we make the search. If there's nothing there we'll return at once."

M. Ferraud spoke to the young woman who

waited on the table.   " Please find Carlo, the driver,
and bring him here."

Ten minutes later Carlo came in, hat in hand,
curious.

" Carlo," began the Frenchman, leaning on his
elbows, his sharp eyes boring into the mild brown
ones of the Corsican, " we shall not return to Carghese to-morrow but the day after."

" Not return to-morrow? " cried Carlo dismayed.
" Ah, but the *signore* does not understand.   We are
engaged day after to-morrow to carry a party to
Bonifacio.   We have promised.   We must return
to-morrow."

Fitzgerald saw the drift and bent forward.   The
admiral fumed because his Italian was an indifferent article.

" But," pursued M. Ferraud, " we will pay you
twenty francs the day, just the same."

" We   are   promised."   Carlo   shrugged   and
spread his hands, but the glitter in his questioner's
eyes disquieted him.

" What's this about? " growled the admiral.

" The man says he must take us back to-morrow,
or leave us, as he has promised to return to Ajaccio

to carry a party to Bonifacio," M. Ferraud explained.

" Then, if we don't go to-morrow it means a week in this forsaken hole? "

" It is possible." M. Ferraud turned to Carlo once more. " We will make it fifty francs per day."

" Impossible, *signore!* "

" Then you will return to-morrow without us." Carlo's face hardened. " But —"

" Come outside with me," said M. Ferraud in a tone which brooked no further argument.

The two stepped out into the hall, and when the Frenchman came back his face was animated.

" Mr. Ferraud," said the admiral icily, " my daughter has informed me what passed between you. I must say that you have taken a deal upon yourself."

" Mr. Ferraud is right," put in Fitzgerald.

" You, too? "

" Yes. I think the time has come for Mr. Ferraud to offer full explanations."

The butterfly-hunter resumed his chair. " They will remain or carry us on to Corte. From there

we can take the train back to Ajaccio, saving a day
and a half. Admiral, I have a confession to make.
It will surprise you, and I offer you my apologies at
once." He paused. He loved moments like this,
when he could resort to the dramatic in perfect
security. "*I* was the man in the chimney."

The admiral gasped. Laura dropped her hands
to the table. Cathewe sat back stiffly. Coldfield
stared. Hildegarde shaded her face with the newspaper through which she had been idly glancing.

"Patience!" as the admiral made as though to
press back his chair. "Mr. Fitzgerald knew from
the beginning. Is that not true?"

"It is, Mr. Ferraud. Go on."

"Breitmann is the great-grandson of Napoleon.
By this time he is traveling over some mountain
pass, with his inheritance snug under his hand.
You will ask, why all these subterfuges, this dodging in and out? Thus. Could I have found the
secret of the chimney — I worked from memory —
none of us would be here, and one of the great conspiracies of the time would have been nipped in
the bud. What do you think? Breitmann pro-
poses to go into France with the torch of anarchy

in his hand; and if he does, he will be shot. He prosposes to divide this money among his companions, who, with their pockets full of gold, will desert him the day he touches France. Do you recollect the scar on his temple? It was not made by a saber; it is the mark of a bullet. He received it while a correspondent in the Balkans. Well, it left a mark on his brain also. That is to say, he is conscious of what he does but not why he does it. He is a sane man with an obsession. This wound, together with the result of Germany's brutal policy toward him and France's indifference, has made him a kind of monomaniac. You will ask why I, an accredited agent in the employ of France, have not stepped in and arrested him. My evidence might bring him to trial, but it would never convict him. Once liberated, he would begin all over again, meaning that I also would have to start in at a new beginning. So I have let him proceed to the end, and in doing so I shall save him in spite of himself. You see, I have a bit of sentiment."

Hildegarde could have reached over and kissed his hand.

"Why didn't he tell all this to me?" cried the

admiral. "Why didn't he tell me? I would have helped him."

"To his death, perhaps," grimly. "For the money was only a means, not an end. The great-grandson of Napoleon: well, he will never rise from his obscurity. And sometime, when the clouds lift from his brain, he will remember me. I have seen in your American cottages the motto hanging on the walls — *God Bless Our Home*. Mr. Breitmann will place my photograph beside it and smoke his cigarette in peace."

And this whimsical turn caused even the admiral to struggle with a smile. He was a square, generous old sailor. He stretched his hand across the table. M. Ferraud took it, but with a shade of doubt.

"You are a good man, Mr. Ferraud. I'm terribly disappointed. All my life I have been goose-chasing for treasures, and this one I had set my heart on. You've gone about it the best you could. If you had told me from the start there wouldn't have been any fun."

"That is it," eagerly assented M. Ferraud. "Why should I spoil your innocent pleasure?

For a month you have lived in a fine adventure, and no harm has befallen. And when you return to America, you will have an unrivaled story to tell; but, I do not think you will ever tell all of it. He will have paid in wretchedness and humiliation for his inheritance. And who has a better right to it? Every coin may represent a sacrifice, a deprivation, and those who gave it freely, gave it to the blood. Is it sometimes that you laugh at French sentiment?"

"Not in Frenchmen like you," said the admiral gravely.

"Good! To men of heart what matters the tongue?"

"Poor young man!" sighed Laura. "I am glad he has found it. Didn't I wish him to have it?"

"And you knew all this?" said Cathewe into the ear of the woman he loved.

Thinly the word came through her lips: "Yes."

Cathewe's chin sank into his collar and he stared at the crumbs on the cloth.

"But what meant this argument with the drivers?" asked Coldfield.

"Yes! I had forgotten that," supplemented the sailor.

"On the way back to Carghese, we should have been stopped. We were to be quietly but effectively suppressed till our Napoleon set sail for Marseilles." M. Ferraud bowed. He had no more to add.

The admiral shook his head. He had come to Corsica as one might go to a picnic; and here he had almost toppled over into a gulf!

The significance of the swift glance which was exchanged between M. Ferraud and Fitzgerald was not translatable to Laura, who alone caught it in its transit. An idea took possession of her, but this idea had nothing to do with the glance, which she forgot almost instantly. Woman has a way with a man; she leads him whither she desires, and never is he any the wiser. She will throw obstacles in his way, or she will tear down walls that rise up before him; she will make a mile out of a rod, or turn a mountain into a mole-hill: and none but the Cumæan Sibyl could tell why. And as Laura was of the disposition to walk down by the

cemetery, to take a final view of the sea before it
melted into the sky, what was more natural than
that Fitzgerald should follow her? They walked
on in the peace of twilight, unmindful of the
curiosity of the villagers or of the play of children about their feet. The two were strangely
silent; but to him it seemed that she must presently
hear the thunder of his insurgent heart. At length
she paused, gazing toward the sea upon which the
purples of night were rapidly deepening.

"And if I had not made that wager!" he said,
following aloud his train of thought.

"And if I had not bought that statuette!" pick-
ing up the thread. If she had laughed, nothing
might have happened. But her voice was low and
sweet and ruminating.

The dam of his reserve broke, and the great current of life rushed over his lips, to happiness or to
misery, whichever it was to be.

"I love you, and I can no more help telling you
than I can help breathing. I have tried not to
speak. I have so little to offer. I have been lonely
so long. I did not mean to tell you here; but I've
done it." He ceased, terrified. His voice had

diminished down to a mere whisper, and finally refused to work at all.

Still she stared out to sea.

He found his voice again. "So there isn't any
hope? There is some one else?" He was very
miserable.

"Had there been, I should have stopped you at
once."

"But . . .!"

"Do you wish a more definite answer . . .
John?" And only then did she turn her head.

"Yes!" his courage coming back full and strong.
"I want you to tell me you love me, and while my
arms are round you like this! May I kiss you?"

"No other man save my father shall."

"Ah, I haven't done anything to deserve this!"

"No?"

"I'm not even a third-rate hero."

"No?" with gentle raillery.

"Say you love me!"

"*Amo, ama, amiamo* . . ."

"In English; I have never heard it in English."

"So," pushing back from him, "you have heard
it in Italian?"

"Laura, I didn't mean that! There was never any one else. Say it!"

So she said it softly; she repeated it, as though the utterance was as sweet to her lips as it was to his ears. And then, for the first time, she became supine in his arms. With his cheek touching the hair on her brow, they together watched but did not see the final conquest of the day.

"And I have had the courage to ask you to be my wife?" It was wonderful.

Napoleon, his hunted great-grandson, the treasure, all these had ceased to exist.

"John, when you lay in the corridor the other night, and I thought you were dying, I kissed you." Her arm tightened as did his. "Will you promise never to tell if I confess a secret?"

"I promise."

"You never would have had the courage to propose if I hadn't deliberately brought you here for that purpose. It was I who proposed to you."

"I'm afraid I don't quite get that," doubtfully.

"Then we'll let the subject rest where it is. You might bring it up in after years." Her laughter was happy.

He raised his eyes reverently toward heaven. She would never know that she had stood in danger.

"But your father!" with a note of sudden alarm. And all the worldly sides to the dream burst upon him.

"Father is only the 'company,' John."

And so the admiral himself admitted when, an hour later, Fitzgerald put the affair before him, briefly and frankly.

"It is all her concern, my son, and only part of mine. My part is to see that you keep in order. I don't know; I rather expected it. Of course," said the admiral, shifting his cigar, "there's a business end to it. I'm a rich man, but Laura isn't worth a cent, in money. Young men generally get the wrong idea, that daughters of wealthy parents must also be wealthy." He was glad to hear the young man laugh. It was a good sign.

"My earnings and my income amount to about seven-thousand a year; and with an object in view I can earn more. She says that will be plenty."

"She's a sensible girl; that ought to do to start on. But let there be no nonsense about money.

Laura's happiness; that's the only thing worth considering. I used to be afraid that she might bring a duke home." It was too dark for Fitzgerald to see the twinkle in the eyes of his future father-in-law. "If worst comes to worst, why, you can be my private secretary. The job is open at present," dryly. "I've been watching you; and I'm not afraid of your father's son. Where's it to be?"

"We haven't talked that over yet."

The admiral drew him down to the space beside him on the parapet and offered the second greatest gift in his possession: one of his selected perfectos.

The course of true love does not always run so smoothly. A short distance up the road Cathewe was grimly fighting for his happiness.

"Hildegarde, forget him. Must he spoil both our lives? Come with me, be my wife. I will make any and all sacrifices toward your contentment."

"Have we not threshed this all out before, my friend?" sadly. "Do not ask me to forget him; rather let me ask you to forget me."

"He will never be loyal to any one but himself. He is selfish to the core. Has he not proved it?"

Where were the words he needed for this last defense? Where his arguments to convince her?
He was losing; in his soul he knew it. If his love
for her was strong, hers for this outcast was no
less. "I have never wished the death of any man,
but if he should die . . .!"

She interrupted him, her hands extended as in
pleading. Never had he seen a woman's face so
sad, "Arthur, I have more faith in you than in any
other man, and I prize your friendship above all
other things. But who can say *must* to the heart?
Not you, not I! Have I not fought it? Have I
not striven to forget, to trample out this fire? Have
you yourself not tried to banish me from your
heart? Have you succeeded? Do you remember
that night in Munich? My voice broke, miserably,
and my public career was ruined. What caused
it? A note from him, saying that he had tired of
the rôle and was leaving. It was not my love he
wanted after all; a slip of paper, which at any time
would have been his for the asking. Arthur, my
friend, when you go from me presently it will be
with loathing. That night you went to his room
. . . he lied to you."

" About what ? "

" I mean, if I can not be his wife, I can not in honor be any man's. God pity me, but must I make it plainer ? "

Here, he believed, was his last throw. " Have I not told you that nothing mattered, nothing at all save that I love you ? "

" I can not argue more," wearily.

" He will tire of you again," desperately.

" I know it. But in my heart something speaks that he will need me; and when he does I shall go to him."

" God in heaven ! to be loved like that ! "

Scarcely realizing the violence of his action, he crushed her to his heart, roughly, and kissed her face, her eyes, her hair. She did not struggle. It was all over in a moment. Then he released her and turned away toward the dusty road. She was not angry. She understood. It was the farewell of the one man who had loved her in honor. Presently he seemed to dissolve into the shadows, and she knew that out of her life he had gone for ever.

CHAPTER XXV

THE DUPE

THE next morning Fitzgerald found Cathewe's note under his plate. He opened it with a sense of disaster.

" MY DEAR OLD JACK:
" I'm off. Found a pony and shall jog to Ajaccio by the route we came. Please take my luggage back to the Grand Hotel, and I'll pick it up. And have my trunk sent ashore, too. I shan't go back to America with the admiral, bless his kindly old heart! I'm off to Mombassa. Always keep a shooting-kit there for emergencies. I suppose you'll understand. Be kind to her, and help her in any way you can. I hope I shan't run into Breitmann. I should kill him out of hand. Happiness to you, my boy. And maybe I'll ship you a trophy for the wedding. Explain my departure in any way you please.

" CATHEWE."

The reader folded the note and stowed it away. Somehow, the bloom was gone from things. He was very fond of Cathewe, kindly, gentle, brave, and chivalrous. What was the matter with the woman, anyhow? How to explain? The simplest way would be to state that Cathewe had gone back to Ajaccio. The why and wherefore should be left to the imagination. But, oddly enough, no one asked a second question. They accepted Cathewe's defection without verbal comment. What they thought was of no immediate consequence. Fitzgerald was gloomy till that moment when Laura joined him. To her, of course, he explained the situation.

Neither she nor Hildegarde cared to go up to the forest. They would find nothing but a hole. And indeed, when the men returned from the pines, weary, dusty, and dissatisfied, they declared that they had gone, not with the expectation of finding anything, but to certify a fact.

M. Ferraud was now in a great hurry. Forty miles to Corte; night or not, they *must* make the town. There was no dissention; the spell of the little man was upon them all.

Hildegarde rode alone, in the middle carriage. Such had been her desire. She did not touch her supper. And when, late at night, they entered the gates of Corte and stepped down before the hotel lights, Laura observed that Hildegarde's face was streaked by the passage of many burning tears. She longed to comfort her, but the older woman held aloof.

Men rarely note these things, and when they do it has to be forced upon them. Fitzgerald, genuine in his regret for Cathewe, was otherwise at peace with the world. He alone of them all had found a treasure, the incomparable treasure of a woman's love.

Racing his horses all through the night, scouring for fresh ones at dawn and finding them, and away again, climbing, turning, climbing round this pass, over that bridge, through this cut, thus flew Breit-mann, the passion of haste upon him. By this tremendous pace he succeeded in arriving at Evisa before the admiral had covered half the distance to Carghese.

How clear and keen his mind was as on he rolled! 'A thousand places wove themselves to the parent-stem. He even laughed aloud, sending a shiver up the spine of the driver, who was certain his old *padrone* was mad. The face of Laura drifted past him as in a dream, and then again, that of the other woman. No, no; he regretted nothing, absolutely nothing. But he had been a fool there; he had wasted time and lent himself to a despicable intrigue. For all that he outcried it, there was a touch of shame on his cheeks when he remembered that, had he asked, she would have given him that scrap of paper the first hour of their meeting. Somewhere in Hildegarde von Mitter lay dormant the spirit of heroes. He had made a mistake.

Two millions of shining money, gold, silver, and English notes! And he laughed again as he recalled M. Ferraud, caught in a trap. He was clever, but not clever enough. What a stroke! To make prisoners of the party on their return, to carry the girl away into the mountains! Would any of them think of treasures, of conspiracies, with her as a hostage? He thought not. In the hue and cry for her, these elements in the game would fall to a minor place. Well he knew M. Ferraud: he would call to heaven for the safety of Laura. Love her? Yes! She was the one woman. But men did not

make captives of women and obtain their love.   He
knew the futility of such coercion.   He had committed two or three scoundrelly acts, but never
would he or could he sink to such a level.   No.   He
meant no harm at all.   Frighten her, perhaps, and
terrorize the others; and mayhap take a kiss as he
left her to the coming of her friends.   Nothing more
serious than that.

Two millions in gold and silver and English
notes!   He would have his revenge for all these
years of struggle and failure; for the cold and callous policies of state which had driven him to this
piece of roguery, on their heads be it.   Two thousand in Marseilles, ready at his beck and call, a
thousand more in Avignon, in Lyons, in Dijon, and
so on up to Paris, the Paris he had cursed one night
from under his mansard.   In a week he would have
them shaking in their boots.   The unemployed, the
idlers, thieves, his to a man.   If he saw his own
death at the end, little he cared.   He would have
one great moment, pay off the score, France as well
as Germany.   He would at least live to see them
harrying each other's throats.   To declare to France
that he was only Germany's tool, put forward for

the sole purpose of destroying peace in the midst
of a great military crisis. He had other papers,
and the prying little Frenchman had never seen
those; clever forgeries, bearing the signature of certain great German personages. These should they
find at the selected moment. Let them rip one another's throats, the dogs! Two million of francs,
enough to purchase a hundred thousand men.

"Ah, my great-grandsire, if spirits have eyes,
yours will see something presently. And that poor
little devil of a secret agent thinks I want a crown
on my head! There was a time . . . Curse
these infernal headaches!"

On, on; hurry, hurry. The driver was faithful,
a sometime brigand and later a harbor boatman;
and of all his confederates this one was the only
man he dared trust on an errand of this kind.

Evisa. They did not pause. They ate their supper on the way. With three Sardinian donkeys,
strong and patient little brutes, with lanterns and
shovels and sacks, the two fared into the pines.
Aïtone was all familiar ground to the Corsican who,
in younger days, had taken his illegal tithe from
these hills. They found the range soon enough,

but made a dozen mistakes in measurements; and it was long toward midnight, when the oil of the lanterns ran low, that their shovels bore down into the precious pocket. The earth flew. They worked like madmen, with nervous energy and power of will; and when the chest finally came into sight, rotten with age and the soak of earth, they fell back against a tree, on the verge of collapse. The hair was damp on their foreheads, their breath came harshly, almost in sobs.

Suddenly Breitmann fell upon his knees and laughed hysterically, plunged his blistered hands into the shining heap. It played through his fingers in little musical cascades. He rose.

" Pietro, you have been faithful to me. Put your two hands in there."

" I, *padrone?* " stupefied.

" Go on! Go on! As much as your two hands can hold is yours. Dig them in deep, man, dig them in deep! "

With a cry Pietro dropped and burrowed into the gold and silver. A dozen times he started to withdraw his hands, but they trembled so that some of the coins would slip and fall. At last, with one desperate plunge, the money running down toward his elbows, he turned aside and let fall his burden on the new earth outside the shallow pit. He rolled beside it, done for, in a fainting state. Breitmann laughed wildly.

"Come, come; we have no time. Put it into your pockets."

"But, *padrone,* I have not counted it!" naïvely.

"To-morrow, when we make camp for breakfast. Let us hurry."

Quickly Pietro stuffed his pockets, jabbering in his patois, swearing so many candles to the Virgin for this night's work. Then began the loading of the sacks, and these were finally dumped into the donkey-panniers.

"Now, Pietro, the shortest cut to Ajaccio. First, your hand on your amulet, and oath never to reveal what has happened."

Pietro swore solemnly. "I am ready now, *padrone!*"

"Lead on, then," replied Breitmann. Impulsively he raised his hands high above his head. "Mine, all mine!"

He wiped his face and hands, pulled his cap down firmly, lighted a cigarette, struck the rear donkey, and the hazardous journey began.

Seven men, more or less young, with a genial air of dissipation about their eyes and a varied degree of recklessness lurking at the corners of their mouths; seven men sat round a table in a house in the Rue St. Charles. They had been eating and drinking rather luxuriously for Ajaccio. The Rue St. Charles is neither spacious nor elegant as a thoroughfare, but at that point where it turns into the *Place Letitia* it is quiet and unfrequented at night. A film of tobacco smoke wavered in and out among the guttering candles and streamed round the empty and part empty champagne bottles. At the head of the table sat Breitmann, still pale and weary from his Herculean labors. His face was immobile, but his eyes were lively.

" To-morrow," said Breitmann, " we leave for France. On board the moneys will be equally divided. Then, for the work." His voice was cold, authoritative.

"Two millions!" mused Picard, from behind a fresh cloud of smoke. He picked up a bottle and gravely filled his glass, beckoning to the others to follow his example. At another sign all rose to their feet, Breitmann alone remaining seated, "To the Day!"

Breitmann's lips grew thinner; that was the only sign.

Outside, glancing obliquely through the grilled window, stood M. Ferraud. He had not seen these worthies together before. He knew all of them. There was not a shoulder among them that he could not lay a hand upon and voice with surety the order of the law. Courage of a kind they all had, names once written gloriously in history but now merely passports into dubious traffics. Heroes of boulevard exploits, duelists, card-players; could it be possible that any sane man should be their dupe? After the strange toast he heard many things, some he had known, some he had guessed at, and some which surprised him. Only loyalty was lacking to make them feared indeed. Presently he saw Breitmann rise. He was tired; he needed sleep. On the morrow, then; and in a week the first blow of

the new terror.   They all bowed respectfully as he
passed out.

The secret agent followed him till he reached the
Place des Palmiers.   He put a hand on Breitmann's
arm.   The latter, highly keyed, swung quickly.
And seeing who it was (the man he believed to be
at that moment a prisoner in the middle country!),
he made a sinister move toward his hip.   M. Ferraud was in peril, and he realized it.

"Wait a moment, Monsieur; there is no need of
that.   I repeat, I wish you well, and this night I
will prove it.   What? do you not know that I could
have put my hand on you at any moment?   Attend.
Return with me to the little house in Rue St.
Charles."

Brietmann's hand again stole toward his hip.

"You were listening?"

"Yes.   Be careful.   My death would not change
anything.   I wish to disillusion you; I wish to prove
to you how deeply you are the dupe of those men.
All your plans have been remarkable, but not one of
them has remained unknown to me.   You clasp the
hand of this duke who plays the sailor under the
name of Picard, who hails you as a future emperor,

and stabs you behind your back? How? Double-
face that he is, have I not proof that he has written
detail after detail of this conspiracy to the *Quai
d'Orsay,* and that he has clung to you only to gain
his share of what is yours? *Zut!* Come back with
me and let your own ears testify. The fact that I
am not in the mountains should convince you how
strong I am."

Breitmann hesitated, wondering whether he had
best shoot this meddler then and there and cut for
it, or follow him.

" I will go with you. But I give you this warning: if what I hear is not what you expect me to
hear, I promise to put a bullet into your meddling
head."

" I agree to that," replied the other. He did not
underestimate his danger; neither did he under-
value his intimate knowledge of human nature.

With what emotions Breitmann returned to the
scene of his triumph, his self-appointed companion
could only surmise. He had determined to save
this young fool in spite of his madness, and never
had he failed to bring his enterprises to their fore-
arranged end. And there was sentiment between

all this, sentiment he would not have been ashamed
to avow. Upon chance, then, fickle inconstant
chance, depended the success of the seven years'
labor. If by this time the wine had not loosened
their tongues, or if they had disappeared!

But fortune favors the persistent no less than the
brave. The profligates were still at the table, and
there were fresh bottles of wine. They were laughing and talking. In all, not more than fifteen
minutes had elapsed since Breitmann's departure.
M. Ferraud stationed him by the window and kept
a hand lightly upon his arm, as one might place a
finger on a pulse.

Of what were they talking? Ostend. The ballet-dancers. The races in May. The shooting at
Monte Carlo. Gaming-tables, empty purses. And
again ballet-dancers.

"To divide two millions!" cried one. "That
will clear my debts, with a little for Dieppe."

"Two hundred and fifty thousand francs!
Princely!"

And then the voice of the master-spirit, pitiless,
ironical; Picard's. "Was there ever such a dupe?
And not to laugh in his face is penance for my sins.

A Dutchman, a bullet-headed clod from Bavaria, the land of sausage, beer, and daschunds; and this shall be written Napoleon IV! Ye gods, what farce, comedy, vaudeville! But, there was always that hope: if he found the money he would divide it. So, kowtow, kowtow! Opera bouffe!"

Breitmann shuddered. M. Ferraud, feeling that shudder under his hand, relaxed his shoulders. He had won!

"An empire! Will you believe it?"

"I suggest the eagle rampant on a sausage!"

"No, no; the lily on the beer-pot!"

The scene went on. The butt of it heard jest and ridicule. They were pillorying him with the light and matchless cruelty of wits. And he, poor fool, had believed them to be *his* dupes, whereas he was *theirs!* Gently he disengaged himself from M. Ferraud's grasp.

"What are you going to do?" whispered the hunter of butterflies.

"Watch and see."

Breitmann walked noiselessly round to the entrance, and M. Ferraud lost sight of him for a few moments. Picard was on his feet, mimicking his dupe by assuming a Napoleonic pose. The door opened and Breitmann stood quietly on the threshold. A hush fell on the revelers. There was something kingly in the contempt with which Breitmann swept the startled faces. He stepped up to the table, took up a full glass of wine and threw it into Picard's face.

"Only one of us shall leave Corsica," said the dupe.

"Certainly it will not be your majesty," replied Picard, wiping his face with a serviette. "His majesty will waive his rights to meet me. To-morrow morning I shall have the pleasure of writing finis to this Napoleonic phase. You fool, you shall die for that!"

"That," returned Breitmann, still unruffled as he went to the door, "remains to be seen. Gentlemen, I regret to say that your monetary difficulties must continue unchanged."

"Oh, for fifty years ago!" murmured the little scene-shifter from the dark of his shelter.

CHAPTER XXVI

THE END OF THE DREAM

IT took place on the road which runs from Ajaccio to the *Cap de la Parata,* not far from *Iles Sanguinaires;* not a main-traveled road. The sun had not yet crossed the mountains, but a crisp gray light lay over land and sea. They fired at the same time. The duke lowered his pistol, and through the smoke he saw Breitmann pitch headforemost into the thick white dust. Presently, nay almost instantly, the dust at the left side of the stricken man became a creeping blackness. The surgeon sprang forward.

" Dead? " asked Picard.

" No! through the shoulder. He has a fighting chance."

" The wine last night; my hand wasn't steady enough. Some day the fool will curse me as a poor shot. The devil take the business! Not a sou for my pocket, out of all the trouble I have had. But for the want of a clear head I should be a rich man to-day. Who thought he would come back?"

"I did," answered M. Ferraud.

"You?"

"With pleasure! I brought him back; thank me for your empty pockets, Monsieur. If I were you I should not land at Marseilles. Try Livarno, by all means, Livarno."

"For this?" asked Picard, with a jerk of his head toward Breitmann, who was being carefully lifted on to the carriage seat.

"No, for certain letters you have *not* sent to the *Quai d'Orsay*. You comprehend?"

"What do you mean?" truculently; for Picard was not in a kindly mood this morning.

But the little Bayard of the *Quai* laughed. "Shall I explain here, Monsieur? Be wise. Go to Italy, all of you. This time you overreached, *Monsieur le Duc*. Your ballet-dancers must wait!" And with rare insolence, M. Ferraud showed his back to his audience, climbed to the seat by the driver, and bade him return slowly to the Grand Hotel.

Hildegarde refused to see any one but M. Ferraud. Hour after hour she sat by the bed of the injured man. Knowing that in all probability he would live, she was happy for the first time in years. He needed her; alone, broken, wrecked among his dreams, he needed her. He had recovered consciousness almost at once, and his first words were a curse on the man who had aimed so badly. He could talk but little, but he declared that he would rip the bandages if they did not prop his pillows so he could see the bay. The second time he woke he saw Hildegarde. She smiled brokenly, but he turned his head aside.

" Has the yacht gone yet? "

" No."

" When will it sail? "

" To-morrow." Her heart swelled with bitter pain. The woman he loved would be on that yacht. But toward Laura she held nothing but kindness tinged with a wondering envy. Was not she, Hildegarde, as beautiful? Had Laura more talents than she, more accomplishments? Alas, yes; one! She had had the unconscious power of making this man love her.

To and fro she waved the fan. For a while, at any rate, he would be hers. And when M. Ferraud said that the others wished to say farewell, she declined. She could look none of them in the face again, nor did she care. She was sorry for Cathewe. His life would be as broken as hers; but a man has the world under his feet, scenes of action, changes to soothe his hurt: a woman has little else but her needle.

All through the day and all through the night she remained on guard, surrendering her vigil only to M. Ferraud. With cold cloths she kept down the fever, wiping the hot face and hands. He would pull through, the surgeon said, but he would have his nurse to thank. There was something about the man the doctor did not understand: he acted as if he did not care to live.

The morning found her still at her post. Breitmann awoke early, and appeared to take little interest in his surroundings.

"Why do you waste your time?" his voice was colorless.

"I am not wasting my time, Karl."

His head rolled slowly over on the pillow till he

could see outside.   Only two or three fishing-boats were visible.

"When will the yacht sail?"

Always that question!   "Go to sleep.   I will wake you when I see it."

"I've been a scoundrel, Hildegarde;" and he closed his eyes.

Where would she go when he left this room? For the future was always rising up with this question.   What would she do, how would she live? She too shut her eyes.

The door opened.   The visitor was M. Ferraud. He touched his lips with a finger and stole toward the bed.

"Better?"

She nodded.

"Are you not dead for sleep?"

"It does not matter."

Breitmann's eyes opened, for his brain was wide awake.   "Ferraud?"

"Yes.   They wished me to say good-by for them."

"To me?" incredulously.

" They have none but good wishes."

" She will never know? "

" Not unless Mr. Fitzgerald tells her."

" Hildegarde, I had planned her abduction. Don't misunderstand. I have sunk low indeed, but not so low as that. I wanted to harry them. They would have left me free. She was to be a pawn. I shouldn't have hurt her."

" You do not care to return to Germany? "

" Nor to France, M. Ferraud."

" There's a wide world outside. You will find room enough," diffidently.

" An outlaw? "

" Of a kind."

" Be easy. I haven't even the wish to be buried there. There is more to the story, more than you know. My name is Herman Stüler . . . if I live. There is not a drop of French blood in my veins. Breitmann died on the field in the Soudan, and I took his papers." His eyes burned into Ferraud's.

" Perhaps that would be the best way," replied M. Ferraud pensively.

"What shall I do with the money? It is under the bed."

"Keep it. No one will contest your right to it, Herman Stüler; and besides, your French, fluent as it is, still posseses the Teutonic burr. Yes, Herman Stüler; very good, indeed."

Hildegarde eyed them in wonder. Were they both mad?

"Will you be sure always to remember?" said M. Ferraud to the bewildered woman. "Herman Stüler; Karl Breitmann, who was the great grandson of Napoleon, died of a gunshot in Africa. If you will always remember that, why even Paris will be possible some day."

Hildegarde was beginning to understand. She was coming to bless this little man.

"I do not believe that the money under the bed is safe there. I shall, if you wish, make arrangements with the local agents of the Credit Legonnais to take over the sum, *without question,* and to issue you two drafts, one on London and the other on New York, or in two letters of credit. Two millions; it is a big sum to let repose under one's bed, anywhere, let alone Corsica, where the amount might purchase half the island."

"I am, then, a rich man; no more crusades, no more stale bread and cheap tobacco, no more turning my cuffs and collars and clipping the frayed edges of my trousers. I am fortunate. There is a joke, too. Picard and his friends advanced me five thousand francs for the enterprise."

"I marvel where they got it!"

"I am sorry that I was rough with you."

"I bear you not the slightest ill-will. I never have. Herman Stüler; I must remember to have them make out the drafts in that name."

Breitmann appeared to be sleeping again. After waiting a moment or two, his guardian-angel tip-toed out.

An hour went by.

"Hildegarde, have you any money?"

"Enough for my needs."

"Will you take half of it?"

"Karl!"

"Will you?"

"No!"

He accepted this as final. And immediately his gaze became fixed on the bay. A sleek white ship was putting out to sea.

" They are leaving, Karl," she said, and the courage in her eyes beat down the pain in her heart.

" In my coat, inside; bring them to me." As he could move only his right arm and that but painfully, he bade her open each paper and hold it so that he could read plainly. The scrawl of the Great Captain; a deed and title; some dust dropping from the worn folds: how he strained his eyes upon them. He could not help the swift intake of air, and the stab which pierced his shoulder made him faint. She began to refold them. " No," he whispered. " Tear them up, tear them up! "

" Why, Karl."

" Tear them up, now, at once. I shall never look at them again. Do it. What does it matter? I am only Herman Stüler. Now! "

With shaking fingers she ripped the tattered sheets, and the tears ran over and down her cheeks. It would not have hurt her more had she torn the man's heart in twain. He watched her with fevered eyes till the last scrap floated into her lap.

"Now, toss them into the grate and light a match."

And when he saw the reflected glare on the opposite wall, he sank deeper into the pillow. The woman was openly sobbing. She came back to his side, knelt, and laid her lips upon his hand. There was now only a dim white speck on the horizon, and with that strange sea-magic the hull suddenly dipped down, and naught but a trail of smoke remained. Then this too vanished. Breitmann withdrew his hand, but he laid it upon her head.

"I am a broken man, Hildegarde; and in my madness I have been something of a rascal. But for all that, I had big dreams, but thus they go, the one in flames and the other out to sea." He stroked her hair. "Will you take what is left? Will you share with me the outlaw, be the wife of a disappointed outcast? Will you?"

"Would I not follow you to any land? Would I not share with you any miseries? Have you ever doubted the strength of my love?"

"Knowing that there was another?"

"Knowing even that."

"It is I who am little and you who are great.

Hildegarde, we'll have our friend Ferraud seek a priest this afternoon and square accounts."

Her head dropped to the coverlet.

After that there was no sound except the crisp metallic rattle of the palms in the freshening breeze.

THE END

www.ingramcontent.com/pod-product-compliance
Lightning Source LLC
Chambersburg PA
CBHW030355030726
47497CB00002B/356